LENGTH OF DAYS –
THE AGE OF SILENCE

LENGTH OF DAYS – THE AGE OF SILENCE

Doris Gaines Rapp

The first novel in a series of three

Daniel's House Publishing

Copyright © 2011 by Doris Gaines Rapp
2nd Edition released in 2014

Daniel's House Publishing
P.O. BOX 623
Huntington, Indiana 46750

Biblical Passages:
THE HOLY BIBLE, NEW INTERNATIONAL VERSION®, NIV®
Copyright © 1973, 1978, 1984, 2011 by Biblica, Inc.™ Used by permission.
All rights reserved worldwide.

Library of Congress Control Number: 2014934058

ISBN: 978-0-9637200-2-3 (paperback)
ISBN: 978-0-9637200-4-7 (eBook)

Contact Daniel's House Publishing at
www.danielshousepublishing@gmail.com

Table of Contents

<u>Dedication</u>

To Bill

ACKNOWLEDGMENTS

I thank God for giving me Christiana Applewait and her story, *Length of Days - The Age of Silence*. A reverence for life is a reverence for the giver of life.

To Bobbi Ray Madry, "Thank you! Thank you!" With more than thirty-five years experience as a published author and Senior Editor of Novels, Textbooks, Teaching Guides, and Audio-visuals, I value your belief in me and *Length of Days - The Age of Silence.* For your friendship, again, I thank you.

To our Writers Group (SDG), thank you for your encouragement each month. I value you all as writers and friends. You included me when I was still "practicing" my writing craft—which I continue to do to this day. Blessings!

To my family—my husband Bill, our children: Vicki, Donna, James, Vonn, Katy, and Mandi, I thank you so much. Your support has been wonderful and I cannot tell you how much I appreciate and love you all.

To all my friends, thank you for being there, praying with me, and caring about what I do and what I have to say.

Thanks to Bob Clayton (Robert A. Clayton) for his wonderful picture of the snowy mountains on the cover. You have enhanced the book beautifully. Your gift of photography blesses us all.

Victoria Borgman, book reviewer and dedicate Christian teacher, a big thank you for reading *Length of Days - The Age of Silence.* Your suggestions were priceless!

9

Proverbs 3:1-2 (NIV)   My son, do not forget my law but let your heart keep my commands, for length of days and long life and peace they will add to you.

PROLOGUE

I had no idea what Silas Drummond wanted from me.

He seemed to appear everywhere. In 2112 people didn't approach Legacy Citizens, but Silas continued to interrupt the tranquility of my days.

It was Gift-giving Season, during *The Age of Silence*. The emergency policies established during the crises of the previous century were still in place. That meant my dear grandparents would soon enter the never-ending-sleep, terminating their *Length of Days*. Even though there were atrocities all around us, none of us knew the evil at the core of our society.

No one saw the gathering darkness. It came slowly, like a fog that shimmers on the horizon before the dense veil overtakes the light. But then, few people were free to seek the glow of truth. In my day most walked in muted tones of gray.

Had I known what evil lurked in the shadows, I would have sought the light. If I had paid attention to my books, I would have seen when the flame began to dim. The last spark of truth was a dying ember, buried but not snuffed out.

Maybe if Silas had explained the true activities at the mountain, a little at a time, I would have been braced for the horror. Had I known the depravity that forced the silence on our people, I would have listened for the angels' song. But, powers stronger than I could imagine, controlled the darkness and closed our hearts to the light.

Indifference can silently steal our will and freedom. Sometimes, when life is too much to bear, we simply turn our eyes away. Had I known what Silas was trying to tell me, I would have been terrified, unable to stop the terrible fate that awaited us all. I had until the end of December to find a way to overturn the despicable law. Will the solution come in time?

Lady Christiana Applewait

CHAPTER ONE
Capitol City, Central Zone, U.S.A.

8:00 a.m. Friday, December 23, 2112

Only seven days left! How could that be? I knew that my loss would be coming soon, but I had avoided thinking about it for a long time. Now, I felt overwhelmed. My heart ached as I struggled with words to explain what I was feeling. Feeling words had vanished from our vocabulary decades ago. No one felt anything anymore, good or bad. I simply couldn't bear to think about what was coming, so I decided to bury myself in the library, the one safe place where I could always hide . . . where books had the power to release me from the gnawing pain inside that could not be expressed.

As I hurried up the steps to the main entrance to the library, a strange little man charged into my path. "Christiana . . . Miss Applewait . . . My Lady, I must talk to you!"

"What?" I was startled.

"Please," he begged as he touched my arm.

"Do yourself a favor, Buddy—move along." The Blue Guard Officer assigned to my protection reached for his prodding stick as he boldly studied the man who appeared to be about forty years old.

"Please My Lady . . ." the man tried to speak again.

"You are free to go, Ma'am," the officer waved me on. "This man is finished here."

From behind me, I could hear a struggle but I didn't look back. The man called out my name again as I dashed into the building. I slipped past the front desk and went directly to the forbidden back room of the library. I felt safe in there. Marge Cummings, the curator, and I were the only ones permitted access to the books, files, and documents locked away there.

I closed the door behind me, leaned against it, and caught my breath. *Why did the man on the steps frighten me so? What did he want?* I trembled as I latched the door to the back stacks before I went to my favorite brown leather chair. The smooth worn armchair reminded me of the old ones—my grandparents. They had a leather sofa. But it hurt too much to think about them.

This month of December 2112 had come too soon. It was the month of Grand-mère and Grand-père's final birthdays, when they would be forced into the never-ending-sleep, terminating their Length of Days. Why should my dear grandparents be part of the discarded, the forsaken? Why should they be among the unwanted, defective and overpopulate infants and children? They certainly weren't unproductive adults like some. No! Not my grandparents. I, Christiana Applewait, was one of the Privileged Legacy Citizens. But, what could I do?

"Christiana, dear, though we are Legacy, your grandfather and I have accepted this edict," my grandmother had assured me.

"You should fight it, Grand-mère. You have the power."

"Power, yes, but we are no better than others."

From beyond the inner door of the library, I thought I heard another scuffle and loud shouts. Did that odd little man call my name again? I recognized the fear in his voice, an emotion everyone still possessed. What was he trying to say? The very thought of discord startled me out of my world of books. Then—I heard nothing more. The man must have managed to get away from the officer, sneak into the building, only to be discovered and forcibly ejected again.

I tried to concentrate on my books, but foreboding thoughts kept tugging at my mind. I knew the chaos of the previous century had set the world spinning into social collapse. In the current era, it was becoming more obvious that life was no longer valued, and empathy had ceased to exist. What was left from the whirlwind of global chaos was an amoral society in which Grand-mère and Grand-père would soon be terminated, cast aside into the chamber portal to the great sleep.

"Grand-mère, please," I had begged her, "do something."

"It wouldn't be proper, Christiana. We're not above the rules."

"Acceptable principles of conduct and rules no longer exist, Grand-mère. I know —"

"What do you know, Christiana?"

"You know I practically live in the library. I—just know." What could I say? I didn't know how to respond to her calm acceptance of the Length of Days laws or the unexplained never-ending-sleep in which no one could visit or know if they would ever return.

One day, around Grand-mère's warm kitchen table, it all seemed so clear. I knew that thousands of years of history had been erased from our books one-hundred years ago with the stroke of a pen. The leaders of the revolution had banned everything written before that point. Only rewritten and newly crafted, politically conforming, texts remained. I could still see Grand-mère's sad eyes in my mind, as if she felt she had let me down.

What did that man want? Why couldn't I shake the sound of his pleading voice?

"Lady Applewait!" There was urgency in his voice that had made my body tense with fear.

Doesn't the man know how dangerous it is to stalk a Legacy Citizen? What does he want from me? Then, I had to reassure myself. *You're safe, Christiana. The door is locked and no one but you and Marge can get in.* Now, that strange, frightened man had drawn me into an intrigue by simply calling my name. Somehow, the world from beyond the library walls had found me.

Until now, I had flooded my mind with images from the books I had been reading so I wouldn't have to think about my grandparents' fate any longer. Today, too many questions had intruded into my thoughts and wouldn't let me escape, as I longed to do.

I wanted to save my grandparents, but I didn't want to be brave. I felt like a walking contradiction, and I didn't know the real *me*. I wanted to be counted on, to help my grandparents in some way. I had thought about it all year, then I had procrastinated for months and now it was December already. I had done nothing but bury my head in my books. Here in the library, in my secret place, I had always been able to lock myself away from reality and the staring public. But, today, reality had found me.

Here in the back stacks, in a place far removed from everything else, I could be alone with the feelings I experienced while reading. Once beyond the maze of closed, locked doors, the dark, dimly lit hallway led the way to a mysterious inner sanctum. This part of the library testified to the secretive nature of the old volumes but revealed nothing about the reason for the labels of *evil* and *forbidden* they had acquired. I had wondered about all the secrecy concerning the old books and why they had been banned as *corrupting literature*. Then, I thought of the little man. Was someone trying to reach me because I have access to illegal material? *No, I must not allow such thoughts to upset me.*

Here, inside the back room, it wasn't dark or sinister at all. December morning sun streamed through the high, crimson and blue stained-glass windows that faced the east and sent dancing rainbows across the floor. I settled down in my chair and soon became engrossed in the characters in the novel. Chills ran down my back, not from the coolness of the dawn, but from the warmth of the words and excitement of the images that flooded my thoughts as I read. The beauty the images created in my mind mesmerized me as I devoured the vivid descriptions and strong characters on each page of the books now locked away and forbidden.

"I know you have been reading a lot," Grand-mère had ventured cautiously that day in her kitchen. "What books do you enjoy the most?"

"Oh, I love to read everything I can find—but the novels—they are wonderful! People had such deep feelings."

"And religion and philosophy, Christiana?"

I hadn't responded to that question. I'd rambled on about a novel I'd read and didn't really answer her properly. I had been so starved for the love and affection that the books of fiction had described; they were the ones I had been devouring.

The world inside my books and the reality I tried to avoid, were nothing alike. The present era was so different from anything the books of times past described. I knew that few people had read the wonderful old volumes. Most people had never learned what had happened before the current epoch. Initially, I had only been interested in the everyday lives of people, as played out in the wonderful old stories. I didn't know what I should, or what I could have known, about history or governments and the rest.

I didn't have an excuse. I was privileged to be able to explore all the knowledge hidden here; yet, I had squandered the opportunity that my special position had given me. But then, I was privileged in every way.

Like royalty of old, I had inherited a favored place in society, not earned it. I was a Legacy Citizen.

"My dear," Grand-mère had cautioned, "you were given a wonderful chance to be of service the day you were born."

"I know Grand-mère," I had mechanically agreed.

She had taken both my hands in hers. "Christiana, look into my eyes. You were born a Legacy Citizen, not a better person. You were born for service, dear, not entitlements. Do you understand?"

I did. Had I not been born a Legacy Citizen, it would have been impossible to have achieved anything significant enough to merit a place in society in the present age. The masses of people were kept in a controlled state, satisfied with the most mediocre existence possible. Currently, there was no incentive for hard work, no merit pay, only everything equal in every way, including nothingness.

Having access to the forbidden areas of the library, I had soaked in all the knowledge and emotions that were written on the secret pages of many of the books stored here. For fear of detection, I had to hold the mysteries close to my heart. That morning, I hadn't even told Grand-mère anything more about what I had been reading.

I had recently earned my Master's degree in Library Science and that, coupled with my Legacy status, had qualified me to carry a master key to the library when I began my research. Members of the Blue Guard escorted me around campus but, once alone in the library my master key gave me access to rooms that held the old texts, documents, and novels of ages past. Even though the old books were not on the bibliography of my University-approved thesis topic, *An Argument for a New Form of Cataloging Books,* there was no one who really knew what I was reading while tucked away in the back recesses of this old wing.

Oh, to have lived in those olden days talked about in the books of fiction, to have experienced those emotions: desire and hope, expectation and surprise. The more I read about the past, the more I longed to be truly alive as the characters seemed to have been then.

Why didn't I know I had not been living to the fullest of my emotions? Why hadn't I noticed that others seemed even flatter in their feelings than I? I had begun to realize that my experience was different from most. I had been living my life inside the pages of books other people never saw or read.

I wondered about the people who lived in my building. They seemed to feel joy, in spite of their drugged state, and I wondered if I was every really happy. What I had read about in the books was more joy than I, and probably others, had experienced.

I was learning about passion and commitment, of people living and learning into advanced old age. People died of natural causes in the arms of their family, not as my beloved grandparents were doomed to leave me, by being locked away in endless sleep.

As I sat there in the library trying to sort out what to think and do, a little pull on the back of my blouse interrupted my thoughts. *That spot on my back is catching again.* I reached over my left shoulder and scratched at the snaggy spot. *A vaccination isn't supposed to tear at your clothing.* Tossing my hair to one side, I reached back again so I could feel around on my old scar. Children were vaccinated when they were infants, but there was a tiny, hard piece of something protruding from my old inoculation site. *I'll have it checked,* I promised myself.

I tried to take my mind off my shoulder. But, I had read too many stories about the illnesses in the old days to stop worrying about it. *There is definitely a lump. What could it be?*

CHAPTER TWO

The Sanctuary

"Christiana Applewait, what are you doing here so early?" Marge smiled as she breezed into the room, as if the morning had just occurred to her.

"What ya readin'?" Marge asked as she glanced at the book I was holding.

"*A Woman of Substance,*" I answered. "In this novel, Emma Harte falls in love, makes mistakes, works herself out of them and lives to an old age, with all her memories gathered around her like a down comforter on a winter morning." I closed the book and inserted Grand-mère's old pink-and-white crocheted cross bookmark in the place where I had left off. I remembered asking her once what the cross meant. She said she would tell me sometime.

"Very romantic, I know. I've read Bradford's books," Marge paused. "Did you hear all that ruckus earlier, out there in the entry hall? Someone was all agitated and looking for you."

"I'm sure it must have been a mistake." I pretended I knew nothing about the man who had tried to get my attention.

Marge leaned in toward me as if someone might hear her. "It was no mistake. He was calling out your name. Then the guard threatened to lock him up if he didn't go away."

"I don't want to think about that now."

"Okay," she agreed. "I've found something you will be interested in though. No one else knows this stuff even exists."

Marge inserted a key into a massive wooden case nearby and removed a small, metal box.

"What is that?" I asked as she placed the box on a stand.

"It's an old operating system of some sort that runs on electricity. Since our generator supplies the alternative energy we need for some of our older devices, I imagine we're one of the few places that would be able to play something like this . . . our library and the hospital." She plugged the box in and inserted a disk of some sort into the opening. A moving picture burst forth on the surface with a lilting musical accompaniment.

"I've never seen anything like this before," Marge whispered. "Our telecommunications messages are so stiff. '*What to do in case of an emergency.*' '*How to rear your children.*' You know, the same old stuff."

"And all the games, Marge, thousands of games. People don't even see the buried images in the game grids." I threw up both hands, trying to express my disgust with the kind of censorship and indoctrination now forced on the population.

"One book I just finished reading," I remembered, "described news programs with dozens of commentators, who talked all day. If people weren't informed back then, it wasn't from lack of a messenger. It was because they didn't want to know."

"That's why the society stopped all those broadcasts," Marge nodded. "They said people were restless all the time and anxious about things they didn't need to think about. The Lawmakers thought no one should spend time worrying about finances, scandals, or the workings of government. They also banned programs that filled the mind with frivolous fluff and programs that told stories."

"Christiana," Marge interrupted, "that's what I found, one of those programs."

"Marge, you mean a story on film?"

"Watch," she restarted the little machine.

We sat in front of a small screen and soaked in all the joys and sorrows of the family in the teleplay. The brothers and sisters walked to a friendly grocery in their bare feet, but no one complained. The parents stole a kiss or a hug as they passed each other, just living their lives. My heart stung with unexercised empathy and longing. Stretching it hurt. No one in 2112 demonstrated affection in public.

I shook my head in disbelief. I'd never seen anything so poignant before. "Six children, a mother and father, and two elderly grandparents all lived on a meager income at the foot of a mountain during the Great Depression of the previous International Chapter and yet, they seemed so happy. And, Marge, the old ones! How could they have lived so long?"

"People just lived until they died." Then Marge shook her head. "What a terrible financial drain they were on their families and the country's economy. They were too selfish to get out of the way so the next generation could live comfortably." I knew Marge was speaking out of rote memory, not out of understanding for the dignity of people, or a reverence for life.

"Marge, my grandparents will soon be seventy-five years old. You know what that means."

"The never-ending-sleep," Marge said with an indifferent tone. "My parents reached the end of their Length of Days when they turned sixty years old, not seventy-five like the Council members."

"It isn't fair," I whispered, even though I knew I was one of the lucky ones. I would one day be on the Council of Elders, the Wise Ones, like my great-great grandparents before me. Our Length of Days is longer than the rest of the population. But, it still isn't fair.

"What choice did society have, Christiana? When the decision was made, health care costs were astronomical, insurance was out of reach and the cost for housing prisoners was beyond the average citizens' imagination. Massive public-funded feeding programs, although well intentioned, had swallowed up a huge portion of the national treasury. Our nation's debt had surmounted any ability to repay. So, it was decided that each person would be allocated a Length of Days, based on their worth to society. Then, they were put into the never-ending-sleep. My job as curator is unique, so I'm more valuable than some others. I get to live longer than many."

"But Marge, how can people's lives be judged this way? Birthdays aren't even celebrated after a child turns ten years old. A kind of grief sets in. Since people know when they will pass on, they have no hope for a brighter future. There are no surprises in life, only a ticking of the clock. And, my own grandparents' birthdays are in a few weeks."

"I know, Christiana, but let's talk about it more after Gift-giving." She stood up and bent over to give me a hug. "What's that?" Marge winced. "I scratched my hand on your shoulder." Marge pulled her arm back and inspected the small surface wound on her little finger.

"Oh that," I shrugged it off. "There's something caught in my vaccination scar. It catches on my clothes. I've snagged several shirts on that little piece that is sticking out."

"Christiana, you must have that looked at. It could be serious," Marge turned me around and ran her fingertips around the spot.

"I suppose," I admitted.

"No 'suppose' to it. There's a new doctor in town and he's taking patients."

"Capitol City needed another doctor? With no stress, no worries, and no outliving the energy of our bodies, we were all to enjoy good health." I felt the hair on the back on my neck bristle. "We weren't even supposed to need health care providers."

Marge shrugged. "They thought they could handle the costs of illness for a limited number of years per person, so the weaker, flawed ones are sorted out at birth. But, it's nothing we should think or worry about."

Heaven forbid that we should think. I thought it, but didn't say out loud. "That's only if the flawed baby is not your older brother," I mumbled, then added. "My parents never got over their loss."

"They didn't have to limit themselves to one child. They could have had another baby after you were born," Marge stated dryly. "Families are just prohibited from having more than a total of two children and must abort other fetal masses that may form."

I shuddered as I listen to her. "My parents' case was too complicated," I said but didn't want to share the story. There was too much suffering wrapped up in that one little boy. "Though my family was granted the privilege of living beyond most other people's Length of Days, they had to terminate the life of a dearly cherished child. It was too hard for them."

Marge jumped to her feet and smiled, oblivious to the family pain I was feeling. "Well, I hear there is someone in town that is not too hard to deal with, the handsome new doctor I told you about. You start on over to his office, and I'll call and tell them you're on your way. As a future Legacy replacement to the Council of Elders, you'll receive preferential treatment."

I dutifully grabbed my shoulder bag, red hat, and my green cloak and headed out to do my civic duty by keeping my body healthy.

Outside, the air was crisp, and the earth still clung to the memory of the fall season. It was a glorious winter day. As I walked mechanically up to the corner transit platform, I heard my name again.

"Christiana," a voice rang out behind me. It was the small man who had tried to stop me this morning. As he hurried toward me, another Blue Guardsman stepped between us and pushed the man aside. He fell to the sidewalk and scrapped the side of his face on the concrete.

I thought I should hurry on until I noticed blood dripping into his eyes. There was something familiar about the man I hadn't noticed before.

"Lady Applewait," he called out as he tried to get to his feet.

"Stay down," the Blue Shirt ordered roughly.

I finally recognized the man. He lived in my building, although I had never spoken to him. "Silas, is that you?"

"Yes, My Lady," he whispered.

"I'll keep him down, Ma'am. You can move along," the Guardsman spoke with authority.

"Wait, please," Silas begged. "I wrote it out for you." He pulled a piece of paper from his pocket and started to hand it to me. When the officer reached for it, Silas snapped it back. "No, no!" Fear was in his eyes. "It's only for Lady Applewait."

I saw the urgent look on his face. The same fear that had gripped me when I heard him calling to me rose up between us. Just as the uniformed man touched the paper, I snatched it out of his hand. "Thank you, Silas."

"It's just a few notes about gift giving in the building you had asked me for the other day, Ma'am." Silas's trembling voice threatened to give away his lies. "Tell this Guard he's overreacting, please."

"Let me see that," the Guard insisted.

"No Sir," I assured him with as much royal privilege as I could muster. "I have it." I could see panic in Silas's eyes. I didn't know what he was talking about or what was going on, but I immediately grasped the grave situation Silas was in. He risked his life to get a message to me. I was sure it wasn't a Gifting list.

"Thank you. I'll check it over later. I have an appointment now." I shoved the folded paper in my bag and hurried up the transit steps.

The note was quickly forgotten as my thoughts turned back to the video Marge and I had seen. The happy family's expectation of good things to come was intoxicating. Their hope was contagious. I just couldn't accept the fate of my grandparents. The Length of Days policy was new in the larger pattern of history. I was one of the few who knew that life had been different in the past.

My mind churned as I thought of how the law could be overturned. I didn't know where to begin. I had read something curious a few months back while I was rummaging through the old files doing research for my thesis. In one of the books, there was something about "inalienable rights." *When I get back to the library from the doctor's office this afternoon, after I have seen my grandparents, I'll find the old manuscripts and see if I can understand what I know is there. I have already read it. Maybe wisdom will be gifted to me before the passage of time.*

I had no idea that within another day, I would be facing my rebirth, where wisdom would unfold rapidly.

CHAPTER THREE

The Spot

10:00 a.m.

I knew I had to have the spot on my back checked. I didn't want to go to the doctor, but it was the responsibility of a Legacy Citizen to take care of their health. The Public Transit waiting area wasn't crowded so I sat on a bench in the warm sunshine and tried to make sense of what this day had meant so far. I would have preferred going most anyplace other than the doctor's office. Just as my books allowed me to escape the reality of my grandparents' fate, I also chose to avoid addressing health issues. As a Legacy Citizen, I had been cared for, protected. I didn't have to face life as most people experienced it. That was just the way life was. Now, I needed to protect the lives of my grandparents by finding a way to use my legacy status to save them.

I'll think about that tomorrow. But, the truth was, I was running out of time, and so were Grand-mère and Grand-père.

Just as the inverse trolley pulled to my stop, I heard the piercing wail of a Blue Shirt's strata-car. I thought of Silas Drummond and shuddered. I couldn't remember ever having been frightened before within the bubble I was kept. I hurried on board the Doris Public Transit where I felt safe. Riding above the streets on the P-T felt serene and peaceful, up in the quiet above the fray. The transit cars floated on electrified steel ribbons, silently crisscrossing the city on a grid that covered the entire metropolitan area. Riding across town with other people, even though they kept their distance from me, was usually pleasant, but my thoughts were preoccupied with my grandparents' situation and this spot on my shoulder.

Maybe I have cancer, I worried. According to my books, people used to have a disease that destroyed healthy tissue in the body. It often started with a lump.

When the Transit reached my stop, I bounded down the steps from the disembarking area, pretending there was nothing wrong. I had learned a long time ago that Legacy Citizens are constantly under surveillance, not in a threatening way, but I knew to present myself to the public as calm and organized. That day, I felt like I was fooling no one.

As I walked up the broad steps of the medical center, I kept thinking about my grandparents and the old ones in the program Marge and I had watched. The actors looked much older than Grand-mère and Grand-père. How amazing it must have been for them to go on living as long as nature allowed.

Once inside the office, a woman looked up from her work. "Yes?" The woman at the reception desk, in the physician's suite, questioned in shorthand. She reached in my direction with a detection wand.

"I am Christiana Applewait. Someone called —"

"Yes, Ma'am. I have your information right here. You can come on back."

I saw other patients already waiting for their time with the doctor, but I still accepted my place at the head of the line. It had always been that way. I watched as one mother cradled her sick daughter in her arms. The child's cheeks were red with fever, and her eyes were glazed with pain. I looked away. I had always been taught—it is best to not fill your head with other people's pain. After all, there was nothing I could do about it.

"Come along, Miss Applewait. Let's not expose you to germs unnecessarily." The nurse hustled me out of the waiting room, down the hall and into examination room number two.

I recognized the nurse. She was Dahlia Zoobamba. We lived in the same building, but we had never spoken.

"This is nice," I said as I looked around the small examination room. I had rarely been sick, and I didn't realize that Society had redecorated the entire Medical Complex the previous year. The pictures were somehow different from what was usually displayed. "The animal photographs are wonderful, especially the farm scenes," I remarked.

"Doctor wanted people to remember the animals as they used to be. Many were slaughtered to reduce Carbon Dioxide levels. Look at those brown eyed cows. Can you believe people used to eat those beasts?"

"Thank goodness for chemically processed food," I mumbled. "This picture of the dog is great. Dogs are so rare now."

"The government thought they used up too much of our food supply."

"I saw one the other day," I reminisced as I remembered the happy, frisky little dog peering at me from a window I had passed.

As the nurse prepared her charts, I noticed the newness of the equipment and the room. Perhaps I could ask a question I had wondered about while she methodically went through her routine. They said this building needed major renovation as a normal part of maintenance. There was a rumor that other motives were at the bottom of the paint cans. "Is the epidemic over?"

"Epidemic? There's been no epidemic." Nurse Dahlia's answer was flat and crisp.

"A friend said two of his cousins needed to be in the hospital but there were no beds," I said. "It sure sounds like an epidemic to me." I knew what I had been told.

The hospital had been filled with people so distraught, they couldn't function. Marge and I had looked in an old medical book for symptoms we had heard about. Depression met all the criteria. It was a disease that had nearly been eradicated by endorphin boosters in the water supply that controlled the old disorder.

"I've noticed people arguing in the library, and I've seen people crying for no apparent reason," I told Dahlia. "My friend told me that six young women had made a suicide pact, but the superintendent in their building had discovered their plan and stopped them before it was too late."

"Suicide? That's an archaic term," Dahlia bristled. "People just don't do that any more. We . . . never mind." The nurse straightened her glasses and turned to leave. "The doctor will be with you in a moment."

She bowed out of the conversation with a dismissive tone I didn't appreciate. I stood there for a moment and wondered if I should leave, but I felt my shoulder again and reconsidered. I gazed out the window and watched the morning move toward noon day. Beyond the building, in the park below that fronted a small, old-fashioned shopping village, a young woman hurried along the sidewalk, then disappeared over a little rise near a wooded area by a fish pond.

Just then I caught sight of a man as he jumped out of his red car. He started to cross the street in the direction of the Medical Center but was stopped by a Blue Shirt who swung his baton with a blow to the back of the man's knees. As he buckled to the ground, his body turned and I could see his face.

Oh no . . . it's that man. It's Silas again. Fear suddenly gripped my heart. *Why has he followed me? What is so important he would risk his life to touch mine?* I fumbled with my bag until I found the note. It was still there.

CHAPTER FOUR
Silas Drummond

Earlier that morning - Before Sunrise

Silas Drummond was never seen around town in the daytime. What had happened that morning to cause him to risk danger to talk to Christiana Applewait? He had never dared speak to her before.

Just hours before he had suddenly appeared in town, Silas Drummond was deep in the bowels of Howard Mountain, going through the routine of his despicable job. He had shuffled as rapidly as his aching legs could carry him, along the sterile tile floor that led back to his post. The bell had rung announcing another delivery for the furnaces. There were arrivals almost around the clock, every day of the week. Silas had been warned not to leave the place or reveal anything he knew, or about his duties there. Some bodies arrived already deceased, needing only to be discarded. The cases that were hard for Silas were the breathing ones who seemed to expect a bed and pillow to rest on, for their never-ending-sleep.

Dark smoke rose from the peak above the vast tentacles of crematorium chambers that were buried in the caverns underneath the once majestic mountain, miles from Capitol City. While death stalked below, purifying snow draped a blanket of white across the slopes above. Death had become so common place the few people who lived near the sickening foulness paid no more attention to what was going on, than those who had lived near the Nazi death camps, more than a century and a half ago. It didn't matter. Silas had gotten used to the stench long ago. The year 2112 was a new time, but an old evil lurked below the mountain like a putrid mold, while seasons came and went on the surface above.

A wide desolate road ran at the base of the mountain and stretched several miles to the edge of the city. One of Silas Drummond's jobs was to check the driver's list of end-travelers as they emerged from luxury vehicles, much like the limousines from the previous era. The list contained the names of those who had reached the age for entering the long sleep that ended their Length of Days. Silas knew that the end-travelers thought they were riding in luxury, like sophisticates of old, to a restful place to sleep for a while, but, Silas knew it was their journey's end.

Blackened clouds from the mountain top blocked the morning light, as another driver pulled his black stretch limo to the gate and hopped out.

"Watch your step folks," the driver cautioned. "You don't want to sleep away your days with a broken leg." He chuckled to himself but his humor was lost on his passengers.

The tall iron gate swung open and two white-coated burly men helped the travelers into several small electric cars that would deliver them to the processing center.

"You got time for coffee, Silas?" the limo driver spoke into the gate speaker.

"I'll be able to take a break in a few minutes, Harry. Come on in with the group and then have a seat in the lounge. Be sure to take the back hallway as usual, not the main one. No one's allowed in that part of the complex."

"Then why do they call it the main hall?" Silas heard Harry mumbled to himself, but said no more.

Silas stepped away from the communicator and waited near the elevator for the newest arrivals. He longed to leave, to get away from the wretched place, but the new group of end-travelers would have to be processed immediately, before reality had time to register.

The huge ornate doors opened, allowing the citizens to enter the pleasant reception room where Silas was waiting to check them in.

"Silas, I didn't know you worked here." A petite blond girl who appeared to be about twenty recognized him. She walked with a severe limp with the aid of crutches.

"The leg still bothering you, Mari?" Silas asked. He knew what that kind of disability meant.

"Some. On rainy days it's the worst. My medical counselor said it would be best for me to get a long rest." She smiled as she hobbled along after Drummond's scuffling steps. "It'll be okay. It's not like the endless sleep of the aged. It's like . . . a long nap."

Silas was speechless as Mari and the group followed behind him like sheep. Bitter bile rose in his throat where it mixed with fear and anger. "But . . . but," he stammered and then saw the guard at the enrollment station glare at him.

Silas had little contact with the travelers as he escorted them to the door from which no one returned. His main responsibility was to make constant rounds, checking all of the gages in order to keep the furnaces firing at the right temperature. He wanted to know nothing and to see even less.

I could not strap her to the tray. He shuddered at the very thought of it. *Much less keep the flame under her young body at a steady, even temperature. I know her . . . I like little Mari.*

They have lied to her. He screamed inside his mind. *And, she's not the only one.*

Later, safely concealed inside a locked restroom, he grabbed his pocket knife and scratched another inch-long jagged red mark on his already scarred arm. His dark blood dripped into the bowl then pooled near the drain as he blindly carved on his own body until the knife penetrated deeply enough that he could feel again.

Control yourself, he demanded. If he complained to his superiors about putting his young friend in the furnace, they might place a stripe against him in his employment jacket. If he were caught giving out information, it would mean certain death. He knew the attendants would take Mari's time piece, belt buckle, and shoes. They took jewelry and anything of value and promised it would be stored. That was something, this time with Mari, he could not accept.

The long nap is a lie. It's not temporary. It's permanent! And, the never-ending-sleep is not a gift. It's extermination. Silas knew, little Mari, these elderly citizens, and many others had been duped and were totally unaware of the real process they were facing.

Silas returned to his desk to pick up his belongings as eerie music lilted through the subterranean lair. These despicable chambers are the only place left in society where music was still played. It was intended to quiet the victims' fears. Silas muttered to himself, "It's not a lullaby. It's a dirge of death." The ghastly songs were not just for the end-travelers, but also for those whose jobs were to carry out the daily procedures or be eliminated along with their families if they didn't.

"Silas, there you are." The limo driver looked up as Silas hurried toward the exit.

Gotta get out of here. Silas hardly knew he was muttering to himself. *Gotta tell her. It has to stop. I know I'll be in trouble for leaving early. If I don't clock out, maybe I can claim I forgot to have my time card punched. Maybe I can be gone long before they miss me.* Then he rushed out, leaving the driver alone in the lounge.

She is the one person who might be able to stop this madness, Silas thought. *Lady Christiana is a Legacy Citizen.* She was the only person he knew who might listen to him, and perhaps believe his story.

Silas hobbled to his car, always bent in a hurried stance. He deposited something large and wrapped in the old blanket from his resting chamber in the back seat, got in and sat in silence while he fumbled nervously with the car's ignition. Then he whispered, "It'll be okay. We'll get to my sister's place before everyone starts stirring."

He would leave the mountain and the stench behind him. As he drove along the road toward the city, he was unaware that another vehicle had pulled away from the mountain at the same time and cast a long shadow behind them. Silas was not alone.

CHAPTER FIVE

The Doctor

I stood and watched Silas Drummond through the medical office window as I waited for the doctor to come in. I was unable to stop studying the little man. He surely knew what would happen if he continued to pursue me. He had been warned more than once that very morning. I had seen him in the apartment building a few times but we had never even shared a glance. It would not have been proper. In fact, it was unthinkable for someone to try to step into the space of a Legacy Citizen.

Suddenly, my attention was drawn from Silas and back into the doctor's examining room. "Good morning," a friendly voice, the texture of warm chocolate, greeted me from behind.

Startled, I spun around to see a tall, athletic man enter the room. I jammed the paper Silas had written more deeply to the bottom of my tote. My heart was pounding. *What does Silas want with me?* "Good morning," I said as the attractive, white coated man came toward me.

"I'm Dr. O'Reilly," he nodded but didn't extend his hand. "I'm happy to meet you."

I knew I was trembling from the events of the morning. My world was usually cushioned with the cotton of quiet solitude, above the stratum on which others lived. My bubble had been invaded many times that morning. I tried to control the anxiety that gripped me.

Dr. O'Reilly smiled. His expression was soft as he studied me.

"Have we met? You seem familiar to me."

I didn't remember having met him—and I would have remembered. There was something in his eyes that was different. He exuded an appeal I could not identify.

Dr. O'Reilly motioned to the examination table. "Jump up here, please. It's your shoulder that's bothering you, right?"

I slipped up on the table and removed my outer jacket. "My shoulder, specifically . . . the vaccination site." My voice sounded shaky to me. *Get control of yourself!* I didn't want to have to explain the reason for my anxiety . . . the Blue Guard . . . or the note Silas Drummond had passed to me.

Doctor O'Reilly moved in closer to examine my shoulder. I could smell a faint scent of aftershave, something that had nearly gone out of custom.

"Let's have a look." He raised his arms as if ready to help remove my blouse but he didn't touch me.

I realized he was being respectful of my station in life, so I slipped the sleeve down by myself. I unbuttoned the top of my garment and slipped it off my shoulder. I twisted and turned again but I still couldn't see the spot.

"You would have to be a pushmi-pull-yu to see the back of your own shoulder," he smiled.

"A what? A push-pull-what?"

"Just a fictional animal from a book I read. Dr. Doolittle," he smiled.

"But if the animal was not real, it was not a book of facts or a book of science. I know books. You had to have read a book of fiction, Doctor."

"Fiction books were banned a long time ago," he protested with that special tone of authority that medical people often use to claim an expertise on more subjects than just medicine.

"What books have you been reading, Dr. O'Reilly?" I was impatient. I had to know and I certainly wasn't intimidated by his education. "Which ones?"

"Oh you know, just the usual," he offered lamely, avoiding the topic and redirected the conversation to the examination.

I could feel my heart pounding inside my chest. There was another stash of books somewhere, outside of the library. I was not going to be dissuaded.

Dr. O'Reilly paused near my ear. "I know this could be risky, but since you know about books of fiction, you may have read some. Books seem important to you." He paused and looked at me. "It's not necessarily a secret but few people know the old wing of the hospital has a library."

I felt my heart catch in my throat. How did he know I lived for my books? "You read them . . . the books?" I kept my voice low and tried not to show any emotion.

His fingers rolled over the lump on my shoulder. "I can feel the sharpness beneath your skin."

I would not let him change the subject that easily. "Do you read the books, Dr. O'Reilly?" I knew I sounded somewhat demanding and I didn't want to draw unusual attention to myself, but I had to know. "Please . . . do you read the books?" I couldn't believe there may be another stash of novels somewhere.

Dr. O'Reilly paused. "They are wonderful," he whispered.

The door handle rattled and Nurse Dahlia reentered the room. The conversation returned to talk of the bump under my skin. Discretely, Dr. Riley pulled back slightly while still examining the lump on my shoulder.

"Do you need any help Doctor?" the nurse questioned politely but had a puzzled look on her face. "Your voices were not clear over the room monitor."

"We are fine, Nurse." Dr. O'Reilly dismissed any concern Dahlia may have had by involving her in the exam. "Come here and take a look at this?" He stepped back and motioned for Dahlia to examine my mysterious lump.

Dahlia looked at me and I sensed by her expression that she

recognized me too. Suddenly, I was aware of all of the apartment building neighbors I had never spoken to. They talked and joked between each other but I was always on the outside. Since they would have been forbidden to speak to a Legacy person first, my isolation was of my own making.

"Ma'am, have you fallen or been hit by something?" Dahlia's questions were professional, and she was careful not to actually touch me. "I haven't heard of any injury you may have sustained."

She was right. If a Legacy Council member, or those who would inherit that position through benefit of their birth, had tripped over a curb, all of the people would have heard about it. We were watched, emulated, guarded, secretly envied, and were socially positioned within the circle of the elite, set apart from the masses.

"No, Nurse Dahlia, never. I know I haven't had any kind of accident, unless I was sleepwalking and didn't remember it."

The nurse stepped back quickly and stared at me. She seemed to be surprised that I used her name.

"I know who you are, Dahlia," I reassured her. "You live in my building."

"Yes, Ma'am. But I didn't know —" She caught herself before she completed that thought. Then she added, "It is a great neighborhood building, isn't it?"

"It's nice to finally speak to you." I looked directly at this woman I saw every day, but had never been in her world of friends and neighbors.

"Yes, Ma'am." She looked back at my shoulder. "Actually, it doesn't look like an injury. It looks as if something is trying to work its way out of your body."

"Oh Dahlia, that sounds awful." I recoiled at the thought of a foreign body under my skin, trying to emerge to the surface. I thought of the alien beings that possessed the bodies of Earthlings in the old science fiction books I had read.

"You're right, Nurse," Dr. O'Reilly concurred. "I found that very curious."

"Yes, Sir." She turned and started to leave, "Oh, I reviewed her chart, Doctor. Miss Applewait is twenty-four years old now."

"Thank you, Nurse." He turned back to me and patted my shoulder. "Let's carefully remove that sliver. It shouldn't leave any more of a mark than the original vaccination did. Then we will address the issue of your age."

"What issue?" I asked. When Dahlia closed the door again, I whispered, "Tell me about the books."

Dr. O'Reilly's words and his gestures suddenly didn't match. His mouth said, "Well, your age isn't an issue so much as a milestone," but his hands were pantomiming another message. He put his index finger to his lips and then opened his hands like he was holding a book.

I nodded and added. "I had a birthday recently but I didn't know it was any major event."

"Do you need any instruments?" Dahlia intruded over the room's two-way monitor.

Dr. O'Reilly muffled a chuckle. "Thanks Dahlia. No, I have what I need." He applied a cool gauze pad over the site and waited a second. "It will be numb in a moment." He pointed to his watch, threw up six fingers and mimed sipping a cup of coffee. Then he pointed out the window to the low row of buildings across the street beyond the park.

I knew the little coffee shop. I had been there several times. I especially liked the quaint, old-fashioned design of the entire cluster of businesses. I nodded and smiled that I understood.

Dr. O'Reilly covered the spot on my shoulder with an anti-bacterial solution and draped the area in order to keep it sterile. As he approached me with the scalpel, I turned my eyes away. He made a tiny incision and skillfully removed a small piece of something from my shoulder.

"Well, there it is," he offered as he held the object with tweezers. "Are you sure you weren't accosted by a communications monitor? It looks like a little component of some sort."

"No attacks or encounters of any kind." I studied the strange, tiny piece in the doctor's hand. "It looks like a bitty chip, doesn't it? Why on earth would that be in my shoulder?"

"Perhaps your parents had you tagged when you were a small child, to insure a measure of protection against kidnaping."

"Tagged?"

"It evidently is the usual practice with children. I was talking to a pediatrician at lunch the other day. He said he had tagged six babies that morning." Dr. O'Reilly shrugged. "Not being in pediatrics, I wasn't aware of the practice." He started to throw the chip in the hazardous waste container and then stopped. "Do you want this thing? It could be an interesting souvenir."

"Sure. I'll ask my parents about it. It's nice that they may have wanted to keep me safe. I could have it mounted. It'll be a conversation starter. Goodness knows I could use one." I knew my face had become red because I could feel my cheeks grow hot. My books called it blushing.

Dr. O'Reilly cleaned the chip quickly and wrapped it in a clean tissue. "There you are, My Lady." He bowed slightly.

Few people addressed me as Lady Applewait. Silas had. Most people, however, didn't speak to me at all. It was illegal to intrude on the privacy of the Council of Elders and those, like me, who would ascend to that position. I put the tiny piece in my tunic pocket. "Now, what is this about my age?"

"Oh yes," Dr. O'Reilly remembered. "None of us in this practice has treated a Council member before, but bulletins have come through regularly to remind us of the protocol. When Legacy members turn twenty-four, they are to begin a regimen of fresh water, eight glasses a day. Since we have additives in our water system, to purify it and to add necessary nutrients, you are to begin diluting your water supply, flushing out the additives. It seems that Legacy Citizens are not to ingest chemicals of any kind and the little pills will turn your tumbler full into fresh water."

"How?" I asked. "I was never told about this." It all seemed incredible to me. With all the books I have read, I should have read something about diluting the water.

"With every glass of water, you must drop in a highly soluble tablet. This is a fairly new process. It was only begun a few years ago." The doctor went to the cabinet and unlocked a small compartment. "Once the pills are started, you are to get them from the same source, so there is a clear record of your taking them. You will need to come back to see me for refills. They are tiny, so there are a lot in each package." Dr. O'Reilly handed me a small paper envelope full of infinitely small, white tablets.

"What is this all about?" I was beginning to wonder if I had reason to mistrust the doctor.

"As I said, the practice is rather new to this office. I've heard not everyone agrees with the policy. Alister Bedlam is not in favor of the detoxification process."

"Alister Bedlam—the wealthy man who thinks he's the Master of the Universe? How is he involved in all of this?" I was confused. Bedlam was neither Legacy nor a governmental official.

"It is my understanding Alister Bedlam is not in favor of the detoxification process for anyone. So far, his protests have been over ruled by the Council of Elders." The doctor patted my arm.

"Bedlam is always behind the scenes, pulling the strings. That's what great wealth can do for those who are power hungry. At least, that's what I've heard from my grandparents. Bedlam may be the richest man in the world but he isn't Legacy."

"Apparently, the Council of Elders wants to insure that none of the side effects of the additives in the water we all are supposed to drink, affect your body. The Legacy Citizens of your parents' generation began the detox process about four years ago. Even I . . ." Dr. O'Reilly stopped abruptly, then continued. "Bedlam wants everyone to continue with the chemicals, the water additives. He says it is a fair and equal treatment. Up until now, the Council's support of the detoxification program has kept it going." Again, he put his finger to his lips. "Just make sure you put a pill in every glass of water."

I knew the gesture meant that the tablets were important. While I may not have known why I needed to take them, I would follow the doctor's orders. There was something about his manner that caused me to sense the seriousness of the tablets.

"Nurse Dahlia will check you out," Dr. O'Reilly instructed. Then, he tapped his watch and pointed his thumb over his shoulder in the direction of the shops.

I didn't hesitate. I returned the gesture with a nod and a smile.

Before I had time to hop down from the table, Dahlia breezed back in the room. "Here, My Lady, drop one of those tablets in this glass of water before you leave. We are supposed to make sure you begin detoxification immediately." She handed me the glass and added, "Drink all of it. The full effects of the pills build up quickly. You will soon reach the therapeutic level. And, make sure you take them regularly. There can be no drug holidays with these pills. The full detoxification process takes time, so drink it all."

All? Detoxification? I thought to myself and then mumbled, "I didn't know I was *toxified* in the first place."

CHAPTER SIX
The Note

10:30 a.m.

It was a short walk back to the transit stop from the doctor's office. I didn't mind. I had a lot to think about—detoxification—coffee with the young doctor—and Silas Drummond. I was afraid Silas would pop up again, and I looked around anxiously. I didn't see him anywhere and felt some relief. As I sat on the transit waiting bench, I pulled Drummond's note from my bag.

> "Dear Miss Applewait,
> I must talk to you immediately. Be very careful.
> We have been linked together since I tried to contact
> you at the library. I'm sorry. Now, we are both in
> grave danger. You may be the only person who can
> help expose this evil. The entire endless-sleep program
> is a sham!"

What is he talking about? I jammed the paper back in my tote. *I'll read the rest of it later.* Fear crept in again, like a mountain lion that stalks the shadows, waiting for a weakened prey. I had to think. My mind raced in circles, from my grandparents, the doctor, the note, the mountain people from the old video Marge and I had viewed—to the beautiful day.

I looked out over the city below the transit platform and drank in the beauty around me. We were well into December and snow was beginning to cover the distant mountain peaks. The frost that had covered the ground earlier in the morning lingered in the lower spots.

I had missed many seasons while buried away with research for my thesis. Now, I only wanted to enjoy the holiday Gifting lights, and the colors that dance off the glittering frost.

My thoughts went to the video we'd seen, because it had taken place around this time of year. That family had celebrated Thanksgiving and gave thanks to their favorite Deity. Yet, they had so little to be thankful for . . . except love. In November 2112, we too had celebrated what Society has provided for us. So you see, in some ways, we are the same . . . and yet.

I was surprised by the glorious December day. The bright morning sun was warm. I took off my tunic and laid it over the back of the bench. It was not possible that cold weather was upon us . . . but it was.

Lost in my own daydreams, I thought of Dr. Jason O'Reilly and smiled. *Don't be silly,* I admonished myself. *I just met him. We're not even friends, not yet.* When the cross-town transit car arrived, I jumped to my feet and boarded quickly.

"Ma'am," the driver commanded softly, "you didn't pay."

"Pay?" I was confused. I had never been asked to pay for a bus ride. Then I remembered my cloak. "Oh, wait, I left something on the bench." I jumped off the bus and grabbed up my tunic, then skipped back on.

"Oh, I'm sorry Ma'am," the driver corrected himself. "I thought. . . . Please, just have a seat."

I moved past the currency exchange as an older woman quickly got out of her seat. "Here, take my place," she offered. "I'll be getting off soon." Her face was drawn and her color seemed pasty white.

"Thank you." Surprisingly, a feeling of gratitude stirred within me. "Are you all right?" The woman seemed frail. Perhaps she wasn't well. Maybe she was the one who should be sitting.

"Yes, dear," she smiled briefly and then her face fell again as if she remembered something sad.

I started to sit down, then asked again, "Are you sure you're okay?"

"I am sure, thank you," she added, but this time her face was flat, expressionless.

"Maybe you'd better go home and rest. What are your plans today?"

"Plans? I haven't had any plans since my Harold died." The little woman's eyes were empty and distant. I studied the old woman as she moved toward the exit and waited.

At the next station, the woman got off and a young man bounced up the steps. He moved quickly with a spring in his steps. I thought him odd. He had more energy than most people my age. *Everyone else lacks zip, why not this fellow?* The man's eyes met mine, and he didn't look away. Why? People always averted my gaze. It was protocol. Why was he different? He looked familiar but his stares made me feel uncomfortable. I turned to the passing scene beyond the window. The calcium reinforced stone on the passing buildings glistened like jewels as the sun bounced off the surfaces. Regardless of what was out there to see, Silas's words whispered in my ear, "Danger . . . danger!"

I tried to focus on my destination, not the people inside or outside the tram. The trip to the stately old homes on the other side of the city wound past sleeping gardens tucked behind white fences. The orange and yellow mums of the last season had been replaced by red and green Gifting lights that peeked out from brightly decorated windows.

Many of the homes had two stories, a tradition that had been banned in newer construction. Recent structures were designed to occupy a minimal footprint and stood tall against the city's skyline. The multi-family buildings lacked the beauty of the rambling homes that lay on both sides of this street. The old houses reminded me of the home I had seen in the teleplay, large and roomy with space for everyone.

My parents had a single family home that was more modest than these. Mother and Daddy had one large gathering room, a kitchen and eating center, three sleeping cubicles, and two bathing areas. It was quite adequate for them. They both worked long hours. Mother was the Chief of Staff to the Center Chair of the Council of Elders and

Daddy was the Director of the Schools. While most people spent their spare time after work at the Social Centers around town, where they played games and listened to lectures, Mother and Daddy spent quiet evenings with friends and family.

When Legacy Citizens turn twenty-one, after we graduate from University, we move out of our parents' home and into our own apartment where we can begin to live independently and solve our own problems. We are supported by our trusts, but we must work or go to graduate school before taking up a career. It never occurred to me to be thankful for all I had. I was simply entitled.

As the transit passed through the Victorian subdivision of Oakwood, the lines dropped down to ground rails, like a trolley of old. People on wraparound porches smiled and waved at us. Surprisingly, the driver waved back. I guess he felt free to be friendly there. These were my people, Legacy and Council of Elders members. I closed my eyes and enjoyed the renewed sensations of warmth and neighborhood.

"My Lady," the driver prompted, "I think this is your stop."

It was the end of the line. The stop had to be mine. As I walked along, I had the eerie sensation of being watched. I had led such a sheltered life, I was not prepared for this intrigue, and I was frightened.

In my grandparents' block, no one was in adjoining yards that cuddled up to the sidewalk, but the street out front was busier than usual. In the time it took me to walk from the bus stop to my grandparents' front door, two Blue Guard strata-cars drove past slowly. They seemed to be searching for someone as they scanned right and left. I thought of Silas Drummond's letter that was stuffed in my pocket and his desperate warning. We had been seen together earlier and that had frightened him and me. The officers looked right past me and then looked back again. Were they looking for Silas? Or, were they looking for me?

CHAPTER SEVEN
Grand-mère and Grand-père

11:30 a.m.

When I arrived at my grandparents' sidewalk, I just wanted to be inside, away from whatever was happening outside. The neighbor's yard had a pair of stuffed dogs that barked and wagged their tails when I passed. Except for the prowling Blue Guard cars, the stuffy dogs were the only movement in the neighborhood. Even with the warm winter day, no one sat on their porch at the houses around my grandparents' home.

As I walked up the sidewalk, the old house I loved so much seemed to be wrapped in goose down, all soft, comfortable, and warm. The heavy wooden door, with its beveled glass panes down both sides, let light flood the entry beyond. I tapped on the door then opened it with a shove of my hip.

"Christiana!" Grand-mère sang out and threw her arms open to welcome me. She was just crossing the entry hall from the kitchen when I walked in. "I didn't know you were coming."

"I took the chance that the Council of Elders wasn't meeting today Grand-mère. I wanted to visit the two of you. Where is Grand-père?" I looked around the familiar room where the family had gathered each December for Gift-giving. It was a joyous holiday when we thought of ways to please other people rather than cater to ourselves. Gifting Day was full of promise and joy.

"Come, Baby, sit here with me." Grand-mère patted the sofa beside her as she sat down. "Grand-père is puttering in his garden out back, clearing away the dead plants that gave up blooming several weeks ago."

I snuggled close to her. She always smelled like flower petals or cinnamon and other spices, a sign that her cookie jar was full. For me, that cookie canister was a symbol of Grand-mère's love for her family and neighbors.

"Now you stay right here and I'll bring us some lemonade and a plate of cookies. I just made some this morning." Grand-mère patted my hand and hurried toward the kitchen.

Sometimes, I felt a little guilty for being closer to my grandparents than to my own mother and father. But, Grand-mère was able to demonstrate so much more love than Mother did. I guess Grand-mère had memories from the old ways that Mother never experienced, just like the story I had seen on the small screen that morning. Grand-mère's love oozed from every love pat and hug.

I am sure Mother felt that she was loved as she grew up. Grand-mère was always Grand-mère. But, Society was severe in their edicts on demonstrations of affections. During those years, when Mother was a child, people were told to drink plenty of water. I thought about that as I waited for the cookie tray. But, Dr. O'Reilly said the detoxification tablets were only started four years ago. So Mother had been exposed to the water everyone drank all of her life, into middle-age. If the pills dilute the additives, I wondered what the chemicals did to people's bodies, including hers. When I was small, my mother and father would have been fully medicated. Now, there was evidently a reversal of thought, at least for Legacy Citizens. According to Dr. O'Reilly's timetable, my parents would have probably undergone that transformation in the last few years. They would have begun detoxification after I was already out of their home and on my own. As I think about it now, I guess I had noticed a change in my parents. They were warmer, more loving, more interested and attentive.

As a child, I had my grandparents, the generation that was not medicated. I know how fortunate I was. None of my friends still had their grandparents. Most of the older generation had already gone into the never-ending-sleep, which made me think of Silas Drummond again. What was his note trying to tell me?

"What brings you way over here?" my grandmother asked as she came back with the treats, eager to entertain. Those in her neighborhood rarely had drop-in visitors.

The Oakwood area wasn't banned, but casual sightseeing in the neighborhood was discouraged. All of the Council of Twelve lived in that section of town. Their privacy was strongly protected. Among my grandparents' neighbors were high-ranking government people, bankers, all those, whose Length of Days extended beyond that of the common person.

"I've been thinking Grand-mère. At the end of the month, right after Gift-giving Day, you and Grand-père turn seventy-five."

"Yes, dear . . . seventy-five."

"How old were your great-grandparents when they died?" I was cautious. I wasn't sure how she felt about the inevitable which was to come.

"Christiana, you're worried about the never-ending-sleep aren't you?" Grand-mère moved closer and took my hand. "It is a natural occurrence. It's not something to worry about."

"It is not natural. I've read enough books to know there is nothing natural about it. Today, someone called it a sham."

"A sham? What on earth are you talking about?"

"Oh, I don't know. Somebody just . . ." I hadn't finished reading Silas's message, so there was little more that I could say. "Grand-mère, it's important to me. Truthfully, do you know how old your great-grandparents were when they entered the sleep?"

"The truth? Honey . . . well, some day you will be a member of the Twelve. I guess there are things you need to know. Let me see. Both of my great-grandparents were still living when I was small. Great-Grandma died when she was, ah, eighty-seven and Great-Grandpa was ninety-one."

"Died? I've read about dying. That's when they just . . . pass on, isn't it. My friend Rachel fell from a top terrace and ceased to live. She must have died too because she didn't enter the permanent sleep chamber." I knew Rachel's passing was different from most. People my age were so sheltered and protected, they rarely died an accidental death and most diseases had been eradicated.

"Yes, Honey, but back then, when they just . . . died, sometimes people suffered with physical maladies and serious illnesses. They may have been in pain and . . . no one would want that."

"Grand-mère, would you rather have no pain or live more years with Grand-père?"

"Sweetheart, I would rather be unable to walk or be in constant pain, than to lose one precious moment with your dear grandfather." My grandmother's eyes glowed as they often did when she spoke of Grand-père.

"I'm going to research the never-ending-sleep. It's new to society. I have . . . well . . . I've read many books. Across eons of time, there was never something like the never-ending-sleep. It wasn't imposed until the last one hundred years. It is not natural. It is calculated murder."

"Christiana!" Grand-mère gasped. "Don't let anyone hear you say such a thing."

I could see the fear in her eyes. "I cannot just wait for you two to be . . . terminated, Grand-mère. I have to do something."

"It won't be in time, Honey. We will be seventy-five in two weeks, after Gift-giving time."

"It has to be in time! You have a right to live as long as you can. I saw an old document in the library Grand-mère. It read in part, *We hold these truths to be self-evident, that all men are created equal, that we are endowed by our Creator with certain inalienable rights that among them are life, liberty, and the pursuit of happiness.* We have a right to life, Grand-mère, an inalienable right, a right that cannot be repudiated. Our *creator* gave us that right. Now, Grand-mère, please tell me, who is the creator? I will contact him." I picked up her hand, pressed it to my lips and silently pleaded for the answer.

"Christiana, it is forbidden, dear. I . . ."

"But, I'm Legacy, Grand-mère. I'm supposed to grow in wisdom and wisdom requires as much knowledge as can be learned in a lifetime."

"Christiana, I . . . it's been so long since Great-Grandpa told me about God." She seemed to search for words again. "He said . . . if you seek God, he will come in and make his home within you.

"He said that the creator is . . . God, the Holy One, he who created everything, even you and me. God is *other*, not anything within our understanding. He is the all-in-all and his most precious gift to all of us, is a reverence for life, for he is Life."

"Where can I find him Grand-mère? Maybe he will tell me how to reverse this terrible edict of Society." I had to know where he lived. God may have been the only one who would have known how to accomplish what seemed impossible.

Grand-mère smiled sweetly. "He lives in the *other* place, Honey, just as he is *other*."

"Other what?" I couldn't fit it all into my unstretched, unpracticed, untouched mind.

I was overwhelmed with all the new information, but maybe I already knew. Something or someone had been tugging at my heart for months as I read the old books. It was a force that was strong enough to call to me from the pages of man's writing and move within my being, like a fog that overtakes a meadow of wild flowers and blankets it, while doing no harm, then leaves a light nourishing mist on the surface of all that lives there.

"What more did Great-grandfather tell you," I pressed.

"Great-grandfather taught me about the ways of the Lord. He told me . . . ," Grand-mère hesitated but she seemed to want to tell me all she knew. Finally, she went on, "There is a special book about him—God—but all those books were destroyed, their contents long forgotten. Great-grandfather had much of it memorized and quoted from it often." Grand-mère looked away from me. "No," she began again quietly, "that's wrong. They weren't all destroyed. Society had entrusted a copy of the book with Great-grandfather since he was the great philosopher, the Wisest One."

"Grand-mère, if he was so wise why did he vote to institute the Length of Days policy?"

"He did not vote for it, Honey. He cast a black ball, not a white. But, the *yeas* won out. There is nothing that can be done now." Again, Grand-mère seemed to accept the inevitable.

"Maybe there is, Grand-mère. What about the book you talked about and the old Bill of Rights? I just know there is something." I could not accept the required sleep. Exposed to life through the old volumes and the harmless teleplay I had watched earlier in the day, hope had begun to take root in my heart. I felt an awakening of my spirit that somehow felt familiar, but I couldn't remember having experienced it before. It was like being surrounded by a sweet life-force that I neither understood nor could describe.

"Let's go into the study, my dear," my grandmother offered as she rose and steadied herself. Large wooden pocket doors, which vanished into the wall and reappeared with a pull on the recessed ring of a brass plate, were parted for the two of us to enter. "Over here," she directed.

I followed her into the wonderful old office with its elegant oak desk. Shelves of books that reached from floor to ceiling stretched around the entire room. "You haven't let me come in here very often," I whispered in awe.

"Now that will have to change, won't it Christiana."

"Why now, Grand-mère? I have been Legacy since I was born."

"Yes, dear, but now you are twenty-four years old. You've started your detoxification process, haven't you?" She asked as though she already knew.

"Yes, in fact, I came here from Dr. O'Reilly's office. I had this thing on my shoulder."

"What *thing* on your shoulder?" My grandmother seemed concerned. My health and well-being were important to all.

"There was something in my vaccination site. It turned out to be no big deal. More curious than anything. Dr. O'Reilly removed it." I reached in my pocket and pulled out the tissue containing the small piece he had returned to me.

"Christiana, that looks like your chip. That was not to be removed." Grandma Constance picked up the piece from my hand and turned it over. "Jason O'Reilly should have known better than to remove the chip. He's Legacy too. This little chip contains the proof of your linage."

I was surprised and amused. The doctor almost bowed in my presence and all along, he was Legacy too? "Dr. O'Reilly is a Privileged Citizen? Why didn't he tell me?"

"With you, Legacy identifies your position. With Jason, his occupational title hides his privileged status. Rather than Lord O'Reilly, he is by education and examination, Dr. O'Reilly. As a physician, he should have known not to remove the chip."

"Have all physicians been trained to know about the device?" I folded the little piece over in the tissue and replaced it in the pocket of my cloak.

"Well, perhaps I'm wrong. I may have been too harsh on Dr. O'Reilly. I imagine only the pediatricians would need to know, since the chip is implanted in an infant immediately after birth." She paused for a moment in her conversation while she searched the upper book shelves. "I only know that everyone is supposed to have one. It's like a permanent census card." She stopped and held the back of her neck as she craned to see the books on the top shelf near the ceiling. "There it is. Christiana, would you climb up there and fetch it down? It's a little beyond my reach these days, my dear."

"Sure," I offered and pulled the library ladder over that was attached to a track that ran along the ceiling and in front of the shelves of books. From the higher elevation as I climbed the rungs, another thought struck me. "Grand-mère, how does it happen that you and Grand-père were both of Legacy Linage?"

"Well, I don't really know," she responded slowly. "Over a little to your left, dear. It's that black leather book between the two red volumes." I fingered the book spines and then she exclaimed excitedly, "That's it." She watched for a moment then added. "Your grandfather was the only man I was ever attracted to. Just Oliver

Richly. He made my socks droop."

"Grand-mère!" I gasped and laughed until I nearly dropped the book.

"Christiana, have you never met a man who absolutely turned your heart into a field full of butterflies?"

"Not yet, Grand-mère." Then, the face of Jason O'Reilly flashed before my eyes and I began to giggle. "Why are we talking about this?" I laughed out loud. As I descended the ladder and handed the book to my grandmother, I felt the warmth of a blush.

"We're discussing this topic, because you asked . . . sort of." Grand-mère took the book to the brown leather sofa that sat in front of the window. I smiled as I thought of my cozy spot in the library.

"Yes, this is it. I've never read it but Great-grandfather told me it had been a very popular book at one time." She took a handkerchief from her pocket and dusted off the cover. After patting it for a moment, she handed it to me. "Now you must protect it. Great-grandfather said it is sacred. This is the one book that Alister Bedlam has not only banned but has also attached the punishment of imprisonment on anyone who possesses it."

"Bedlam? Grand-mère, he's not in the government. What does he have to do with decisions that impact all the rest of us?"

"Oh, Christiana, he has never been elected but he pulls the strings. He's like the supreme head of a shadow government that influences all aspects of life without ever holding office."

"You said, *prison,* Grand-mère. One could go to prison for just possessing this book. I don't like the sound of that. Besides, I thought the prisons had been emptied a long time ago."

Grand-mère leaned toward me and lowered her voice. "There is one prison, outside of our zone, that houses . . . political detainees."

"Political prisoners? You mean, owning this book could threaten the very fabric of our government?" My mind raced. "As docile as people are in this Age of Silence, how could anyone be a threat? Besides, you've had the book a long time. You and Grand-père have been safe."

"That's what I am hoping, for you," she whispered. "It is absolutely necessary that this book lives on. I am so sorry, my dear, that I have to pass it on to you. But you're the only one I can trust. Besides, no one else in your world will know of its importance."

"Thank you Grand-mère, for your confidence in me. I'll protect it." I thought for a moment. "I'll need to find a safe place for it."

"It may be safe out in the open but above or below eye level, as we have stored it."

"Did Grand-père read the book?" I wondered out loud.

"No, I —"

A familiar voice joined the conversation from the door. "Yes, I have read the book, several times, and replaced it in the same spot after each reading." Oliver Richly removed his wide-brimmed gardening hat and slapped it across his leg.

"Oliver, dear, the dust," Constance scolded softly.

"I'm sorry, Honey. *Dust to dust,* some people say. If people were really passing through on dust beams, I guess we would all have to stop using the vacuum cleaner." He smiled and winked his eye. Then his voice softened and his eyes shone with a spirit of light.

"Christiana, dear," he began as he took my hand that cradled the precious book, "promise that you will read it word for word, chapter by chapter, cover to cover. And, when you've finished, read it a second time, for a clearer meaning and greater understanding."

"I will, Grand-père. I promise." His words charged me with the power of purpose.

"Oliver? Why didn't you tell me you read the book? Would I have liked it?" She sounded surprised, hurt, as if her love had betrayed her heart.

"Oh Connie, you would have loved it. But, you saw me reading it many times. Since you didn't say anything, I didn't push it on you." Grand-père was taken aback. "I never intended to leave you out."

"Perhaps, I should leave the book with you Grand-mère, until you've had a chance to read it." I was embarrassed. It felt like I was taking something of great value from my own grandmother who had only weeks to live.

"No, no, Christiana," Grand-père corrected, "you must take it. And, you cannot reveal anything about what I'm about to say."

"Of course," I said as layers of intrigue piled up like cordwood around me.

"My dears," Grand-père's voice lowered to a whisper, "I made a copy of the book a few years ago when we still had access to personal copy machines."

"You mean you actually had a copier here in the house? I don't think I remember that. Why are those things no longer available to everyone?" I asked.

"When the country converted the energy source from electricity, they said it wasn't fair that everyone should have to buy a new computing machine and printer. And, since everyone's personal space is much smaller than it used to be, they decided to have computing centers for communication and use the home models exclusively for gaming. It seemed reasonable at the time."

"And now?" I couldn't imagine why decreased reading and communication would be considered something to be praised.

"I don't know any more. It seems like people have lost interest in life, in each other, in everything," my grandfather admitted, but had no explanation for the phenomenon.

"*They* said? Grand-père, who are *they*?"

"The government, honey. The Council of Elders only advises the government. The decisions belong to the governmental officials unless it is a constitutional issue."

Then his eyes brightened again and he added, "You take this one." He patted the leather bound book in my hand with reverence. "And, I have something for you, dear." He pulled a manuscript from a high shelf and handed it to Grand-mère. "You may have this one Connie."

I cradled the book in my arms and drew it to my chest. It seemed precious to me, at least that's the impression I got from my grandfather and I believed him. "I'll have a safe installed in my apartment."

"No!" both of my grandparents admonished me at once. "They will suspect you're hiding something."

"They?" Their sudden outburst startled me.

"Society . . . the government. It would be best if you put it in a grocery sack and simply carried it into your building along with vegetables and fruits. You can remove it from the sack and put it somewhere in your apartment. When you move over to this end of town, they won't be curious. They wouldn't dare. The homes of the Council of Elders are off limits."

Grand-père gave me a hug and kissed my forehead. It felt like he was anointing me as I ascended into the Lower Council where future members are exposed to the vast wealth of knowledge available to the few.

"Gotta run, Sweeties. I have an appointment," I chuckled and started toward the door.

"A meeting?" Grand-mère questioned.

I thought for a moment and wondered if I should reveal my afternoon coffee time with an interesting man. "I'm meeting Dr. O'Reilly in a while for a cup of coffee, and I want to take this book home first."

"Here's a little shopping bag, Honey." Grand-mère offered one from the corner of the desk. "I brought a new pillow home in it. Put the book in here," she offered. "We'll get some celery and apples to put on top of it." Then she smiled mischievously, "You're meeting Jason O'Reilly for coffee?"

"I'll get the food camouflage while you two have some girl-talk," Grand-père winked.

I studied the impish look on my grandmother's face. "Now, don't make something out of this," I laughed softly. "It's just coffee."

"Yes, dear," she agreed but it sounded like she was only humoring me. "I'll try not to ask any questions."

"There isn't anything to say, Grand-mère. I just met the man this morning," I protested.

"But, you're having coffee with him already, my dear. It seems to me like there is something to say. If nothing else, you could say, 'He seems like a very nice man.'"

"Okay Grand-mère—Dr. O'Reilly seems like a very nice man." As we laughed together, the giggles warmed my heart. I knew how much I will miss our time together once Grand-mère enters the sleep.

"Here you are." Grand-père returned with the food and placed it in my sack. Then he did something he had never done before. He placed his right hand on the top of my head. "Now, may the peace and safety of the Lord go with you, my child."

I felt blessed and overcome with awe. I didn't want to leave. I wanted to stay in the glow I was feeling. But, time was moving on. I breezed back through the house with the musical laughter of my grandparents tickling my ears from the warmly paneled office. *Those two Rascals, they are probably in their hugging and laughing with the sheer joy of life. I have so much to learn.*

As I stepped out onto the porch and started down the walk, another strata-car pulled to a stop and then the driver-side window opened. "Excuse me Ma'am. We're looking for a man in a red car that has darkly tinted windows. Have you seen the vehicle or the man?" The Blue Guardsman asked.

"No," I answered but that one word caught in my throat like a seed and I could scarcely breathe. *They are talking about Silas Drummond. They're looking for him. He's in danger. I may not be safe either.*

There was something to fear and I didn't know what it was. As the squad car moved on, I turned for one last look at Grand-mère and Grand-père's stately old home and wondered where my family would gather next year on Gift-giving Day. I had to find a way to save them. *I want them around forever, and if not forever, then when their bodies wear out, not when they wear out their time.*

CHAPTER EIGHT

Inspector Stoner

Out on the streets, other forces bustled about the city. It was the season that brought most people out of their little apartment cubicles and into the world of shops with holiday trappings. Extra police were on patrol. The masses had to be supervised.

An official Blue Guard, four-wheeler strata-car, with a unique black stripe down the side, passed by one of the many transit entrances. The strata-car windows were tinted black and the whole thing had a dark, menacing look, like a rolling crypt. But the strata-car was no burial place. The vehicle had multilayers of assault and defense technology that made it nearly impenetrable and unstoppable.

Busy, busy, busy little people, the strata driver mocked. Inspector Tombstone was what his men called him, never to his face, but he knew it. Inspector Stoner would never have permitted it. He stared blankly at the holiday shoppers as they passed. *A bunch of rusty robots, every one of them,* he mumbled to himself. *How can they drag about like lazy mice in a maze?*

He had been driving around all morning. With Gifting Day not far off, security had been increased in town. And now there was this business of Silas Drummond going AWOL at work. Drummond had to be found. Everyone, from boot officers to Ward Stoner, the Chief Inspector of the Blue Guard, was on the streets.

Most people were afraid of the Blue Guard and crossed to the other side of the street when they encountered one. The officers' behavior was just too unpredictable. One day they might help a child up the steps to the transit platform, another day they might not be helpful at all and could even be abusive. If the walk-paths were congested, a member of the elite division thought nothing of jabbing someone in the ribs with a prodding stick to move them aside. If accused of a crime, a handcuffed person could arrive at Guard Headquarters bloody and broken. Now, during the holidays, even the Guard had joined with the regular police patrol and Inspector Tombstone didn't like it one bit. He was above having to deal with babysitting women in shopping cart brawls.

He gripped the steering wheel tightly and stirred restlessly on the seat. He saw a young family begin to cross the street and turned on the siren, as much to scare them, as to hurry them along. *That's right—take your time,* he groaned sarcastically. *There's always somebody dragging their sorry carcass across the street, getting in everybody's way. Why don't they stay at home in their tired little apartment if they can't move about the streets with more power than that?* The chief inspector of the Blue Guard sneered at the world around him.

"Inspector?" His communication device interrupted his thoughts.

"Of course," he snapped back.

"I'm sorry to break into your patrol, but there's no one else to send. There has been some sort of situation on a Public Transit car this morning."

Stoner sighed and pulled away from the curb. As he listened to the details, he headed toward Capitol Square.

When he arrived up town at the City Transit office, Ward Stoner—skilled detective and Chief of the Blue Guard's entire investigative division—burst through the door with the might of one who had no problem seizing authority. He had no time to waste and was in no mood for nonsense. He was a man ruled by his own power. Power was his master and he controlled others by the strength of that small Kingdom of Stoner, his own world, his own power, his own rules. No one got in his way.

Stoner burst through the door of the transit system office. He would make the frivolous stop but he didn't have to like it. "What is all of this about?" His question was crisp. His tone was bored.

"Yes, Sir." The woman in the outer office jumped to her feet. "Follow me, please," she said as she led the way through a swinging gate that separated the inner rooms from the public space, then down a hall to the manager's office. The woman entered the room first and attempted to introduce the Chief to the transit line manager. "Mr. Munson, the Inspect—"

"Stoner," the Inspector interrupted. "We are nearly upon Gift-giving Day and you have me running around chasing a—a what—a ghost?" Stoner laughed rudely as though his time could be better spent somewhere else, doing almost anything besides talking to Munson.

"I don't know what it was, Sir," Munson whispered as he shooed the woman out of his office. He checked the hall for eavesdroppers and motioned to a chair for his guest.

Stoner waved him off and remained standing. "I have no time to get comfortable." He squared his shoulders and tried to remain calm in a situation that was making him more irritated by the moment. He blinked his eyes three times, tilted his head to the side and worked his jaw with gritting anger. "Again, speak up Mister. What is this all about? Invisible intruders? Maybe it's the jolly Gift Giver." Once more, his jaw tensed and he ground away at apparently nothing, except Munson's tired explanation.

"Sir," Munson stood up, leaned his knuckles on the desk and stared the inspector in the eyes. "I do not know what was there. I am reporting a . . . situation."

"Well now," Stoner drew out his words in mocking disbelief. "Why don't you tell me about the . . . situation?"

"My driver on the midtown line called in a strange . . . situation. I'm sorry, Sir. I don't know what else to call it."

"Go on . . . ." the inspector's boredom was evident in his voice. He wanted information, not irrelevant details and he wanted it faster than it was being delivered.

"The driver reported that a woman boarded a bus this morning and didn't set off the buzzer, just a . . . swish . . . you know . . . a . . . swish . . . like when a cat passes in front of a sensor."

"A cat . . ." Stoner could feel his pulse beating behind his eyes and knew his blood pressure was rising. He was wasting time. He still had a few Gift Day presents left to buy and time was running out.

"Sir . . . you are making me feel a little foolish. I was ordered to report any irregularities." The manager stood as tall as he could. What power he didn't have in authority, he seemed to be trying to make up for in height.

"Go on," Stoner moaned. His jaw flexed as his eyes darted from the window to Munson and back again.

"A cat . . . or a dog . . . anything other than a person makes when it passes." Munson cleared his throat. "The driver said that a woman got on the bus and didn't set off a buzz, just a swish, and then got off to get something she forgot. When she got back on, the buzzer sounded like it was supposed to. He didn't think anything more about it, but he thought he'd better report it when he got to the end of the line." Munson said his piece and waited.

Stoner's eyes snapped back at Munson. "Did he check the mechanism? Was it defective? There has to be a more logical answer than a *swish*."

"He pulled the bus into the garage so we could check it out. There was nothing. The tone trigger worked just fine." Munson crossed his arms. "We have done our job here, Sir."

"Did he say who the passenger was?" Stoner didn't acknowledge Munson's unspoken message. *Now you do your job* seemed buried beneath the surface. The Inspector didn't take orders from anyone.

"The driver said he was busy this morning and couldn't say for sure who it was."

Inspector Stoner gripped his hat in his hands several times, then, controlling himself again, he smoothed it with his fingers. "It happened only one time and yet, he was too unobservant to notice who the patron was."

"He noticed that it happened but not who it was, Sir. That's why he reported it." Munson's teeth sounded clenched.

Stoner ignored the man's mounting anger and walked toward the door. "You did the right thing, Munson. I'll look into it." He started to leave without looking back, then turned and shook the man's hand. Stoner respected a man who could hold his own in a good argument.

He shook his head and tried to clear his thinking. *No guilt here. Toughness is what's needed, what's always needed*, he thought. He had to remain hard and rigid on the job. He was sure, if he didn't use fear to intimidate others, he would lose the power that came with his office. He battled with himself daily. One side of his head was at war with the other, as if good whispered in one ear and evil writhed in the other. *Chatter on—I will win this battle.*

CHAPTER NINE

The Horror in the Note

1:30 p.m.

After leaving my grandparents' home, I rode the transit back to my apartment, but I couldn't focus on the city as it passed. *There is that same man again.* I was very uneasy with his constant presence. *He was on the bus earlier today. His stares make me feel uncomfortable. He didn't even look away when I caught him looking at me. Does he know I'm carrying the secret book?* A chill over took me, and I shuddered. I could not appear anxious or secretive. No one could have known that I was carrying a banned volume. I had to make sure my behavior and attitude didn't create suspicion. I tried to ignore the man and maintained an empty gaze out the window.

Rather than being concerned with the scenes as they passed, or the penetrating gaze of the other riders, I was caught up in the words and images I had just experienced at my grandparents' home. I was determined to do whatever I had to do, to find a solution for overturning the Length of Days policy that would seal their inevitable fate.

As I thought of the Length of Days policy, I pulled Silas's note from my bag and picked up reading where I left off.

"The entire endless sleep program is a sham!
Lady Applewait, people either reach their allotted days,
are ill or injured, and then are told they will enter into
an endless sleep. Some people actually believe they will

be awakened at some time in the future. Some have even
left a wake-up-call for a specific date and time. They
thought they were staying in a fine hotel. The saddest
people, My Lady, are the ones who would have healed
on their own but are told they will heal more quickly if
they take a long nap. All of those people, the timed-out,
the sick and the tricked, have the same fate. Ma'am, they
are taken alive to the mountain where they are placed in
the furnaces and their ashes are disposed of."

I gagged on the words and fear rose in my throat like vomit. I
wanted to scream, but I knew people would be watching me. I had to
hold myself together. The man on the front seat stared at me intently
as I tried to control the waves of sickening nausea. I trembled at the
thought of the danger the information had put me in and the fate
awaiting Grand-mère and Grand-père. I had to finish reading the note,
but I also had to control myself. I breathed in and out slowly several
times. I wasn't finished with the letter. What more could Silas have
written?

"Their bones," Drummond continued, "are ground into
calcium powder that is used in the mortar of our
buildings and epoxied into large chunks for carving
statues and other works of art. Please, My Lady, I
didn't know anyone else I could tell. You are the only
one who can stop this abomination. I will contact you at
the apartment building soon.
Respectfully,
Silas Drummond"

No, I whispered bitterly. *It is all a lie!* I had to regain composure.
Control, calm, peace—I repeated it over and over. Suddenly I felt a
light touch on my shoulder. The little boy who sat with his mother on
the opposite seat patted my shoulder.

"Don't cry, Miss," he soothed. "It'll be all right."

I buried the note in my tote again and wiped my eyes. "Yes,
honey, I think it will be." I jumped up, eager to get away where I
would not be observed. I patted the boy on the head with a sincere,
"Thank you." Then it was my stop, and I bounded quickly from the

transit.

I know it's not true. It can't be true. I will get to the bottom of it. I'll track Silas down. He'll pay for this. If I find it is true, if this evil exists, I'll absolutely do something. What? I don't know . . . but something.

CHAPTER TEN
A New Way of Being

2:00 p.m.

I ran from the transit and down the platform staircase with Silas's note in my bag and Grand-père's precious book held tightly in the sack with the vegetables. Near the entrance to my residential building, I heard a faint whimper coming from the shadows under a low bush near the door.

"Well, what's this?" The little puddle of fur was not much larger than my hand. "A real kitten," I marveled as I stroked the fur. For a brief moment, I was transported from the danger I was in. "I never noticed any of you little mouse patrollers before. Where did you come from?" As I picked her up, I looked around, but no one was nearby.

I walked to the corner and looked down the side street for a possible cat owner in search of a kitten. No one.

"Amazing," I purred to the little creature in my arms. "I never knew your kind would be so soft and cuddly." I had never held a kitten before. Her fur was as smooth as the silkweed from the grassy meadow behind Grand-mère's house. As I petted the kitten's head and belly, a quiet calmness came over me.

I knew the kitten's ancestors had been feral for decades, but I wanted to keep it. "I don't think you'll eat much. Would you like to come home with me?" I whispered. The little creature nestled in the crook of my arm, balanced on top of the grocery sack with the precious book inside. Carefully, I carried her into my building.

My mind raced, one thought canceled out the other. The kitten was soft and cuddly, a stark contrast to the rage that coursed through my body. A new purpose flooded my mind. Emotions I had never known before collided and demanded my full attention. I felt terrified and energized at the same time. Despite the vileness of the information Silas had passed on to me, a feeling of joy mingled with fear and disgust. Courage had ridden in on the back of all that anger. I was determined. I would do something to help my grandparents.

As I walked through the apartment lobby, I felt exposed. Maybe I had been reckless, drawing attention to myself with the kitten. I felt sure the people around me could see the entire contents of my bag with x-ray vision. I knew that made no sense, but my insides knotted like a Gifting bow. I was relieved when everything in the lobby seemed cheery. Colored lights and a festive wreath hung from the walls. Everything looked brighter, more vivid. The biggest change must have been within me.

How can so many opposing feelings survive in one mind? Tender feelings, fear, anger, hope, courage. And just as amazing, I have a new energy. It felt as if I could actually fly or I'd fly apart from the tornado of emotions within me.

"Hi, Mrs. LaGassi," I sang out as I passed a longtime resident of the modest building.

"Good afternoon Ma'am," the woman responded. She appeared startled that I had noticed her along the way.

"How is your son, Tony? He was sick, wasn't he?" I stopped for a moment with my foot in the elevator door and continued to enjoy my contact with the middle-aged woman.

"Yes, he was, but, I wasn't aware that you knew. He is much better now. Thank you for asking," Mrs. LaGassi added with an air of surprise.

"You tell him, I like the hat he had on the other day. They used to call those, ball caps." I stepped onto the lift and continued to hold the door with my foot. "Baseball was a game they used to play, on teams, with other players . . . outside . . . in the field."

"Oh," was all the woman could say as the elevator door closed.

All the way up to the tenth floor my mood was erratic. It was a strange experience. My insides rattled. I understood the fear and anger, but they were mixed with good feelings as well. Pounding waves of emotions rolled within me. *I'll research these symptoms when I get back to the library. My books will tell me what I need to know.* I looked at my timepiece. It was already a little after 2:00 p.m.

I pushed the door to my apartment open and entered my sanctuary, my sweet solitude from the world. The kitten scampered playfully around the kitchen when I put her down. The white furry ball of fuzz wrapped her body around, in and out and through my legs.

"I think I'll call you Shakespeare," I said. "No one now knows who Shakespeare was, so you'll be my own private bit of culture in a dull and drab world." I poured her a little saucer of milk as my mind darted to what the events of that day could mean. *First, this book must be hidden.* But the other . . . *I don't know what to do with Silas's note.*

Gripping fear clouded the outer edges of my mind, as I went to my desk and research area. *Where should I put this strange Bible? My friends have never understood about me and my love of books. They thought I was nuts for having any of them. Now, I'm even crazier for bringing a banned book into my home. A banned book, a banned cat, and a note that could inflame a revolution. Citizens' lack of interest may be the very thing that will protect me from the danger I could be facing.*

My collection of books was innocent enough. Many of them were a group of uninteresting volumes about rules and policies of the Populous. Yesterday, I felt privileged to have four rows of unimportant books. Now, they had become the very camouflage to conceal the book that held such mystery and danger.

My communication instrument flashed its blinking light. "Hello?"

"Christiana, dear —"

"Grand-mère! Twice in one day, how wonderful!"

"My dear, I have been so worried about you since you left."

"Worried? Why?"

"The . . . the box of candy we gave you today, dear. Possessing chocolate is very dangerous for you—it could draw in neighbors you don't even know." She spoke in code and faked a little chuckle. "Have you hidden the box as we said?"

My mind raced to catch up. Grand-mère was talking about the Bible. The communications line—it may not be secure. We would not know who could be listening. "I was just about to."

"Where, Sweetheart?"

"Well," my stomach started to tighten and my heart pounded. Where was I going to hide the Bible and how could I tell Grand-mère, to ease her mind, without revealing much? "I was just going to shelve it in the pantry. Maybe I'll wrap the box in brown paper and put it behind Great-grandpa's favorite cereal. No one would see it or know it's there."

"Yes, yes . . . no, wait —"

"Grand-mère, you're frightening me."

"I'm sorry." Her voice became low and full of regret. "Maybe we shouldn't have given the candy to you."

"No, it'll be all right. It will be well hidden behind my other foods."

"But, what if someone finds the box wrapped in paper? If it's discovered, then they'll wonder why it's so important that it needed to be camouflaged and concealed."

"Oh, Grand-mère." Fear gripped my chest like a vice. "What's in that candy?" I couldn't believe my grandparents would have had anything vile or sinister.

"Christiana, it is a box of chocolates full of love and promises."

"Love? What's so subversive about love?" Fear and joy clanged inside me, both at the same time. All of my new emotions were bombarding my mind with contradictory messages.

"Love, my dear, can change the world, even more surely than the arms of war. You must be careful. Chocolate is the stuff that inspires revolution." Grand-mère tried to sound light and bubbly but there was an intensity in her manner that let me know her concern.

"Mutiny? Grand-mère . . . anarchy? In that box of chocolate?" I laughed nervously.

"A revolution of the heart, sweetheart. Just hide it well. Perhaps out in the open is still the best place to put it. Just another box of food among many. Besides, most people have no interest in sweets anymore. Anyone who visits won't even see it."

I wanted to ask her more about the never-ending-sleep. But, it wasn't safe to talk about such things over the communication lines. I decided not to question her but imagined what Grand-mère would say.

"Sleep dear. Just a very long sleep," is all that she would say. I dared not ask her more.

"Well okay, Grand-mère. It was nice talking to you. I'm fine. Everything will be all right. Bye-bye."

Grand-mère didn't know the horror that Silas wrote about. *It must be a lie*, I told myself.

I sat down in front of the large window and watched the day. Some of the Gifting lights were on even though it was the middle of the day. Still, they were beautiful. I sat there and allowed my mind to empty of all of the evil images Silas's note had imprinted on my mind.

• • • • •

I have no idea how long I had napped. But, I felt a little better when I awakened. Still, I had to hide the book.

I looked over my shelves of books for a good spot to place the leather edition. On the top shelf, to the left, was a series of leather bound philosophy books my great-grandfather had written. I had been so proud of the volumes. I had always thought of them as objects of beauty or artful room decorations. Now, something had changed within me.

"I'll devour every page right after Gifting Season, Shakespeare," I mumbled to the scampering toenail tapper in the otherwise silent room. "I want to know the legacy he left to me, and not just to me. He had willed it to all of us."

I pushed the book that was shelved beside the set of six, farther down the shelf, and placed the precious one I had just brought home on the shelf beside them. At a quick glance, it looked like a cluster of seven, rather than six, and would go unnoticed, certainly by the uninterested eyes of my friends who usually passed unaware. It had to go unseen.

Possessing revolutionary materials would have meant an indictment for treason. Although no one is allowed to violate the privacy of a Legacy Citizen or enter their living space without the written consent of a zone judge, they often did. My hands trembled as I thought about the gravity of the situation I was in. I had to know what threat waited within its pages. Why was it banned? What made it precious? *I'll begin reading it later,* I promised myself.

Even while Grand-mère's frightening words still hung in my mind, I felt I had to avoid facing them as I always had. *I'll quickly splash some water over my face and apply a small dab of lip rouge. At least I'll feel refreshed.* I started toward the sink and then I thought of Dr. O'Reilly and decided to apply a little color to my cheeks as well.

I fumbled with the compact that refused to open. "Oh, stop it, Christiana," I snapped at myself out loud, but my hands would not stop shaking. Their trembling only made me more anxious—I was anxious over being anxious. In my usual form, I tried to ignore my fear.

"You are being melodramatic," I admonished myself. Life simply isn't that deep or complicated. "Who do you think you are— some international spy?" I grumbled into the mirror. "Don't make yourself that important at a time like this. Fear won't be your credentials, but it may be your undoing. Snap out of it. Get some courage." Trepidation continued to fight a battle for my mind, so I chose to focus on happier thoughts. As I applied the lip rouge and brushed some color over my cheeks, I remembered blushing in the doctor's presence without the help of cosmetics, and for a moment, I smiled to myself. Then, I remembered the seriousness of my task.

I'll hurry over to the library and begin researching the subject of death. I also want to review the change that was made to our laws regarding the Length of Days policy. There will still be enough time to meet Dr. O'Reilly at 6:00 at the Demitasse Coffee Shop. I grabbed my tunic and darted out the door, relying on my name and position alone to protect the Bible book. *No one is allowed to violate the privacy of a Legacy Citizen—yet rules have been broken.*

CHAPTER ELEVEN
Seeable but Unheard

3:30 p.m.

On board the Public Transit, again, I moved to the first seat, sat down and resumed my gaze out the window. The scenery that passed outside was very different in that part of town from the picturesque, old section where Legacy Members and the Council of Elders lived. A tired looking woman of nondescript age sat down beside me.

"It's not as colorful in this part of town is it?" I said but didn't expect her to answer. The woman glanced in my direction then back to nothingness.

"The buildings are all the same, one apartment building after another."

She said nothing, but I noticed her breathing had changed.

I tried again. "It seems we have high taxes for infrastructure, community centers and parks, but nothing to brighten up people's homes."

She leaned slightly in my direction and whispered, "People have no money left to personalize their own homes—just sameness everywhere. That's why I love the lights at Gifting time." She then faded back into the vacant space from where she had just come. Like the surroundings, she had merged her *self* with the masses.

When we got to the woman's bus stop, she started to get up, then turned back to me and whispered. "Funny how those in the government and other professionals can maintain a measure of uniqueness for themselves, isn't it My Lady?" Then she was gone. I rode on in amazement. The woman had learned to move in and out of mob dullness at will.

The transit bus stopped again at the corner near the library. As I disembarked, I stepped into a day that seemed brighter and more glorious than any December afternoon I could remember. It was as if I were seeing the world through new eyes. How could anyone be in danger in that bright world? The colors were more vivid and sparkling than I had ever seen them. Why? Why was the sky so high? Why did it have such a vast expanse? Why did the whole world suddenly come alive? All of that beauty had the power to lift my spirits higher than I had ever known.

On a mission, I hurried into the building. "Good afternoon, Frank," I sang out as I breezed past the guard who was stationed at the portal, near the archive room.

"Afternoon, Ma'am," he smiled back without looking up from his row of monitors. "Funny, I didn't see you come in," he remarked dryly.

"I am invisible today, Frank," I teased.

"Most likely," he yawned. "Or in-hearable," he added.

I didn't know what he meant, but I didn't linger around to ask questions. I floated through the swinging gate and stopped at the Reference Desk.

"May I leave my bag and stuff here, Mary?" If I had to leave the back recesses of the library in a hurry, I didn't want to leave anything behind. Mary, the Research Librarian, was always helpful.

"Sure, Christiana, just stash them under there." Mary pointed to a low shelf in the checkout desk, out of vision and out of touch.

"Thanks," I added and moved on through the outer reading room and into the back stacks. My shoes clicked and echoed on the concrete floors. I had left my purse behind and had taken only a small pencil, some paper to take notes, and my keys. Unlocking the side door, I slipped into the archival room. It was a tense adventure into my beloved books, since I knew I would only have a few minutes before someone would come to check on me. After all, I had already checked out of the library for the day when I left for the doctor's office in the morning. I had been thinking of an excuse that I could use for being in the room if someone came back. The only thing that came to mind was an explanation about having left something in the room when I was researching other materials. The misplaced item could not be my tunic I decided. No, I had left it with my purse. *I'll have to think about it as I look through the papers and texts. Maybe it won't matter. It could be anything. No one else knows what's in the room anyway.*

I couldn't help thinking how I had amazed myself. Where had I gotten the nerve to be on this dangerous quest in the first place? Silas's note, if true, was motivation enough to speak out, but it was also reason for fear. Now, suddenly, I felt new strength to follow through, to find the truth, to do something about the terrible policy of termination, even though I didn't know yet what to do. Did I really grasp the seriousness of the cause and the danger I was in? Would I succeed . . . and at what cost?

CHAPTER TWELVE
The Precious Document

4:00 p.m.

The long rays of afternoon light were still streaming through the western window of the library when I walked into the back sections. The light was so beautiful that lamps were not needed. Besides, I preferred natural light to the dreary blue haze cast by energy efficient lamps. I moved directly to the document case I had noticed when I had been in the archives before and stopped in front of a large glass-covered display box. I paused and listened for the guard to come to see who had gotten too close to the case and had activated the sensors. No one came. I was still alone.

The document was clearly visible through the glass, in spite of its faded condition. It was considered to be one of the few copies made of an original document. School children no longer filed past to view the archive. The top of the case had only gathered dirt. No one studied its contents. Few people were even aware of its existence anymore, but still it remained, sealed up in an environmentally controlled case, safe in its own cocoon.

I pressed as closely as I could, wiped the dust of the ages from the surface, and read the words that I had only glanced at before. An odd sensation overtook me as I began to read. Excitement and awe bathed me like anointing oil.

IN CONGRESS, JULY 4, 1776

The unanimous Declaration of the thirteen

United States of America

When in the course of human events it becomes necessary for one people to dissolve the political bands which have connected them with another and to assume among the powers of the earth, the separate and equal station to which the laws of nature and of nature's God entitle them, a decent respect to the opinions of mankind requires that they should declare the causes which impel them to the separation.

So, when the people decided to make their own country, under the authority of their God, they believed they should list the causes for their decision to separate.

We hold these truths to be self-evident, that all men are created equal, that they are endowed by their Creator with certain unalienable Rights, that among these are Life, Liberty and the pursuit of Happiness. — That to secure these rights, governments are instituted among men, deriving their just powers from the consent of the governed. — That whenever any form of government becomes destructive of these ends, it is the Right of the People to alter or to abolish it, and to institute new government, laying its foundation on such principles and organizing its powers in such form, as to them shall seem most likely to affect their safety and happiness.

Wow! Everyone is equal—there are no elite—no Legacy Citizens, and everyone has a right to live, to be free, and to pursue their own happiness. These people are to govern themselves, and when the government interferes with the right of the people to self-govern, that government should be abolished. It is their responsibility to do so. It is all here—every bit of it—especially my grandparents' right to life.

Prudence, indeed, will dictate that Governments long established should not be changed for light and transient causes; and accordingly all experience hath shown that mankind are more disposed to suffer, while evils are

78

sufferable, than to right themselves by abolishing the forms to which they are accustomed. But when a long train of abuses and usurpations, pursuing invariably the same Object evinces a design to reduce them under absolute despotism, it is their right, it is their duty, to throw off such government, and to provide new guards for their future security. —

It says when a government, even a long-standing one, becomes tyrannical and their abuses are evident and numerable, it is the duty of the people to abolish that government and create a new one. The colonists had reached the limit of their patience. They would act. And we have reached the limit of ours.

Such has been the patient sufferance of these Colonies; and such is now the necessity which constrains them to alter their former Systems of Government. The history of the present King of Great Britain is a history of repeated injuries and usurpations, all having in direct object the establishment of an absolute Tyranny over these States. To prove this, let facts be submitted to a candid world.

My heart leaped within my body. I grabbed my chest and felt the beat of it. Self-evident truths. *Our Creator . . . our Creator . . . God. God is the Creator*! I couldn't stop rolling the thought around in my head. A sweet cloud of Presence filled the room, and I knew . . . I knew. I read it over and over, until I had satisfied my soul that the words were buried in my heart.

The *truths*, that we are all created equal, that we have inherited from God—the right to life, liberty, and the pursuit of happiness—took my breath away. *We are guaranteed the right to life, the right to live. Why had it been changed?* With mood altering additives in our water there were fewer disturbed individuals and fewer still who disturbed others. People rarely got angry. But then, they rarely felt anything at all.

The people were to be self-ruled. If they were not and those who governed, repeatedly abused their authority, that government should be taken down and replaced by one that will govern by the will of the people. The colonists listed their grievances for all the world to see.

I had to move on. The other materials I wanted to see were

further back in the room. No one went into the old manuscript room, not even the cleaning staff. The books within that space were now forgotten.

I walked freely through the room. Books and papers were shelved haphazardly everywhere. It looked as if someone had shoved the last bit of knowledge away from sight, slammed the door and locked it. Nearly a hundred years later, I had unlocked the rooms full of old novels, and the history, philosophy, and religious texts that had been banned years ago. Newer versions of those books had been cannibalized beyond recognition. The new editions, re-written texts, no longer spoke truth but were rendered utterly impotent with their lies. Marge had alluded to a time when information flowed like honey from the hive, then its comb was cut down and thrown behind locked doors where it buzzed in silence, still living but unheard.

I checked my time piece. There was still time to do more research before going to meet Jason at the coffee shop. Against the back wall was a long series of history and legal volumes. *Let me see*—I fingered my way through the books until I found historic references that were previous to the last one-hundred years. I leafed through the index. *The New Bill of Rights.* It was right there. On page 384 I began comparing the old with the new first ten amendments to the United States Constitution. The first and fourth amendments tugged at me more strongly than the others. I wasn't able to let go of those two.

1. Freedom of Speech, Press, Religion and Petition.

4. Right of search and seizure regulated.

What I read seemed unbelievable compared to the policed restrictions of the new society. Citizens used to have the right to speak their mind in public, get accurate information from newspapers and news outlets, and were free to worship their God. There he was again, the Creator, God. What on earth had happened?

Then, the *New Bill of Rights* glared at me from the pages. During the upheaval of one-hundred years ago it was determined, in order to control the people, there had to be fewer citizens and a smaller territory. So, the country was separated into four political zones/states, each with their own government and president, which was all controlled by a central government and Prime Minister. A new government was established with a new set of rights. *Let me see, Preamble to the New Bill of Rights.* I read on:

> "The Constitution of the United States made certain introductory statements that can no longer stand in a modern thinking society. In particular, individuals have a right to life, liberty, and the pursuit of happiness. An enlightened society recognizes that life is a privilege and should be available to those viable souls who participate the most, for the greatest good of all. In light of the cost of living, education of the masses, health care, incarceration of those in opposition to society, and financial entitlements and support for those who will not be productive, it is evident that each individual's Length of Days should be planned and terminated before the cost of care begins to be a burden on society. No one has a right to expect society to care for an individual for an undetermined and lengthy period of time. Therefore, an individual's Length of Days will be calculated as follows:
>
> twenty-two (22) years to graduate from college
>
> two (2) years beyond education to form a family unit
>
> two (2) years from the beginning of the family unit to the arrival of the first child
>
> two (2) years until the second child is born and thus replace the two parental units
>
> twenty-two (22) more years to rear the youngest child and support them through four years of college
>
> six (6) years to give ample time for the youngest child to be reared, educated, construct a family unit and have their first and second children
>
> four (4) years until the youngest grandchild is established in a society supported preschool
>
> A total of sixty (60) years equals an individual's Length of Days, with the exception of certain professions that require additional education and length of service, such as medicine, space, and politics. Those professionals will live until age sixty-five (65), in order to serve society with their knowledge.

81

The members of the Council of Elders will live until age seventy-five (75) to take advantage of their wisdom.

In addition to these citizens, families who initiate fetuses over the allotted two per family will terminate the gestation of the third and any that may follow.

In the event a couple may want to swap out an existing child for another, the first child will enter the sleep chamber by eighteen months of age, thus keeping the family unit to three or four in total.

I was stunned. It was all there, a planned termination of each individual citizen into the endless sleep. With a few strokes of a pen a century ago, people had moved from a right to life, to a right to a speedy termination, with no suffering, just a simple sleep. Some people called it *putting a citizen down*. Silas Drummond's message didn't confirm the long sleep however. He called it extermination.

According to the older documents, life was not all we had a right to. People had a right, given to them by God, to liberty or freedom, and the pursuit of happiness. Now, it was becoming clear to me that society had translated the last right, to a guarantee that all people would be happy. In order to guarantee happiness, our ancestors who were in control of society had started putting additives into the water supply. The antidepressants and chemicals that restrained people's behavior through mind control were loaded daily into the water supply. It had a less than desirable effect on everyone however. While people would not say they were sad, they couldn't say they were happy either. Their emotions and energy were flat. They were neither unhappy, nor happy, just maintained.

Of course this explained why their need for intimacy and sexual contact was without desire. It was just strong enough in the early years of the formation of their family unit, that they were able to consummate and create a pregnancy to insure the next generation. The chemicals were modified for each couple through the conception of a second child. By eliminating the sex drive, society thought they could control the root cause of violence and successfully eradicate competition and aggression.

But, why was a free press so important? It was listed early in the document, right up there in the first Amendment. Then, it came to me. *When people are informed, they'll not allow their freedoms to be stripped from their grasp. But, their televisions dispensed news all day long. Had the news casters lied to the people?* It hardly seemed possible.

My mind whirled around my *new understandings*. I had studied the New Bill of Rights in school and had always had an innate sense of there being something more, something beautiful, energetic. The novels had also taught me about romance, love, a fuller life.

I was aware of my time in the back stacks and felt panic overtake me as I tried to read all I could. The Original First Amendment stated:

> "Congress shall make no law respecting an establishment of religion, or prohibiting the free exercise thereof; or abridging the freedom of speech, or of the press; or the right of the people peaceably to assemble, and to petition the Government for a redress of grievances."

So, under the original Constitution, the government could not set up a National religion or keep the people from exercising the religion of their choice. I would need another book to pursue my second question.

I got out the dictionary. "Abridge: to reduce or lessen in authority; to deprive, cut off." *That's easy. An abridged dictionary is shorter without changing the definitions and meanings.* So, the government could not shorten or change the free speech of people or the press. Then I continued on to the fourth amendment:

> "The right of the people to be secure in their persons, houses, papers, and effects, against unreasonable searches and seizures, shall not be violated, and no warrants shall issue, but upon probable cause, supported by oath or affirmation, and particularly describing the place to be searched, and the persons or things to be seized."

That means, the Blue Shirts simply cannot come into my home and take out books and papers without good reason. That includes the Bible book and Drummond's paper. I looked at my time piece again. I had to be careful in the library. I wouldn't go undetected for very long. Someone would remember seeing me come back to the Library later than usual. I quickly turned to the page that contained those two amendments in the New Bill of Rights.

> "When in the lives of a free people, it becomes evident that the speech of a gentile society has slipped into an inflammatory, prejudicial, and threatening treatise, it becomes necessary to limit the ability of that society to express itself openly. Under penalty of punishment by incarceration and fine, there will be no speech that is prejudicial with respect to age, social class or occupation, nationality, race, sex, sexual orientation, political affiliation, or religion. Within the press and media, there can be no inflammatory words written or spoken in respect to the above classifications. All written and verbally expressed media will first seek governmental approval of their proposed texts, and then file for position equivalence time, so that all represented opinions can be presented at the same time and in the same venue, whether that be private or public, on television or radio programming, in religious locations or public institutions."

I knew I must speak up and speak out, but how was I going to stop them? I wasn't a public speaker or a particularly brave person. It would be easier to look the other way. But, I couldn't. My grandparents' lives were too dear to me.

I finally knew the truth. There was a glorious time in a blessed place, when Freedom had stepped onto the stage of life, inspired the world with her words and gifts and actions, then, like a bored, tired, careless actor, forgot her lines and silently, willingly, drew the curtain closed, turned off the lights, and went home to sleep.

CHAPTER THIRTEEN

Ward Stoner Found a Solution

Also in the library, Ward Stoner walked briskly into the main lobby and thumped his knuckles on the desk. In his mind, as the muscle behind the Blue Guard, he was entitled to fast service. Everyone else could go to the back of the line. A woman and two small children had come in ahead of him to return a stack of books and Stoner was losing his patience. The boy and his sister bounced back and forth arguing over who would carry the books.

"Madam, control your children," he snapped.

"Certainly, Inspector." The woman led both children through the portal. The curly haired five-year-old looked back at Stoner and stuck out his tongue. Stoner deemed the boy a good judge of character.

Stoner took pride in being a part of an elite department of the national police. The Blue Guard was considered a necessary evil. They took their orders from no one and their actions were under the scrutiny of no one. At one time, they had the power to protect the citizens from abuses from the government. They were originally established to derive their powers, not from the government, but from the people. Now, they were too often the source of abuse against the people. Stoner was one of those who perpetrated some of the most heinous abuses, especially in the last year.

Something had been working in Ward's life. His attitudes and behavior vacillated back and forth, from somewhat considerate, to wholly inconsiderate. One day recently he woke to find himself changed. A shroud had lifted from his eyes, and he could see again. That day, he hesitated before lashing out and thought before applying force. Other days, he bent his personality around his old principles as he searched for more power. He was a jagged riddle unto himself, never knowing which side of his personality would emerge at any point during the day, until the day acted upon him. But, he had a job to do. He had shopping to complete . . . and he did not like waiting.

"Thank you Ma'am," he mumbled and tipped his hat at the woman as he went through the library gate.

"May I help you, Sir?" Frank, the portal monitoring guard asked as he watched the inspector approach.

"No, I know the area I'm looking for. I spent many hours in here as a student." Stoner pushed through the gate brashly and covered the length of the hall with great strides. He rarely asked for assistance in anything. He depended on no one.

Science, here we are, he mumbled to himself. Stoner studied in those stacks as an undergrad student intent on becoming a renowned scientist. Then he met Miriam, the counterbalance in his life. But, now she was gone. All he had left was his mother and his son. His true balance had died with his wife.

He walked through the stacks and slowed at the A's. *Astronomy.* There was a large section of books, astrological charts, and other related materials. He ran his eyes rapidly over the bindings until he found what he was looking for. He took the volume to a nearby table and flipped it open to the index.

There it is, Pluto, Discovery. He ran his finger down the page, speed-reading the text and then snapped the book closed. *I knew it,* he sneered as if he had been walking his trap lines all morning and had just caught an unsuspecting animal.

CHAPTER FOURTEEN
Covered Her Tracks

All of the books and papers I had taken off the library shelves, I carefully replaced, so no one would know I had been in the room should someone venture in. My ability to move about in the back section of the library and linger as long as I had, was a stroke of good luck. Earlier, I had logged out for the day and this time I hadn't signed back in. Security guards could have seen me enter, checked on me, and then thrown me out.

I walked cautiously from the back room and locked the door behind me. Even when I hurried along the corridor back to collect my things before leaving, there was no one in the hall or around the next corner. I stopped at Mary's desk to pick up my bag and tunic before I left the back area. I had Dr. Jason O'Reilly on my mind.

"Oh, Christiana, I've been so anxious to get out of here, I had forgotten you were back there." The reference librarian looked up from her work. "I didn't hear you. Wonder why I didn't?"

"What do you mean?"

"Every time someone comes or goes, there's a faint buzz. Nothing happened this time."

"How odd," I agreed then retrieved my belongings and put the paper and pencil into my pocket.

As I hurried down the library's main hall, I saw a Blue Shirt approaching from the left. I could feel my heart beating faster and wondered if my fear was obvious to the officer as well. I had hidden the book at home, but I still carried Silas Drummond's desperate note in my bag. Upset with myself for displaying such a reaction to the guard's presence, I tried to cover my surprise with a comment.

"I see someone else is spending the near holidays in the library." I wondered if I sounded as panicked as I felt. *Christiana, get a grip on yourself!* I was surely going to dissolve into helpless fear or giddy giggles. I didn't know which. I only knew I was nearly out of control.

"Yes Ma'am," the blue-shirted Chief Inspector murmured gruffly, tipped his hat and moved swiftly past me. The clip, clip of his shoes sounded just as rigid as he had appeared.

I exhaled and darted past Frank with a merry smile. "In a hurry—sorry."

"Certainly My Lady," he glanced up and waved me on.

I panicked again but resisted the urge to run out of the building. My leg muscles ached. I felt as if I were fleeing down a marathon course on the inside, while crawling to the finish line in reality. *Did the Blue Guardsman know me? Do I have to jump and run every time one comes near? Will all of this never end?*

CHAPTER FIFTEEN
The Demitasse

5:30 p.m.

By the time I got to the transit, I felt calm and more in control, until I boarded. I was both amazed and irritated. That strange man who had ridden the bus before and stared at me was still on the bus or maybe he had boarded again. Was I being stalked? The thought made my skin knot in fear. My feet were ready to run while my body was forced to remain still. Finally, I took a front seat where I didn't have to look at him. I tried to clear my mind by thinking about the little shops that flanked the medical complex.

The old books would have called the buildings quaint. I liked that word, and I loved the shops. They reminded me of something I couldn't recall, an old picture, or a description from a romantic novel I had read. Each small shop was slightly different in architectural style and painted an array of colors that fed my spirit. They seemed to greet everyone like assorted bobbles on a charm bracelet. Their ambiance of comfortable steadfastness helped to wipe away the anxiety I had felt in the library and on the transit.

6:00 p.m.

Once at my destination, I smiled with anticipation as I entered the *Demitasse*, the popular coffee shop. I was surprised to see Doctor

O'Reilly waiting for me at a corner table.

"You're early." I laughed. "I've finally met a physician who is willing to be kept waiting. It is usually the other way around."

"I was able to leave early." Dr. O'Reilly smiled. He stood and pulled out my chair for me.

I stared at him for a moment. It was unusual to see a man with the old manners most men had forgotten years ago or never had. "Thank you, kind sir." I sat down and wanted to bluster out with question after question. *Tell me about the books. How many have you read? Do you know anything about the Length of Days process?* I decided I had better know a little bit more about the man before I asked too many questions.

"How long have you been here in Capitol City, Dr. O'Reilly?"

Before he could answer, the serving girl came to take our order. My questions had to wait.

"What would you like, Miss Applewait?" Then, he turned to the waitress. "I'd like the steak sandwich and coffee," Jason said.

"Um, I don't think I have eaten all day. I had just a few of my grandmother's fresh baked cookies. That sounds good. I'll have the same." I sat back and looked around the delightful room.

"Right," the serving girl jotted down the order and bustled away.

We dissolved into casual conversation, *small talk,* one of my books called it. It felt natural and comfortable. Even the silent parts, while we took time to eat, were packed full of a closeness that was growing. I was surprised that I was enjoying myself so much.

"You've had a busy day?" I said as I watched him relax and enjoy his food.

"Very busy," he admitted. "Hospital rounds took longer than usual, which put me behind schedule seeing my office patients. Luckily, those in the hospital were all being discharged in time for the holidays. But, there were a lot of them."

"What with the epidemic and all," I teased, reverting back to the morning's conversation I had with Dahlia in the medical office.

"I wouldn't call it an epidemic in the same sense as an illness or communicable disease. But, Christy . . . is *Christy* okay?"

"Sure Jason." I felt comfortable using his first name. He was rapidly becoming more Jason than Dr. O'Reilly.

"It's not like we have an outbreak of an old illness, like influenza, or something. It's . . . I probably shouldn't talk about the office."

"You're not talking about your patients. You're talking about the non-epidemic. You don't have to give me their names."

"True," he paused again. "Christy, I am seeing suicidal young people . . . so many of them. Medicine had eradicated depression and suicide when they put additives in the drinking water. And, there's another curious thing. All of these young people expressed a fear that I would take them back to their previous feeling level, of flat and bland emotions. They wouldn't consider returning to a life of nothingness. Their new found joy of living was worth the possibility of their death."

"Did they have a wound on their shoulder at their inoculation sight, like I did?" Something inside of me was trying to pull together all of the mysterious threads that were emerging in my life.

"No, they had no complaint of itching or something tearing their clothing. A general exam didn't reveal anything either?" He looked intently at me, a curious expression on his face. "What do you know, Christy? I feel I am getting answers to questions I never knew I was supposed to ask."

I reached in my pocket and pulled out the tissue Jason had given me earlier. "Grand-mère said this small coded particle was not to be removed. She said it was my identification chip that has everything on it, including my DNA code."

"I knew we used to tag people, but I had no idea . . ." Jason shook his head. He seemed bewildered. "Why didn't I know that? I'm a physician. I'm sorry, Christiana. I didn't mean to —"

"Jason, I guess I understand your anger. A few hours ago, neither of us knew anything about tagging children nor the true reality of this world in which we live. Of course a doctor should be told about all aspects of their patients' health, like removing the chip from my shoulder. How would you know how to treat any of us if you had not been trained or informed about the I.D. chips?"

He looked at me as if a few of the missing pieces had suddenly fallen into place. "That's what the pediatricians were talking about." He shook his head. "Why didn't I ask?" He stared out the window in silence for a minute. "I am embarrassed. I should have known. Why didn't I?"

"I think the important question is why did they keep the secret from you? Especially, since you're a Legacy Citi—"

Jason's eyes snapped up to meet mine. He didn't seem angry, just surprised.

His eyes squinted and he smiled quizzically. "Now, how did you find out about that?"

"Grand-mère told me." I lightly touched his hand. "I am sorry. I didn't mean to let your secret out."

"Don't worry about it, Christy," he said as he took my hand in his. "It isn't a secret. It's just something I don't tell people. I am already treated differently because I'm a doctor. If people knew I was Legacy as well, they would be spreading laurel wreaths in my path. I don't want any part of that."

"I like that in you," I whispered, then wondered if I should have spoken so honestly. Why was I feeling such a strong and immediate attraction to this man? I changed the subject. "Jason, do you think the chip could have other functions besides identification?"

"I don't know, but I'll tell you this, I'm going to find out." Jason picked up his cup and made a face. The coffee had obviously grown cold. He motioned for the server to come and freshen up our cups.

After she left, I whispered, "If the suicidal kids had a missing or damaged chips that might have told us something. You have removed mine, what if I don't have it put back? What effect would that have?"

"I guess you won't be identified. After I gave you the detoxification tablets and you left, Dahlia told me she had found a lot of pills missing. She couldn't tell me exactly how many since we have never dispensed them before, they've just waited there, locked away in storage. We have no idea who could have taken them."

"Why would someone want to go through the detoxification process? What would they get out of it? What do I get out of it? What is this all about, Jason? Should I put the tablets in my water or not? What about you?"

"Since doctors don't prescribe for themselves, I get my detox pills from another physician. I take them. I advise you to take them too. After you've used the packet of tablets I gave you, you'll be given a second amount with a higher dose, gradually increasing the amount, while you slowly detoxify. Think about it. If these kids used the tablets in a non-prescribed way, I have no idea what the outcome would be. They may have taken larger initial doses than they should have."

"One would think that pure water would be a good thing."

"Christy, it is a good thing. But, we're not really sure what is being filtered out. Maybe pure water isn't the only goal."

A spark of insight flashed through my mind. "Jason! The antidepressants that are in the water . . . maybe the young people are filtering out too much too fast. That may explain the suicide tendencies. They could experience a ricochet of reverberating emotions, bouncing all over the place."

"That is it, Christy! That has to be it. But, why are they using the tablets, and why are they using such a high dose?"

"Well . . . what are some of the side effects one would experience with antidepressant medication? The side effects would be gone too." It made sense to me to see what they would gain back, if they eliminated the medication from their system.

"Sex!" Jason whispered excitedly. He had obviously been too loud when others turned to stare. He lowered his voice and added, "Christy! They would get their sex drive back."

"Sex drive? You mean that I'll get a sex drive? Jason O'Reilly, you tell me the truth and you tell me right now." I blushed at the very idea that we were sitting in a quiet coffee shop talking about sex. Not that it was taboo. It wasn't. In fact, no one seemed to care about sex anymore. Maybe the additives in the water were the reason everyone stopped caring.

"Christy, I think you may have hit on the cause of several situations, the etiology of the *epidemic* as you called it and the reason for the low libido in everybody else. As I read the old books, I wondered what they were talking about when they spoke of passion and longing. As I explained, I began my detoxification several years ago, but I have never been attracted to anyone before. Now, Christy, with you —"

"Jason, I'm attracted to you too and I've only had one dose of the detoxification tablets. It's all happening so fast." I sat back in my chair but could not take my eyes off his handsome face.

"Maybe, as we detoxify, we become drawn to others who are also medication free, or at least have begun the process. In that way, Legacies are attracted to each other." Jason leaned in even closer. "Did you just say you're attracted to me?" His smile was mischievous and compelling.

There was an amazing excitement I had never experienced before. It made my heart rate increase. I actually thought I was beginning to perspire . . . in December!

"Christy?" Jason murmured lowly. He cupped his hand under my chin so my eyes would meet his. His warm smile spread from his eyes across his face.

"Yes, you heard correctly, Dr. O'Reilly." I blushed and then cooled my passion by turning the conversation to the books he had talked about. "Wait a minute. What do you mean you read about passion in the old books? You were going to tell me about those books."

He hesitated. "You switched tracks on me pretty fast that time." Then he smiled, "The books . . . okay." He lowered his voice and looked around to see if anyone was close. "I'm feeling a little paranoid talking about the books in public."

"I know what you mean. When I am in the back rooms of the library, I'm afraid someone will come in unexpectedly. I am constantly looking over my shoulder."

"Is that a bad thing? Is the library a dangerous place?"

"The back rooms, the ones all the way down the back hall, are totally off limits to everyone else, except Marge, the curator of old books and documents, and me."

"What's back there, Christy? The Constitution?" Jason smiled as if he had just made a joke. "Christy?"

"Among other things . . . yes." I patted his hand, hoping we could move on. "Your books? Let's talk about your books."

"Well, they aren't my books. Maybe . . . I guess they are *like* mine," Jason said. "No one else knows they are kept there. That must make them mine. And, I'm the only one who brings them home."

"Home? Jason, where are they?" I needed to know about other collections of books, those outside the library, in case there were books there that I hadn't read.

"Christy, they're in the hospital library. People used to read while they recuperated. I take them home, one at a time, and then return them later. That wing of the hospital has been sealed off for many years. Since it also houses the DNA file banks and bears the Bradford family name, our strongest benefactors by the way, that section remains open, even if it isn't open to the public."

"How many books are in there? What kind? Who are the authors? Can I see them?"

"Slow down, Miss Applewait. Drink your coffee." He wasn't ordering me. It was a tease rather than a command.

I watched Jason closely. There was so much to learn about him. "You know I'm going to see those books eventually don't you? Sooner or later." Just then the server brought fresh water, and I remembered the little white tablets and took them out of my bag. "Every glass of water?" I asked as I paused over the water before releasing the pill.

"Every glass," he agreed, then smiled mischievously. "And, let's not forget the side effects, or the elimination of them in your case."

I couldn't believe he had just said that. I had only known him half a day. What I had learned so far, I liked. Admittedly, there was an attraction. I had no idea how to handle the new emotions I was feeling, except to avoid them. So, I changed the subject. "Could we go to the hospital library Jason, so I can see the books?"

Jason looked at me and the corners of his blue eyes crinkled softly. "Yes, I guess that would be all right. There wouldn't be anyone in the DNA lab at this time of day, given the upcoming holiday. We can go there from here, if you have the time."

"Do I have the time? I'll carve time out of my imagination if I have to," I laughed. "But I have just one more question." I scanned the room for safety and then whispered, "My grandparents will be seventy-five in a few days. What is the process with the never-ending-sleep?"

He looked surprised that I was asking about the Length of Days law. "The sleep? Everything we have been taught tells us that it is just that. When a person gets to the end of their Length of Days, they are put into a state of perpetual sleep."

He wasn't confirming what Silas said at all. "Where are their bodies then?" I asked.

"There are storage areas for sleepers within some of the mountains around here." He looked at me carefully. "Why the questions?"

"I read some very disturbing information recently. But we can talk about it later." I knew I shouldn't get the note from Silas out of my bag where someone else might see us exchanging something that appeared secretive.

We left the restaurant and stepped out into the wonderful late afternoon air. The wind from the northeast was chilling, so I drew my tunic around me. A light frost crunched under our feet and the aroma of espresso coffee from inside the Demitasse hung on the cold air like perfume from a fine crystal bottle. It was breathtaking and it was December, nearly Gifting Day. Snow would certainly follow in a few days. The Gift-giving season was upon us and I hadn't even noticed the passage of time. In spite of the frost in the air, I felt strangely warm as Jason took my hand in his.

CHAPTER SIXTEEN
Cameras in the Capitol

In the heart of the city, Ward Stoner pushed his way into the Capitol Building and flashed his badge at the guard. His attitude of entitlement to authority was enough to command domination. He stormed past the entry portal, elbowed an elderly woman out of his way and made a straight path back to the Capitol security office.

"Yes Sir," the duty officer jumped up and snapped to attention. He kept his eyes focused forward like the royal guards of old.

"We may have a small glitch in our security around town." Stoner paced back and forth, both impatient and somewhat bored with the smallness of the task. "Only one incident has been reported. It's rather an odd situation. It may be an anomaly but we're not going to error on the side of laziness."

"No, Sir," the duty officer agreed.

Stoner glanced at the guard. The officer's rigid, fixed gaze irritated him. How could he intimidate someone who never blinked? "Someone has accessed a secure area without setting off a buzzer," Stoner sneered. "While the reported incident happened on a transit bus, we are not going to wait until it happens in a more sensitive area. I will be stopping at the courthouse, the banks, the hospital, and the communication headquarters with a system to get things started before the holiday."

The duty office said nothing. He simply maintained attention.

"Are you hearing me, Mister?" Stoner growled, with his face aggressively thrust out toward the guard.

"Yes, Sir," the security officer shot back with bullet report speed. "The Capitol will be locked up tight during the holiday weekend. No guards will be on duty because no one can get it."

"I'm taking no chances," Stoner snapped. "Then, on December twenty-fifth, while the buildings are closed, I will view the tapes and see if we've caught anything or anyone. The little *swisher* will not get past me."

"The twenty-fifth, Inspector Tomb— . . . Stoner? That's the holiday."

"Yes, it is the holiday." Stoner worked his jaw in impatient anger. He had heard the slip and chose to ignore it. "We cannot wait until we have a serious breach of security before we begin investigating."

"Yes Sir."

Stoner pushed the security guard's papers to the corner of the office desk, plopped his bag down in the middle and unzipped it. "I have some old motion sensor video cameras we're going to use to catch this guy."

"Really Sir? Those haven't been used in years." The officer's interest peaked as he studied the camera. Such stop action picture equipment was no longer available.

"No, they haven't. But, we have a well-stocked arsenal of weapons and instruments, both new and vintage. We use the best weapon for the kill and in a case like this, one of these. I'll set up a camera here at the portal to the Capitol, a few throughout the building, and at the other major locations I mentioned. A second camera will be positioned ten yards past the security check to catch anyone we missed with the first images. We will see anyone who walks through the portal, even if we don't hear a buzz. It won't matter if it's an animal, human, or specter."

CHAPTER SEVENTEEN
A Cache of Books

7:30 p.m.

After leaving the café, Jason and I walked across the street to Memorial Hospital where he would sneak us into the private library. It was dark outside by that hour so the building glowed with glittering lights, an oasis in the dimly lit city. By contrast, the other neighborhoods were allowed only an eerie glow from the energy-efficient, non-heat producing bulbs that cast a pall over the city. Only the Gifting lights provided a colorful break from the drab.

"You walk in first, Christy," Jason whispered. "I'll follow behind you and we'll meet by the elevators. We'll ride up to the second floor, then get off and walk up two more flights. That way, it won't be obvious that we're going to a closed area of the hospital." Jason kissed my cheek and guided me in through the front door.

In the middle of the open hallway on the main floor, a marble topped information desk and communication station commanded a presence. A pleasant looking, middle-aged woman looked up and smiled as I walked past but since I kept on going, she said nothing. I reached the elevators just as the doors opened. Looking back, I didn't see Jason and didn't know what to do next. Another woman, in a green uniform, stepped onto the elevator and stared at me. "Well, Ma'am, are you coming?" Then she seemed to recognize me and looked away.

Up two floors. I rehearsed Jason's instructions and stepped into the car just as he hurried around the corner and slipped onto the lift. I started to smile, when the woman in the green uniform spoke to him.

"Dr. O'Reilly, why are you here at this hour?" She didn't really look at him but faced forward and watched the floor numbers tick off above the door, as people tend to do who need assurance and control.

"I'll just be a little while," he explained, then stepped to the side as the doors opened on the third floor.

I hesitated. He wasn't getting off.

"Ma'am?" the lady groaned again obviously irritated.

"Oh," I feigned absentmindedly, "sorry."

I stepped off without looking back at Jason, and walked toward the drinking fountain. A moment later, Jason darted through the door that led from the stairwell, out of breath and beaming.

"That was fun!" He whispered hoarsely as he touched my back.

"Jason, what happened?"

"I thought I'd better not make a display of getting off the elevator with you, so I rode up to the next floor, waited to the last second, then pretended I'd been daydreaming and nearly missed my floor. I squeezed out through the closing doors. Right or wrong, it was still exciting." He took my hand and led me back into the stairwell so we could walk up two additional flights. Jason paused at the stairway door, checked to make sure no one was in that wing of the hospital and then eased us silently into the hall. We darted through the double doors to the left and into a darkened passageway. "If we stay close to the wall, we can make our way into the back recesses."

We turned at the next cross hallway. A little beam of moonlight was sneaking in through the window at the end of the hall, just enough to lend light to the next turn. Once around the corner, Jason guided us through a windowless door into a room on the right. "We can turn on the overhead lamps in here. The room is positioned in the heart of the building. None of the walls have outside exposure. No one will look in and see us in here."

"Ah!" I gasped as the lights snapped on. I found myself in a richly veined gold mine of precious books. "Oh Jason, look at all of them." I ran my fingers over the first few shelves and moved on around the room. "How many are there?"

"I don't know. I've never counted them."

"How many have you read?" I saw titles of many wonderful old stories from the last centuries. I had read some of these books before, their words strung together like pearls on a string that created a beautifully crafted work of art. Over the years, the language, attitudes and vocabulary changed, but in these books the underlying message was always the same: good won over evil, and love was the redeeming and saving emotion of all time.

"There are hundreds of them locked in here," Jason said. "I've had the ability to safely get them out of the hospital, and since I don't have much to do in the evening, I read." Jason's voice trailed off. I thought it might have been a sad testimony to his loneliness. "We shouldn't take too long," he hurried me along "I usually hear a beep if someone comes through that outer door."

"A beep? Someone else said something about a beeping sound as people passed certain points. I haven't heard any tone."

"Oh sure, there's always a sound. You just get used to it after a while." Jason pulled a book from the shelf. "Here's one I like, *Autumn of Love.*" He opened the small leather bound book and leafed through a few pages and read:

> "Autumn's richest golden days
> held love's promise within their grasp,
> and sending leaves upon the wind,
> whispered, "Death won't win. Love will last."

"Jason," I gasped, amazed at the beauty of the words from lives lived long, with promise and togetherness. "I don't know what to say. I can only feel."

Jason pulled me to him and kissed me tenderly. "I've waited so long," he whispered. I knew what he meant, even though I didn't know I had also been waiting until I found Jason's arms.

He held me close. I could hear the beat of his heart against my chest. I felt safe and at home. I never knew that the love I'd read about between the pages of my novels and the dreams I had dreamed, could have been surpassed by first love. We lingered in our embrace only a few minutes.

"We'd better go," Jason said. "There are no sensors in this old part of the hospital, but they'll soon be aware that X-number of people came into the building and there are two unaccounted for."

"Sensors? The rest of the hospital has a . . . what? Like a census system? They can count people as they come and go in here? Jason you mean they . . ."

"They trace our every move, not just in the hospital. There are sensors everywhere." Jason put the book under his jacket and took my arm.

"Then, there are sensors in the library too?"

"Sure, everywhere, except the oldest buildings. There are only three structures that are so old they probably don't think sensors are needed: here in this original hospital wing, the old sections of the library that you're aware of, and the archival rooms of the Capitol."

"Jason that must account for the buzzing noise we set off as we pass. Maybe that is the key. They are numbering the citizens and checking each person's activities."

"Probably. They used to do a census, now I guess we just buzz." He turned off the lights and guided me out of the room.

"Could I borrow some of those books? There have to be some that aren't in my library."

"Sure, we'll come back another day or if you know the title of a particular book or a favorite author, I can pull several from the shelves and bring them to you."

Our whispers hovered in the hall and seemed to echo off the walls. I thought of that buzzing sound again. "You know, when I was in the library this afternoon, they didn't even know I was there. And, the transit driver thought I had to pay. Then, when I went back and picked up my tunic, he apologized. Jason! It finally came to me . . . The chip! The chip that you removed from my shoulder was in the pocket of my tunic. When I didn't have the wrap with me, I went about unnoticed. Now, I guess, we know why infants are tagged," I gasped. "Jason, they track our every movement, from the time we're born until we reach the end of our days. The DNA code etched in our chip lets them know exactly where we are and who we are. It's like we have an old fashioned easy pass at a highway toll booth permanently implanted in our bodies."

Jason gripped my arm as we stood in the dim hallway. "Don't raise your voice Christy. It was all done in the name of national security. I read about that era, when the revolution of the masses overthrew the rights of the individual." Jason looked beyond the corner of the hallway before we slipped around and into the final hall. "If you're going to have mass rule, you better be prepared to live with mob control. That's us. People aren't living lives of freedom, to pursue our loftiest individual plans," he whispered. "We exist on the lowest plane possible for all to attain, the level of mediocrity through chemical control."

Just then I recognized the double doors at the end of the hall. "Here we are," I said with great relief.

"Wait," Jason spoke softly. "Come here," he smiled.

He kissed me tenderly, sweetly and looked into my eyes. "You're amazing, Christy."

"Jason, I don't even know how to express all the new feelings I'm experiencing. There are no words left in our meager vocabulary."

"The old novels expressed it well," he reminded me.

I knew authors would have used words like *thrilling* and *desire,* but I hesitated. "I know, but I don't think I have the courage to use those words yet."

"You have more courage than you know, Christy," Jason assured me. I wondered if his words would still be right, over the long course that lay ahead of us.

There was one thing I was sure of. This feeling between us could be the kind of love that lingers and lasts, the kind of love that lives are built on—the kind of never-ending love that lasts beyond our present Length of Days.

CHAPTER EIGHTEEN
Stoner's Encounter

After leaving the Capitol, one of Tombstone Stoner's next stops was the hospital. Ever since his Miriam died, he didn't like anything about the place, especially the antiseptic odor that permeated through the never-ending halls of deceptively beautiful marble. It smelled corruptly clean—like all the life had been scrubbed out of everything with a substance so strong it stung his eyes. He shuddered and moved past the front desk into the wide hallway to the right. He knew where the records' office was. Not the current patients' charts. Those electronic documents were at the nurse's station located near each room. The official records' office held information on discharged, discarded, and deceased patients and the necessary data on each citizen to determine their Length of Days.

Stoner knew that each citizen had credits—factors that make them more valuable—that added to their Length of Days, to calculate the exact birthday at which they would enter the never-ending-sleep. In addition, a health record was maintained to determine the viability of each citizen unit. His Blue Guard training also emphasized that every damage to the body was itemized with a specific point value, and the running total was maintained until it reached twenty-five points. Defective persons were eliminated, just like pre-birth masses that needed no points to justify their termination. The family was notified to bring the unwanted and useless to the sleep chamber at an appointed hour. If they failed to show up, a squad of Blue Guardsmen was sent to bring them in. Stoner's mind raced and tumbled with all the faces of those he had forced into the limousine that took them to the sleep center. His head swam a little and he thought he was going to be sick.

Shake it off Stoner! What were those people to you? Then another voice echoed in his head. *But, she was.*

"Yes Sir, may I help you?" A nurse in a white uniform with a round, pleated nurse's cap, approached the inspector.

"No," Stoner snapped when he glanced at her cap. "I want to see your supervisor." Ward Stoner dealt only with the person in charge, no matter where he was.

"Yes, Sir. Certainly."

A woman wearing a smooth, white, nurse's cap with a black band along the upper edge—identifying her as the head nurse—came out of the inner room. "Inspector, what may I do for you?"

"I'm here to place a camera in the records' office. Please lead the way." Short and to the point, Stoner used no more words than were necessary.

"A camera, Sir? I don't understand"

"You don't have to understand, Nurse," he responded gruffly. "Understanding isn't a requirement for you to lead me to the records office."

"This way, Inspector." The nurse's tone showed little respect, but she led the way and said no more. They walked silently to the elevator, rode down to the lower level, and proceeded along the corridor. "May I ask if there has been a problem that we're unaware of?"

"No, you may not," Stoner snapped. "This is a precaution. The files must be protected. Without each citizen record, we wouldn't be able to administer the never-ending-sleep fairly."

"Yes Sir, the endless sleep. We must know exactly when we can legally kill someone, mustn't we?"

Stoner was outraged. He gripped his fists to control his temper. "Hold your tongue, Nurse. We are very fair. You should know that a common cold doesn't carry any point values unless a pattern of chronic upper-respiratory distress becomes evident. Only then is each additional incident noted in the patient's records. That, combined with other indicators, determines the health of an individual. That seems quite fair. I'm sure you'll agree."

"Yes Sir," she reported dryly.

"Nurse, furthermore, it's only the loss of a limb during an accident, or blindness that could automatically reduce a citizen's Length of Days to age twenty-five," Stoner scolded. "You know, if there is compelling evidence of a citizen's ability to contribute to society, well above any financial drain caused by their injuries, their Length of Days can be reinstated with a proper court hearing. Surely, you learned that only a coma of more than three days, or a back injury that results in paralysis, could trigger an immediate placement in the sleep chamber." Stoner gritted his teeth in anger. "I fail to see why I'm explaining myself to you."

"Here we are, Sir. I'll be happy to help you further if needed," the nurse offered as they came to the records room.

"No, Nurse. Just leave. Silence will be the only help I require."

Stoner quickly installed the camera facing the entrance to the large humidity controlled vault-like records office and slammed the door closed. He didn't look back. He was glad to get out of that dreary place.

Stoner took the elevator down and had stepped off near the lobby entrance when he heard shouting. As he rounded the corner, he ran into a gang of five young men who were waving old, last century, guns in the air. Laughing and stumbling over one another, they were behaving in a strange and hysterical way.

"Look, Benny," one of them laughed as he pointed his weapon at Stoner. "We found us a little soldier boy."

"Get that thing out of my face," Stoner ordered with a controlled, calm voice.

"Whoa, man, listen to the little chief," one of the other young thugs yelled. "You tell one of the nurses, they'd better get us some of those little white pills or we'll find them ourselves," he shouted.

"You've had enough pills already, Mister. I'm going to give you the greatest Gift-giving present you will ever receive. I'll give you a chance to leave this hospital under your own power," Stoner barked.

To Stoner's instant analysis, the men appeared to be intoxicated. How that was possible, since alcohol and most other substances were controlled, Stoner had no idea. There had been rumors of a huge increase in the production of an old substance called moonshine. What he saw before him was an out of control mob, of out of control young men, who continued to wave guns erratically in the air and shout obscenities and taunts to everyone who came near. They obviously had no respect for the authority of the Chief Inspector of the Blue Guard and that was intolerable to Stoner. When the young thugs didn't run, he pulled his sting ray from its holster, aimed and fired in rapid, Gatling gun fashion, sending laser point shots of contact-anesthetic directly into their faces. All five dropped where they stood.

"Clean this mess up," Stoner barked at the head nurse as he stepped over the body of one of the young men. He resisted an impulse to kick him in the ribs.

"But Sir," she responded with an expression of bewilderment and fear. "What do we do with them? Can't you arrest them?"

"Scan them for their names, addresses, and contact information while they're still out. You'll be able to get closer to them while they're still unconscious. When they wake up, if they can get themselves under control, send them home to their mamas for the holidays. If they give you even the slightest resistance, call security and the Blue Guard will put them in jail for the holidays, and they'll stay there until the courts reopen."

"But Sir," she tried to protest, "we are used to caring for people in a near comatose state. Most people are in their own world of mumble thinking. We've had little preparation for handling erratic, uncontrolled patients."

"Are you saying you're not up to your job's requirements, Nurse?" Stoner growled.

"No, Sir. I am not saying that at all."

Stoner turned crisply, leaving the nurse standing in the hallway with the anaesthetized bodies of five drooling young men at her feet. As Stoner rounded the corner, he saw a young woman push through the doors of the adjacent hallway.

Well, well, the same female again . . . or she's one of the triplets I've been seeing around town all day. He slipped back around the corner and waited for her to pass. *Now, why is she ahead of me everywhere I go?*

CHAPTER NINETEEN
Dahlia's Secrets

8:30 p.m.

Jason and I had slipped cautiously through the large double doors into what appeared to be an empty outer hall of the hospital. We had been in the off-limits library, but were still not totally out of danger of being apprehended. I thought I had heard noises coming from that area but now I only heard Jason sigh deeply. It must have been a situation around the corner, in the adjacent hall. I wanted to get out of there.

Jason motioned that it was clear to come out. "I'll take the stairway and you go down on the elevator," he whispered. "If there's a problem, I'll meet you back at the coffee shop."

Jason moved silently to the doors that led to the stairwell and disappeared. I stood there for a moment then pressed the down button for the lift. My stomach tightened with a growing awareness of the danger we were in. My thoughts went to Silas Drummond's note. Surely he had lied. All that he described was so grotesque and beyond my mind's ability to take in; it couldn't possibly be true.

"Lady Applewait," Dahlia called to me as I stepped from the elevator car on the first floor, still wrapped in my concern over Silas's warning. "You're here late," she smiled as she came toward me.

I thought fast. "Just doing some research for someone and then realized that I didn't really have the time." I looked at my watch, hoping Dahlia would recognize the social cue to move on. "I'm to meet someone at the Demitasse."

"Really? I love that place. I've finished teaching a seminar and I'm ready to leave. I'll walk over with you." Dahlia didn't wait for a response but fell into step beside me as I started toward the door. Her manner was strikingly different from the morning's encounter in the office.

I saw Jason start to emerge through the stairway door. He stopped and turned to descend the next staircase to the lower level of the hospital. Neither of us was ready to be seen together. We had only been *together* for a matter of hours and had no idea ourselves, where it would all lead, if anywhere.

I didn't look back as we darted across the damp streets. It hadn't been raining, but a fine December mist had settled over the pavement beyond the brightly lit hospital. The water drainage system under the heated streets evaporated moisture as soon as it landed on the pavement, leaving only a wet glaze that sparkled in the holiday lights. The night had grown cold. We moved quickly into the coffee shop and claimed the last remaining booth by the front windows.

"May I join you until your friend arrives?" Dahlia questioned as she slid onto the bench seat.

"Sure." What else could I have said? She was already seated. I knew that Jason wouldn't come in if he saw his nurse with me. Too many questions spoil the mystery. I was glad we had found a table in the front, close to the window. Jason would be able to see us before he came in. But, how was I going to politely get rid of her?

"You look tired," I began. "Did you have a busy day . . . more than usual? I know you're always busy." I tried a professional tactic.

"Yes, very. Even the mammas with the little kids seemed more stressed than usual. One said she had been herding chickens all day."

"More of those suicides and attempted self-annihilations?" I kept my voice low so the people around us couldn't hear, but clearly enough so Dahlia would know I intended to pursue my line of conversation.

"Suicides?" Dahlia gasped in a hushed voice.

"Yes, Dahlia," I lowered my voice to a crisp whisper, "suicides."

"People don't suicide anymore," she denied.

"Most don't, but there is a growing epidemic of young people who are taking their own lives. It's a strange topic for all of us, Dahlia. Most people have never even heard the term, suicide."

"How do you know what it's called?" Dahlia wasn't asking. She seemed surprised that I knew.

"As a Legacy Citizen, I've begun to delve into the wisdom of the ages, to immerse myself in the history of our people." I pressed on. "Suicide is a sin, Dahlia."

"A what?" Dahlia appeared anxious as her eyes scanned the room.

"A sin, you know. It's against Devine law." I heard myself saying words I didn't know that I knew, much less understood. "Life is precious, Dahlia. It's a gift."

"A gift from whom?" She whispered incredulously. "Like a Gift-giving present? A gift implies a giver."

I tried to appear relaxed, but I was a witness, bearing testimony about someone I didn't even know. Dahlia was asking *who*, not as an inquisitor, but as a seeker, and I had no answers for her. I had hoped our conversation would cause her to leave but instead she stayed, and it made me want to flee. "There are things I'm not at liberty to talk about Dahlia." I saw the disappointment in her eyes and added, "We'll talk about it when we can. This isn't the best place" I picked up my bag and started to leave. If she wasn't going to move, I would have to.

"No, Miss Applewait, I'll go. You're waiting for someone." Dahlia drank from the water glass the waitress had placed in front of her and added, "Don't forget your detox pill."

I saw Jason cross the street just as Dahlia stood up. Behind him, two blue guard officers pushed past him and entered the restaurant. The room hushed as the men slowly scanned each table.

"Wonder who they're looking for." Dahlia whispered nervously.

"Dahlia, you're afraid? Of what?"

"I'm always nervous when the Blue Shirts show up and lately I've seen them more often."

"Why are you afraid? If you've done nothing—"

"There's a group of people that . . ." she stopped as the guards came closer to our table.

"What group? Dahlia, what's wrong?"

"Hush," Dahlia begged as she looked down at her water glass and avoided the men who drew closer with each step.

I asked no more as the officers stopped at our table and eyed Dahlia as she slumped and pulled her coat around her. I raised my chin and confidently looked at them both. "Good evening officers. It's a beautiful night isn't it?"

"Yes, Ma'am," one of them mumbled and then they moved on.

"They're gone," I nudged Dahlia on the sleeve. "What is wrong? What group were you talking about?"

"I can't talk now." She jumped up to leave just as Jason entered. I didn't want them to meet at the door so I touched Dahlia's arm to turn her away from the windows.

"Yes, Dahlia, not now, but we'll talk more later. It sounds like we both have some information that needs to be shared. I'm just not ready to talk and it seems you're not either."

"Thanks. Lately it seems, I've had the feeling there's more, and I don't even know what there is *more* of. Those of us in my group are aware of . . . something. I sense a change in you, Miss Applewait. You know what I'm talking about even if I don't." Dahlia sat back down on the edge of her chair and spoke quietly. "Miss Applewait—"

"Please, Dahlia, call me Christiana. Very few people do, you know. Even in school I was Miss Applewait. Since I am Legacy, I was set apart. And, please talk to me when you see me in the apartment building. I may be in my own world, but you are welcome there." I touched her arm to reassure her of my sincerity. Then I thought, *Legacy people don't touch others, and they aren't contacted in return.* The old rules now sounded strange.

"Yes, Christiana," she said with a tremble in her voice. "I would love to sit down with you soon. Maybe we can talk about the *knowing* that's inside of you sometime over the Gift-giving Holidays?" Her voice was pleading as she touched my hand.

"Yes, that would be nice."

"There's a fresh glow in your face, Christiana. When little Hector Montoya fell down the stairs and broke his leg, you showed love and compassion for him. Most people just accept the inevitable."

"Maybe the inevitable doesn't have to be the inescapable."

"My great-grandmother used to say, 'Bless you child,' and for some reason that seems to fit. Bless you, Christiana Applewait."

I watched as Dahlia stepped out into the night. The serving woman came over to the table, paused and stared at me.

"Are you staying?" she asked and slouched with a hand on her hip. "Do you want to order?"

"She will have a cup of cocoa and a glass of water." Jason touched my shoulder as he sat down opposite me. "And I'll have cocoa too. Oh, sorry, do you want anything to eat?"

"I don't think so."

Jason sat back and waited until the serving girl walked away, then asked, "How did you do with Dahlia? Did she ask too many questions?"

"No, she didn't ask much. She started to tell me about a group of friends. Two blue guardsmen came in, and she became really frightened." Christiana paused as the server put the hot chocolate before us.

"Friends? What was she talking about?"

We paused again as the server placed spoons and napkins on the table, then left. Jason repeated, "What friends?

"I don't know. It sounded like a spiritual quest she had recently embarked on. Then she brought up the friends and quickly dropped it."

"Spiritual?" Jason covered his mouth with his hand and whispered into his palm so no one could read his lips. "Like, in God?"

"God?" My words were nearly inaudible. "Do you know about God?" I couldn't believe what I was hearing. To speak the name of the deity of old had been forbidden for more years than anyone could remember.

"Christiana . . . we haven't known each other very long. I'm afraid I'm dragging you into dangerous —"

"It's all right Jason. If you hang, I'll hang right there beside you. They would need two executioners. Besides, our punishment would not be severe, since we're . . . well, you know. We would be in a reeducation program." We kept our voices low, but my excitement was hard to conceal. "Tell me Jason, what do you know about God?"

"I have a book." Jason was hesitating, but I wouldn't let him stop.

My breath caught in my throat. I was nearly unable to speak. Then I whispered, "Is it . . . black?" Could it possibly be that Jason had a copy of Grand-père's book?

"Yes, it's black. It has letters on the front." He paused as if he were gathering permission to say the words. "It says, Holy Bible."

"Where did you get it?" I could feel my heart race to embrace the words I longed to hear again. How could Jason have a Bible? They had all been destroyed.

"I found it in the hospital library. I had never heard anything about a Bible book, so I didn't know what it was." His eyes shone as he talked. "When I read it, Christy, it was like truth had been unfolded in my soul. I don't know how, but I knew. I just knew."

"I know what you mean, and I haven't even started reading it. I have a copy of that Bible book, Jason. I just got it today. It had been Grand-père's. He gave it to me since I've come of age, and they are nearing the end of their Length of Days. He said the Bible book had to be passed on, to be kept safe." I studied his face. I was feeling strangely empowered. Somewhere, in an old text, the haunting words, *and the truth will set you free,* echoed in my mind. But, what truth? Silas' truth . . . or had he lied? If he hadn't, how safe was all this talk of forbidden books and old truths? I was learning that truth had power, but I didn't know what truths would be found. Should I drag Jason into all of this? Could I trust him with things I didn't know about . . . yet?

CHAPTER TWENTY
Chalky Boone

Over in a part of town Christiana rarely visited, Ward Stoner charged into the headquarters of the Blue Guard, ignoring the Desk Sargent's, "Evening Inspector," as he dashed to his office. Chief Inspector Stoner was in his own world of anger with a purpose. *Why do I have to micro-manage this unit?* He sank into his desk chair and snapped around to look out the window. He saw no holiday lights or happy shoppers scurrying about the city looking for a special Gifting surprise for their loved one. In his wounded spirit, he saw greedy children trying to drain another precious dollar from their overworked parents. Through his own anger and pain, he saw overindulgent parents who wanted to pile presents under the Gift-giving tree to buy the love of their selfish children.

Chalky Boone, Stoner's first assistant, poked her head around the corner of the half-opened door. "Is there anything I can do for you, Boss?"

"No," he snapped and then asked. "Where is everybody? The place looks empty."

"Some people had put in for vacation days months ago, Boss." Her comment was an over the shoulder afterthought as she started to go back to her desk.

"Chalky," he shouted after her, "bring me the daily roster."

There was never a *please*. To Stoner's mind, *please* implied a request. He was not asking for anything. He was giving an order and that didn't warrant *please* or *thank you* for having done what was expected in the first place.

"Here you are, Sir," Chalky smiled anyway and laid the file on her boss's desk. After working for Stoner for several years, she had skin as thick as tanned hide, though it masqueraded as young and supple.

The Inspector didn't look up but reached roughly for the file. Only a handful of the guard was listed for that day. Perhaps because the roster was so sparse, one item that would have been buried in the dearth of other activity glared at Stoner from the page. A special contingent of guard was working that day. It mocked at him from the page. There were far more guardsmen on the streets than he had scheduled. He certainly had not ordered out a special detachment of personnel. One, two . . . there were five men at work that day, but their locations were not listed. Beside each guard's name were the words, *Confidential Assignment.*

"What's this?" Stoner yelled as he jumped to his feet. "Boone!" he shouted to anyone beyond his office door. It didn't matter to him who responded.

"Yes, Sir," Chalky stuck her head around the door again, but this time her manner seemed apprehensive.

"What is this . . . this *Confidential Assignment,* some arrogant joke?" His eyes flared with the fire of rekindled anger.

"*Confidential Assignment,* Inspector?" Chalky Boone eased carefully into the gladiator's arena with nothing but her fountain pen to protect herself from the lion.

"I have brought the most modern law enforcement equipment into this office," Stoner bellowed. "Aren't our people outfitted with the latest in light weight, oxford cloth upper torso body armor that wears like your favorite shirt? Didn't I fight for and get the best communication device on the market, the Tiny Fleck, a radio and transmitter so small it can look like your Lodge pin or your favorite tie tack your mama gave you as a Gift-giving present? Even the communications implant was my idea."

"Yes Sir," Chalky Boone responded hesitantly to the obvious questions with the not so obvious meaning under the spoken words.

"Then, will you please tell me how we can have an elite, clandestine unit of Blue Guard . . ." he paused as the anger rose in his chest and threatened to choke all breath from his raging body . . . "which I command!" He seethed . . . "And yet, I know nothing about it?" His voice rose and landed on the ground at Boone's feet.

Chalky Boone was usually able to handle his tirades. This time, Stoner's behavior was different. That day, he was the epitome of that which he loathed, a man out of control. Boone could see it in his eyes. "Sir, let's look at the entire week's schedule and see if a pattern emerges that will explain the mystery."

Boone returned quickly with a 281 Palm Device and set it on Stoner's desk. She flipped it on. The picture glowed like a hologram before his eyes. "There," she pointed to the names, "Shiloh Perkins, C.A. . . . Clause Zunstein, C.A. . . . and there and there. Sir, all five guardsmen were scheduled to work a confidential assignment all of last week. Have they been working undercover?"

"How the blazes would I know!" He shouted. "I'm just the commander around here. It looks like someone else is giving orders as well." He glared at Chalky for a long minute. Then he grabbed his hat again.

"I'll let it ride for today, Boone, given the season and all. But I'll find out what's going on. You can bet your future on that. And when I do, some careers will fall like downed timber, with a mighty crash." He stormed back out into the world of holiday lights. But, inside him, the only sparkle came from the fire that continued to rage within.

CHAPTER TWENTY-ONE

Christmas – a Word from the Past

9:30 p.m.

Jason and I stepped out of the coffee shop and back into the clear evening air. It was cold. I could feel snow trying to move in on the city.

"I'll drive you home, Christy." Jason motioned to a car parked by the curb.

Jason had an individually owned motor vehicle! I slid into the sleek black car and felt guilty, guilty because an automobile ride was for only a few of Society's most valued citizens. Physicians, police, and those on the fire department couldn't wait for Public Transit before responding to an emergency. It wouldn't be quite so tragic if the fire or robbery was at a low-producing citizens' home. But, what if the emergency were in the home of an official of the government or other professional person? Delay wouldn't be tolerated. I shuddered as I heard myself justifying such elitist thoughts. Why were some lives considered more important than others?

I understood Jason's need for a car. Being a physician, he was expected to be on call for emergencies, and his car had to be kept in top condition.

"This is nice," I marveled as I ran my fingers over the hand sewn leather cushions of the expensive vehicle. "It must be nice to drive such a car."

"Yes, it is," Jason said. "Since so few automobiles are made, the old production lines have become a thing of history. Can you believe cars are made by hand now, one at a time? If the government didn't subsidize the exorbitant price, I wouldn't be able to afford it."

We drove through the late evening streets where lights twinkled off the glassy surface of the damp pavement. "Oh Jason, just look at the Gifting lights. They are breathtaking. I hadn't even noticed so many of them had been put up."

"They just finished them late this afternoon. We've both been a little busy today."

How could the evil that Silas described possibly exist alongside such beauty? The poor man was mad.

"It's in the next block." I motioned to the large apartment complex on the right. "You can park out front since you're a doctor and I'm . . . well, all that and . . . never mind . . . right there."

Jason parked in the emergency vehicle space and then reached over and took my hand. "You apparently don't like to refer to yourself as *Legacy* either."

"Jason, you're no different. You hide behind your physician's white coat and no one knows you're Legacy." I stopped. I didn't want to be rude or start an argument. "I'm sorry."

"You can flash those gorgeous hazel eyes at me any time." He took a deep breath and looked out the window. "I've read a lot, Christy. I've discovered that no one is better than anyone else. We are all precious in the heart of the Creator." He looked at the brightly decorated tree in the small space in front of the building. "The lights are great though. I enjoy the Gifting season when everything is bright and full of celebration."

"That's why I enjoy this season so much too. I wonder who started the tradition of lights at Gifting time? I have never even thought about it before." Suddenly, with Jason, I was seeing everything in new ways, and my curiosity was mounting about everything around me.

"The lights may have begun with the Sabbath lights around the Jewish family's evening table. Certainly, from what I have read, there was a light from Heaven that shown the night the Christ child was born. That star led believers to a humble manger in Bethlehem; no doubt that is what inspired the lights at Gift-giving time."

"The Christ, Jason? Who or what is the Christ?" I had never heard that name before.

"He was the promised one, Christy. You'll read about him in the new section of your Bible." He smiled. "The Gift-giving lights are also reminiscent of the lighted tapers in the churches of old, which represented the presence of the Holy Spirit. Look over there at the house across the way," he whispered as if the inhabitants would hear us talking about them. "Those folks are like our early ancestors who put up a tree in their home and decorated it with bright bulbs. See them twinkle," he pointed. "A very long time ago, before people had old fashioned electrical lighting, families carefully placed candles on each branch and lit them only on Christmas Eve. Fire could have taken the tree and the whole house, but the candle light was too beautiful to miss out on."

"Christmas Eve?" I had read about Christmas in some of the novels I cherished the most, but I was surprised to hear the words spoken aloud. The word *Christmas* was forbidden, because it was too exclusive to one group and therefore offensive to a few. "In my books, everyone seemed so happy at Christmas time, so full of love and acceptance." A strange feeling gripped me. The stars of the night were lighting the dark places in my heart. Tears flowed down my cheeks. As I touched my face, Jason pulled me into his arms.

"It's all right Christy. Those are tears."

"Tears? I've never cried before. And I'm not sad. I don't think I have ever been sad enough to cry."

"There were other reasons why people used to cry besides sadness. In fact, joy could bring some people to tears. Also, being touched by the heart of God brought many people to tears."

"God's own heart? The Creator is like us? He has a heart?"

"We're like him, Christy, but he is not like us. He's bigger and more wonderful than our minds can ever understand. He is outside of time and outside of our ability to fully know him. If we could understand him, we would be God and . . . trust me, we are not God."

We sat there a few more minutes. I didn't want to go in. Everything was so new. It was hard to bend my mind around such strange, unheard of shapes and concepts. I wanted to talk more but, what would people say if I brought Jason into my living space? I thought for a minute and it didn't seem to matter what other people thought any more. Not since . . . Could it be possible that things started to change just this morning? "Jason, do you want to come in for a little while?" Then I remembered, "Jason, your nurse Dahlia lives in my building."

"Maybe we won't see her," Jason laughed.

Even with the cold outside, it was nice in the quiet of the car. I squeezed Jason's hand and felt his warmth. "You follow behind me and I'll check the hallway, but I have to tell you, I'm on the top floor. If no one is in the lobby, there may still be people in the elevator."

"I'm game. I can handle another adventure tonight."

We started to get out of the car and then Jason said, "Wait here." He jumped out and walked around the car, opened the door for me and offered his hand to help me to the sidewalk. "My Lady," he smiled.

"Wow, what book did you read that in?"

"None. My father always treated my mother with that kind of respect. He held her chair for her, walked on the curb side of the sidewalk when they were out for a stroll, held her hand, and opened the door for her."

"They remind me of my family, my parents, and especially my grandparents." We hurried along to the front door. The night air was chilled and frost had gathered on the front steps. "Do your parents live here in town?"

"No, Christy, they died two years ago. They were driving in the mountains and the road was icy. They slipped off the pavement and died in the crash."

"Oh, I'm so sorry," I said.

I looked through the large heavy glass window of the front door and saw no one in the hall. As Jason opened the door, I wanted to say words of comfort, but I had no experience to guide me. "Jason, I'm not good at this *feeling* stuff, but I am truly sorry you lost your parents so early. They were Legacy and would have lived long lives."

"Thanks Christy," he smiled.

Not many people in 2112 even remembered any feeling words. But, it didn't matter. The people had lost all empathy for one another by that time.

"The shock has passed," he reassured me, "but the love remains. I miss them every day." He smiled. "I'm glad I found you." The touch of his hand held warmth that had the power to melt my own loneliness.

CHAPTER TWENTY-TWO
The First Christmas Carols

10:00 p.m.

Jason and I looked through the heavy glass windows in the door to my apartment building. When we saw no one between the door and the elevator, we went in. Then we heard them. To the left of the brightly lit entry, a few people had gathered around the piano.

Jason rolled his eyes in surrender. "Caught," he mouthed in silence.

Dahlia smiled from across the room. She looked like someone who had just gotten an inside joke or secret. "Doctor," she sang out in a well, drawn out stream, "and My Lady." She started over toward us. "Sorry. I remember. It's Christiana." As she came nearer, she threw her arms open as an old friend would prepare to embrace a childhood chum.

"I'm so glad to see you two again . . . together." She flung her arms around me and hugged me as a friend. "Does *together* have a different meaning for Legacy Citizens than it does for us common people?"

She touched me. It felt good. Except for my family, and now Jason, I was never in close contact with others. People could have been arrested for touching me.

"I'm glad to see you too, Dahlia." I looked at my new friend and then at Jason. "Please Dahlia, don't . . ."

"I don't tell people everything I know, and nothing of what I suspect." She hugged me again, then stepped back and whispered, "Merry Christmas."

"Dahlia, you know? How?" Jason seemed as surprised as I was. We knew there were only a few Bible books still in existence.

"Yes, Dr. O'Reilly, I know a little bit. I was hoping Christiana could teach me more."

"Me? But, Dahlia, I'm just learning myself."

"But there's something inside of you, Christiana. You glow from within. He's alive in you."

I was shocked, "Who, Dahlia?"

"Come accompany us, Dahlia, so we can sing some more," someone called from the piano.

"They look like they're having so much fun." I watched the people laugh and touch and be together. I had never seen people interact like that before, except for my own family.

"Would you like to join us? We're going to sing more Christmas songs."

"Dahlia, it's forbidden. Aren't you afraid?"

"Not anymore," Dahlia took my hand and led me over to the piano. "Christiana, there are a lot of us now. This is the group I told you about."

"Is Silas Drummond with you tonight?"

"Silas? No. He works nights, but I haven't seen him all day. There were some Blue Shirts in here looking for him earlier."

"Blue Shirts? Why?"

"I don't know, except they said he wasn't at work at 3:00 p.m. as usual."

I gasped as I thought of Silas's warning. What was going on?

"How many are in your group?" Jason asked. He seemed mystified by the gathering. He didn't yet know about Silas.

Could it be possible that there were many seekers? How could a new spiritual revival have gone undetected by anyone, especially the Blue Guard?

"I can't give you numbers right now, but there are a lot of us who celebrate Christmas rather than Gift-giving Day. The number grows all the time."

"How do you know it's safe to talk about these things? If new people are joining your group every day, how do you know whom you're talking to? Maybe you'll say something and someone will turn you in." Jason was concerned for Dahlia as a friend, not just an employee. She could be arrested and jailed.

"We . . ." she studied us both very carefully, "we have a way of identifying each other."

"Can you tell us how?" Jason smiled and placed a kind hand on her shoulder. "I really want to know, Dahlia."

"Two ways," she whispered. "First, we say, 'I'm Thomas's friend,' since Thomas doubted until he saw the Savior's hands with his own eyes. We have been in darkness, too. Then we were told a great mystery which many of us didn't believe at first. But, then the truth grew within us, and we knew, we just knew."

"Dahlia," the singer called again.

"Okay, I'm coming," she laughed and walked away.

"Dahlia, what's the other way?" We followed her as she joined the group.

Dahlia smiled at us and pressed her index finger to her lips. "Come join us."

"I don't know any songs," I protested. Few people sang any more. There never seemed to be anything to sing about, no romance, no disappointment, no longing or striving, no inspiration. Besides, most music had been banned.

"I've heard you humming when you've stepped off the elevator," Dahlia insisted.

"I have heard you, too," the man from the bus chimed in.

"Do you live here?" I knew I recognized him from the P-T that morning, but I hadn't been aware of having seen him before that. I stepped closer to Jason and took his arm.

"No, I don't live here but I saw you at the university when we were both working on our Master's degrees," the man smiled a knowing smile, like he knew me better than I knew him.

A shiver ran up my spine, and I wondered what else I hadn't been aware of.

"What's your name?" Jason asked.

"I'm sorry. My name is Sean." He offered his hand in friendship, an archaic display of nonviolence, known for spreading germs. I reached out my hand and took his. It was warmer and friendlier than I expected. I liked the gesture. "I got my graduate degree in Communications Journalism." Then he stopped abruptly, cautious but confident. He lowered his voice and whispered, "Dahlia said you two can be trusted." He paused and looked from Jason to me. "I . . . publish an underground newspaper."

"A newspaper? I've heard of those," I gasped.

"Where did you hear of a newspaper?" Sean asked suspiciously. Newspapers had been abandoned nearly a hundred years ago when other forms of fast news dissemination flooded the market.

I thought for a moment. "I read about them."

"Come," Dahlia took my arm and led me to the group near the piano. "There is music in your soul, Christiana. Everyone can sing, at least in their own way. Even the angels in Heaven communicate through song."

Angels? My mind was overflowing. I had read about angels and about people who sang when they were happy and sang when they were sad. I had even seen the words of Christmas songs printed on pages of song books I had read, but I had never heard the melodies or felt them resounding in my mind. I didn't know their meaning.

"Your heart will recognize the tunes," Dahlia assured us.

She sat at the piano and ran her fingers up and down the keys, chord upon beautiful chord. I wondered where she had learned how to play.

Obviously, I had seen the piano in the corner of the gathering room before and never gave it further attention. Why had I not wondered about it before? If music had been banned, why was there still a musical instrument in the building? Then I remembered what the building manager had said. She had described it as a work of art. Maybe the manager was right in her thinking but only partially. She may have confused the instruments of music with objects of art, like sculpture or paintings. She had said, "Isn't it a beautiful piano?" like it was a fine art statue. How very strange. For a hundred years, people had rejected the sound but not the form.

It was a wonderful evening of music—Christmas carols Dahlia had called them. We sang about a baby who slept in a manger because there was no room for him in the Inn. Angels sang alleluias from the heavens to announce his birth and to glorify God for his precious gift, just like Jason had described. Dahlia was right. The music went deep within me and then streamed forth from the depths of my soul, and . . . I knew, but I didn't yet know that I knew.

CHAPTER TWENTY-THREE
Forbidden Singing Heard

Out on the streets, people were going in for the night. As Stoner drove through neighborhoods, he noticed a small group of people sitting on the steps of an apartment building, talking. If he had the capacity for enjoyment, Stoner would have appreciated the solitary quietness of the evening as he drove around the city in the frosty air. Sometimes, he just had to get away from people. For someone who worked with the public every day, he had a growing disdain for most everyone. The truth was, he didn't like himself much either. He could only tolerate a short amount of alone-time. He was not his own best company.

The long evening hours had been uneventful, so the silent vibration of his communication device startled him. He tilted his head slightly as a voice spoke quietly in the ear piece buried beneath his skin near the bone behind his ear. "Inspector, I hate to bother you. Your location indicator places you near Indian River Apartments."

"I just passed it," Stoner spoke into the emptiness of the night.

"It's the craziest thing. Someone has reported that they heard singing coming from the building?" the dispatcher reported.

"Singing? You're kidding, right?"

"No, Sir," she apologized.

"Singing was banned a long time ago. No one has sung in nearly a century. How would they know how? Who knows any songs?"

"I don't know, Sir. I'm sorry to have bothered you."

"No, Dispatch. I don't know how they're singing, but I'll check on it." The very thought of songs being sung assaulted his ears. Stoner made a U-turn in the street and headed the few blocks back to the Indian River Apartments.

He didn't hesitate. He parked his strata-car in front of the building and stormed to the entrance. He thrust open both double doors and burst into the apartment building lobby. In the large gathering room to the left, a group of people were sitting around on sofas or chairs, and a few were casually lounging on the floor. A piano art piece was present but no one was trying to play it. Who could have? It seemed to Stoner, they were apparently listening to a speaker who was leading them in a chant of some sort.

"Spending money carefully,
my responsibility.
Gifting Day is nearly here
Raise a cup and shout a cheer.
Hip, Hip, Hay! Hip, Hip Hurrah!
Happy, happy, Gifting Day,
When I spend up all my pay
giving gifts to everyone,
is my duty and my fun.
Hip, Hip, Hay! Hip, Hip, Hurrah!"

"Very good everyone, we . . ." the speaker stopped when she saw the inspector who stood listening impatiently. "May I help you, Sir?"

"There was a report that singing was heard coming from this building," he snapped.

"Singing, Sir?" Dahlia questioned. "Song was banned a long time ago. I would think that most people wouldn't even know how to sing, Inspector."

"Someone reported hearing music and singing nevertheless."

"Oh . . . maybe they heard our chants." She glanced toward the piano. "People don't even know how to play one of those beautiful instruments any more. They are graceful and lovely aren't they?" She smiled sweetly. "The chants may sound silly, but I find they're a good way to remember some of Society's important points." She turned to the group. "Let's chant the one we were doing a few minutes ago."

"Raising children every day,
with the help the People give,
lets me know they're in control,
giving time to work and live"

"Lady . . . shut up!" Stoner shouted as he glared at the group. "Whom do you think you're dealing with?"

"Sir —"

"Enough lady! That sounds like a song to me, a very bad song, but . . ." Stoner's face grew red, and his neck was taunt and rigid. "Why am I wasting my time with this nonsense? Chant if you want— just don't sing—or I'm sending a bus for all of you! Got it?"

"Yes, Sir," Dahlia agreed with polite surrender to his authority.

The inspector shot a caustic glance around the room, mentally recording the faces of each participant. Some looked familiar but at the moment, he didn't care. He had to get out of there. He was not going to run around town chasing ghosts and felonious singers.

He turned with near parade drill formation and shot back out the door. He was not retreating. He was leaving. He was too important for such stupidity. "Every minute I stand here, I lose ten IQ points," he mumbled out loud. *On a night like this, somebody always has a complaint, an observance, or a question to be investigated. If they're not griping about something, they lose their reason for living. Their entire identity is wrapped up in spying on their neighbors and reporting every little remonstrance to someone, anyone. But, I will not be reduced to a baby sitter for these minimal citizens.*

Stoner left the light and went back out into the darkness where shadows provided better cover for his indignant hostility. Back in his patrol car, he tried to remember where he had seen the leader before. Later, he would get the names of everyone who lived in that building.

CHAPTER TWENTY-FOUR
The Spirit inside the Book

11:30 p.m.

That evening, out in front of the apartment building, Dahlia had stationed friends nearby, talking together in little clusters. They watched for anyone the group did not know or trust. Fortunately, Stoner's strata-car was seen in time for Jason and me to move to the back of the group, inside Indian River Apartments. After Stoner left, we didn't expect him to waste his time coming back, so, we sang far into the night. There were songs about sleighs and snowflakes, and choruses about a family who had no place to sleep but a barn. That family was remembered for thousands of years and the baby was the miracle of the ages.

The lyrics and the strains of music, that had the power to penetrate my soul, were something I had never experienced. Some melodies made me feel like I was riding the wind of the sea, lifting me higher and higher. Other music made me think of home and yet, it was the kind of home I had only read about. I finally understood why the angels sing. Music touched my soul in ways mere words could not express.

It was late when the last of the carolers finally gave up and went off to sleep a few hours before the day would dawn again. Jason and I waited until the others had left, to say good night to Dahlia.

"Well, my new friends," Dahlia yawned, "I will fall off this bench into a sleeping ball, and none of us want that." She stood and stretched, then gave me another hug. "I'm happy for both of you."

"Don't bother coming into the office, Dahlia. Morning starts soon," Jason smiled.

"You're very generous, Doctor. Tomorrow is the day before First-day, our day of rest—which also happens to be Gifting Day. We never work those two days."

Jason laughed and kissed her cheek.

"Night, Dahlia," I added. Then I did something I had never done before. I reached out to her with an embrace. Suddenly, I remembered. "Dahlia, what is the second sign that helps us to identify others who believe? You were telling us earlier. 'I'm Thomas's friend,' and what else?"

She took my hands like one sharing a secret with a friend. "Jesus's friend Peter was often called the Big Fisherman, Christiana. Jesus called Peter and two brothers, James and John, also fishermen, to follow him. As his disciples, they would learn from him, so that they could reveal God to the people as well. Jesus said he would make his followers fishers of men. Christiana, watch for the ichthus. Watch for the ichthus." Then she turned to go up to her apartment.

"Ichthus, Dahlia? Watch for fish?" I called after her, but she only waved her hand in the air, smiled over her shoulder, and walked on.

"Jason, remember those happy, laughing faces around the piano this evening? Somewhere on each one's clothing—a lapel pin, a necklace, a design on a ring—there was a fish, the ichthus." I was amazed. "They recognized each other by their brand—the ichthus."

Jason never went to my room. At the door, we lingered for a moment. It had been a wonderful day and we didn't want to let it end. There had been no joy like this in our time, so it was hard to trust there could possibly be a repeat of this glorious day. We said little, but when our eyes met, volumes were hidden behind them. Jason kissed my forehead. I watched him turn and walk slowly out into the night. Snow had begun to fall and I remembered a song: something about a white Christmas. I smiled.

• • • • •

In my apartment, I pushed the button to ignite the flame in the fireplace, a luxury known only to Legacy Citizens. Workers were forbidden to waste fuel. I started to rationalize how added responsibility should earn special perks and then I shuddered. I hadn't even thought about my elite status before. I had taken it for granted. Now, it all felt pretentious. I wasn't better than others. For the first time, I finally felt I was part of a cluster of friends.

As I sat there in the stillness of my apartment, I felt a presence growing within me, an indwelling spirit. It was mysterious yet loving, beckoning and calling gently for entrance into my world. It gave me hope and courage. At that moment, I felt emboldened enough to take a stand against the darkness that seemed to be crowding in around me.

I stretched as tall as I could, pulled the leather bound book from its conspicuous hiding place, and curled up in my favorite reading chair beside the fire.

How could a harmless black book make me feel excited, afraid, curious and indifferent, all at the same time? If I opened that book, would my life change completely? Why were there secrets inside those pages that had been declared unsafe, subversive? *What should I do?* I placed the book on the floor and stared into the fire. *I'll give it back to Grand-père. He'll understand. I don't know why he had given me the dangerous contraband in the first place. What if I get caught with it?*

Unable to move from the spot, I watched the flames leaping in the firebox and thought of my new emotions. I jumped up, paced back and forth, and stole little glances at the book. I turned my back and walked over to the windows. Sparkling snow clung to the trees and bushes creating a kaleidoscope of color as it danced under the multicolored Gifting lights. I thought about Jesus and the meaning of Christmas. I understood something since I'd heard of him. Without him, there is no reason for gifting.

I looked down at the leather-covered book there on the floor near the hearth. What should I do? *Should I, shouldn't I?* Even that sounded silly. I hadn't just found the book lying in the street. My grandfather had given it to me. If I couldn't trust him, I couldn't trust anyone. I picked up the sacred book, ran my hands over the cover, felt the grain of the leather beneath my fingers, and sat down on the edge of the chair. The old volume fell open to the middle where the heading read *Psalms*. Carefully, I leafed through the pages. Jason had suggested that I start reading alternately from the old covenant and then the new. But, as a reason for my reading, he recommended that I read three passages first. I turned to those selections.

> Genesis 1: 1-3. In the beginning God created the heavens and the earth. Now the earth was formless and empty, darkness was over the surface of the deep. And the Spirit of God was hovering over the waters. And God said, "Let there be light, and there was light."

My breath stopped. God spoke light into being! My mind could not grasp the enormity of what I was reading, but my soul soaked up the words it thirsted for. First there was nothing, absolutely nothing, then God spoke and light blazed forth. I tried to imagine what the thunder of creation from the mouth of God would have sounded like!

Then I turned to the second passage.

> John 1: 1-5. In the beginning was the Word, and the Word was with God, and the Word was God. He was with God in the beginning. Through him all things were made; without him nothing was made that has been made. In him was life, and that life was the light of men. The light shines in the darkness, but the darkness has not understood it.

So God wants to shine light into all the dark places. He wants us to understand, even though much of life is not understandable. He wants all of us to have wisdom, every one of us. Jason had said, when we follow God's commands and embrace the wisdom in those laws, we are given promises. He said those promises and the reason for my quest for a solution to my grandparents' fate would be found.

> Proverbs 3: 1-2.
>
> My son, do not forget my law, but let your heart keep my commands, for length of days and long life and peace they will add to you.

Length of days and long life . . . what did that mean? The reference explained, enduring days with warm hours that would be stretched over a lengthy life time and peace for the heart is promised to those who keep God's laws. All of my worry over my grandparents' fate was stripped away. They had a right to live a long and wise life, just as all of God's created souls had the same right. God had given that promise. Light was shining into what I thought had been the shadowed, empty places of my heart. But, I discovered there are no empty places, only foreign lands of the soul that speak another language and have other experiences and customs. It takes time, a life time, an eternity, to travel to the far boundaries of the human soul. Then I knew —and I knew that I knew.

CHAPTER TWENTY-FIVE
Stoner Challenged

Ward Stoner pulled to a stop again in front of the Indian River Apartments. He had been driving around in circles since leaving the building earlier where he checked out a report that music and singing had been heard. He had only encountered a group of chanters. Each time he had passed the building, the same people sat in conversation on concrete steps, laughing and enjoying themselves. *How can they stand to spend an entire cold evening together, doing nothing more than talk, talk, talk?* His skin began to crawl. Had he known they were spotters for Dahlia, he may have had another opinion.

Stoner had felt drawn back to the apartment building, but he didn't know why. Two situations loomed in front of him, the disappearance of a furnace technician and a phantom woman that roamed the transit and the apartment complex and had ties to both. Silas Drummond had to be found. He was totally insignificant, but he knew things that could not get out to the general public.

This time Stoner left the motor running. He wanted to keep the heater on. He had no intention of staying long.

Dispatch whispered in his ear. "Inspector, location monitoring places you back at Indian River Apartments. Is there a problem?"

"No, no problem."

"Sir, I heard the exchange before. I think I dropped IQ points too, just listening to your encounter with those people over the communication device."

"Never mind. I'll build up more IQ points later. I'll not be able to understand people like that. Lack of education is one thing but celebrating ignorance is more than I can tolerate."

"It's late, Sir. Why don't you go home?"

Stoner had used his address pod to check out residents of the building. He made a list of each inhabitant. The inspector vowed to waste no more time that night on ghosts, wayward singers, or on an uppity Legacy Citizen who had the mysterious ability to stay a few steps ahead of him all day. Yes, once he had left the little gathering and cleared his head from the mundane dribble of the chants he had been subjected to, he realized he had recognized her standing almost behind someone else. *Why have you been skipping along in front of me all day, Missy? What are you doing that's so, so important?*

But, there was more. Stoner was a man with a personal force of iron. He was used to intimidating people with a frozen glance. Miss Number-One Citizen was different. There was something about her, a growing presence, a strengthening of her will. *Where does her strength come from? She probably doesn't even know she has it,* he thought as his icy breath came out with his mumblings and hung on the night air.

He had worked in the Blue Guard for many years and had risen in the ranks, like an alley cat leaping to the top of the backyard fence. One day he was on the ground and suddenly he was on the top. The rise to power was too heady for him. It affected his mind and sense of his own importance. At first, he had struggled with balancing power with his family life. While Miriam was still alive, she kept him grounded. However, once she was gone, his equilibrium died with her. He could no longer weigh the importance of each element of his life. All events held equal weight in Stoner's world. Everything was an inconvenience. Everyone was an annoyance. Every incident of his long days made him angry.

He stared up at the building and followed the structure's facade to the very top floor. Lights still glowed from the windows in the high penthouse and would have made others feel warm. Not Ward Stoner.

I'm sure you must live up there, Missy, a fairy princess at the top of her castle. Suddenly, he saw the silhouette of a woman framed in a top floor window beyond the shade. He jumped. He was surprised because it forced him to remember she was real, not an imaginary adversary lurking about in his mind, growing larger and stronger with each antagonistic thought. He shook his head to reshuffle the pictures in his deck of mental face cards. *That's enough of you tonight, Missy. Tomorrow, we'll see who has the greater power, you or me.*

CHAPTER TWENTY-SIX
Silas is Taken

7:00 a.m. Saturday, December 24

I woke up the next morning with Christmas melodies singing in my heart. *I must have been singing them in my sleep, all night long.* I stretched and yawned and smiled at the morning. Light streamed in my windows and bounced off the beveled mirror above my dresser sending prisms of carnival light across the surfaces of the room. Then I remembered, *And God said, let there be light and there was light.*

Rolling over in bed, I felt a furry body near my foot. "Oh it's you, Shakespeare," I purred at the new white ball of feline fuzz. Laying there a while longer, I drew Shakespeare's soft body near me as new and thrilling images of the previous day filled my thoughts.

Everything I had been taught and had experienced up to that Gifting Season was being over-turned or up-righted. Not that my life had been a lie. I had realized in a flash—the last generations had not known about the true history of mankind. The text books had been purged and rewritten many years ago in order to bring stability to a society that had grown lazy and full of entitlement demands. We had been proud people, energetic, creative, prosperous, free people, who had forgotten how to think, how to problem-solve, and how to rejoice with what we had been given. Now, Society took care of us at the most minimal level, feeding our need to be nearly illiterate, uninformed, unmotivated, and volatile. People were left with just enough energy to be good worker bees. Antidepressants and mind dulling drugs in our water supply now controlled us but left our emotions flat, our libido restrained, and all creativity thwarted.

I was no better informed. I only read approved text books while growing up. Emotion was lacking from my life too, so when I found the old books in the back rooms of the library, I preferred to read the novels of the past that overflowed with feelings. Once I found the novels, I neglected the books of history, comparative governments and religions. I was an elective illiterate the same as others.

I shot out of bed with a new resolve. Perhaps there would still be a way to reverse my grandparents' death sentence, the never-ending-sleep. The answers had to be buried in the old texts in the library.

I showered in the open wet area, dressed, and then checked my image in the mirror. For some strange reason, it was important how I looked today. I thought of a red blouse I had bought a few years back and had never worn, thinking that the color clashed with my auburn hair and fair complexion. Today it felt festive. It reminded me of the bright lights that bejeweled the city with celebration. I dressed quickly and dashed out to greet the day.

Outside, it had grown colder through the night and snow covered the ground. The icicle laden trees looked beautiful. The sky was blue and as clear as I had ever seen it. *Maybe God is blessing me with clarity today too.* I hoped I was right.

Another transit ride, I sighed. *I hope there is no stranger staring at me again, like Sean, or no little man to get inside my head with evil dribble.* By the time I got to my stop near the library, my ride had been so uneventful, I nearly forgot about Sean or Silas Drummond.

8:30 a.m.

When I got to the library, it was still early and the sun danced off the window panes. But, just as I entered through the main doors, I heard my name and turned.

"Lady Applewait, wait!"

I could not believe it. Silas Drummond called to me again from the opposite curb.

Every word of the awful letter he had written flashed before my eyes and resounded in my ears. I tried to ignore him as I pushed on the door but his words stopped me.

"Look at the glitter of the building Miss Applewait. Believe me, please. Calcium," he shouted.

I gasped in disgust at the possibility of human bones being ground into a fine powder. I gaged and wanted to run but there was something about the man. His beard had grown scraggly and deep lines etched his face. He looked as if he hadn't slept all night and exhaustion was evident in every motion of his frail body. Just as I was feeling a new empathy for him, two blue guardsmen jumped out of a vehicle, grabbed Drummond and shoved him into the back of their car. I could hear his screams as they sped off.

"Lady Christiana, please . . ."

Fear gripped me as I stood frozen on the steps of the library. What was happening? Had he been caught because he was spreading lies or because he was revealing the truth?

CHAPTER TWENTY-SEVEN

Formation of the New Society

The encounter with Silas Drummond left me feeling vulnerable, exposed. I hurried in through the huge library doors and caught my breath in the main lobby. It was the day before Gift-giving Day and the place seemed empty except for security personnel and a few librarians and other workers. I welcomed the sight of Frank, the guard, and sailed through the front inspection barrier where he sat half asleep.

"Rise and shine, Frank," I called out as I slipped through the gate to the safety of the other side. This time I listened for the sound. I had made sure the chip was in my satchel and, sure enough, I heard a faint beep as I walked through the scanner.

"Oh Frank, I left my book over there." It was not an accident. I was setting up my own experiment. I put my bag, with the chip inside of it, on the desk on Frank's side of the gate and walked back through the portal. I picked up the book I had left over there and started back through the gate again. I walked slowly and listened intently. There was no sound. The guard looked up in surprise.

"That's odd," he observed.

"What's that Frank?" I questioned as I scooped up my satchel again.

"You weren't detected. Everyone is detected when they come in."

"Really? How?" I asked innocently.

"I don't know. I just know we all beep."

"Let me see," I stepped back through the gate with my bag securely in my hand. I turned and swung back through the portal like I was executing a dance move, *allemande left,* one of the books had called it. That time, I heard a beep.

"Well, okay." Frank seemed mystified. "I guess I didn't hear you the first time."

"You were asleep, my friend, and we both know it," I teased. I sighed with relief. My experiment had proven my hypothesis. The tagging chip caused the beep - society's methodical counting of souls.

"You sure are different today, My Lady." Frank studied me carefully.

"Am I?" I thought I'd better move on. It wasn't the custom for Legacy Citizens to have lengthy conversations with workers.

I hurried into the back stacks and was surprised to see Marge sitting by the window reading.

"Christiana? What are you doing here? It's the day before Gift-giving."

"I could ask the same of you, Marge." I sounded a little snippy and wished I had phrased it differently.

Marge didn't seem to notice. Perhaps I usually snapped at people. I did not like that possibility. Actually, I wished she would leave. I wanted to go on back into the inner recesses, unnoticed and unquestioned.

"Do you have company you need to prepare for?" I asked.

"No, not this year. I'll be alone."

Suddenly, a wave of loneliness I'd never felt before swept over me. "I'm sorry, Marge."

She looked up from her book. "You are? Why?"

"No one wants to be alone on Gift-giving Day."

"Are you all right, Christiana?" She was still watching me

closely. "What did the doctor say about your shoulder yesterday?"

"Yesterday? Was that yesterday?"

"Yes," she drew out slowly. "Was it serious?"

"Was what serious?" She startled me but I had to smile. I wasn't sure if she was talking about the doctor and me, or about my seeing the doctor. "No," I stalled with a chuckle, "it was just like a sliver and the doctor removed it."

"And . . . the doctor . . . what did you think about him?" Marge closed the book and laid it in her lap.

How could I tell her what had happened? How could I explain my new emotions, my new understandings, my new awakening, my new friends . . . and Dr. Jason O'Reilly? I didn't even understand it all myself. How could I explain it to someone else?

"He's gorgeous!" I teased playfully as I turned to go toward the back hallway.

"Gorgeous? So men are gorgeous now? Christiana, you are bubbling." Marge started to get up and since I didn't want her to follow me, I turned back quickly.

I thought fast and switched the topic. "They have me on a new medication. I am being . . . detoxified," I said with a tone of resignation.

Laying her book on the side table, Marge eased out of her chair. "Detoxification?" she whispered.

"Yes."

"With tiny little pills?" Marge moved closer, her eyes darted toward the door and back at me.

I couldn't believe how Marge could have known about the pills? She wasn't Legacy and no one else would have had knowledge of them. "Marge, what do you think you know?"

"I read about them, Christina, about the water and the citizen control . . . and —"

"What about . . . the never-ending-sleep?" I held my breath. Could it really be that easy? Was the answer that close? "Where,

Marge? Where did you read about the pills and all of that?"

"Come back here," she said as she led the way down the hallway and into the back stacks. "Over here. I remember exactly where I had seen it because it was so profound." She ran her finger over the books on the shelf about eye level and stopped. "Here it is," she whispered as she studied the spine. *"Formation of the New Society."*

Marge scanned the index and stopped on chapter eleven. "Here, page one-hundred sixteen, *Citizen Control.* It's all right here, Christiana. They have been putting stuff in our water for years, in order to make us calm and cooperative, but it also robbed us, Christina. Yes, we aren't sad or angry anymore, but we no longer have any joy either. The antidepressants control all negative feelings, sadness and anger, which should have brought a measure of happiness. But, the other chemicals that counteracted the side effects of the additives flattened everyone back out again because their ultimate goal had nothing to do with our best interests. It was all about population control. Their motives were twofold. First, they wanted to insure there would be no rebellion, and second . . . here let me show you this."

She turned more pages frantically. "They wanted to decrease the number of citizens. Here it is, *Population Control*—listen to this. 'In order for any society to support the most productive members, there must be a depopulation policy to legally put down its most disturbed, disabled, and infirmed individuals, as well as the elderly, and those citizens considered not capable of rehabilitation. These individual human units will be placed in a sleep chamber where they will drift off into an endless sleep.' It's right there."

"Population Control? Marge, they have lied all along. Their motives were to build their own power!" I could not believe it, but I knew with my heart it was true.

Marge continued reading. "Since a society in the post-industrialized era requires only a modest workforce, it is necessary to limit the number of children produced in each family unit. Given that children born outside a family unit have little potential for success, they will be terminated before they become viable."

"Oh Marge, those poor babies . . . and their grieving mothers . . .

how could they?" I could not believe our leaders were so cruel.

"Here it is, Christiana," Marge went on. "As a proactive policy, additives in the water supply will decrease the human desire to procreate, which will also eventually depopulate the nation. After a passage of time, this present crisis will pass. Then the policy regarding the endless sleep and these other forms of population control will be reevaluated to see if they should continue. Overturning this law will require a referendum from the citizenry."

"What was this great crisis of the past? What happened?" I felt knowledge deprived and that rendered me helpless to change the future.

"I read the old history books as well as the transitional texts," Marge whispered into the solitude of the back library. "The people had gotten complacent and had no longer participated in the republic. They only wanted to play games and engage in all manner of irresponsible behavior. Gluttony and an insatiable need for riches led most people into a totally self-indulgent, self-centered, and self-destructive life style. Families imploded, financial institutions collapsed and while people slept off their drunken stupor, a political faction of those bent on the total control of others rolled into place and shoved the lazy majority aside where they could continue to wallow in their own self-pity."

"How did this come about? Didn't the people try to stop it?" I questioned.

"No, the people paid no attention to their own government, except to complain," Marge responded and then went on reading. "That anti-democratic political movement had been growing beneath the general population's awareness, waiting for the right moment to take over the government while the country slept in their self-induced fog. When the people finally awakened from their apathy, they began fighting back, but it was too late. The movement had become very strong. The emotions on both sides finally exploded into the streets and chaos rained down. No one trusted the other. Those who successfully won the takeover of the government started drugging the water to control the masses of people."

"Marge, how could it have gotten to that point? It seems

impossible that people, who were blessed with the emotions of love and compassion, would give up such jewels for the plastic bobbles of frivolous play?"

"They had become lazy, complacent, Christiana."

"Marge, why hadn't you told me all of this before?" I was both thrilled and disappointed at the same time. Marge knew I had been concerned about my grandparents. She must have known that her information was relevant to my cause.

"I'm sorry." She looked away and whispered, "I was afraid."

"Afraid?" I thought Marge and I were friends. Maybe a Legacy Citizen can have no friends. "Were you afraid of me?"

"No . . ." she hesitated, "well, yes . . . maybe." Marge touched my hand but would not look at me. "I was afraid of everything. If they had found out I had been reading the old books, I could have lost my job. If they thought I was trying to organize or arouse the people, I could have gone to jail."

"Sedition . . . promoting through speech or writing, discontent or rebellion against the country," I clarified out loud, although the warning was meant for me too.

"Yes," she whispered in agreement. "If I lost my job or worse yet, if they put me in jail, I would no longer be a valued citizen. I would have my Length of Days lowered to the status of the common person." Marge's face was strained and tears rolled down her cheeks.

I studied her expression and asked carefully, "Marge, have you been using the pills too? How else could you feel so deeply?" Maybe I was revealing too much. I put my arms around her and hugged her as a friend. "It's okay. But, where did you get the pills?"

"That, I can't tell you, Christiana. Not yet. Please don't ask me again." She was pleading and I couldn't refuse.

"Tomorrow is Gift-giving Day. Do you know another name for Gift-giving Day?" It could do no harm. If she didn't know, she would say so without raising more questions.

She looked at me and smiled. "Christiana . . . am I going to get to say it again? I don't usually get to wish anyone a *Merry Christmas*.

Not very often anyway."

Joy flooded my heart. Though I'd known about Christmas for less than twenty-four hours, it felt like my soul had known forever. "Tomorrow is Christmas, Marge," I whispered. "I have until the end of the month to find a way to halt the evil euthanasia of the infirmed and elderly." I put my hand on the book Marge had just read from. "I have to get this book out of here today. Grand-père has to see it. Maybe if he knew the true history of our country, maybe he wouldn't be so willing to accept the inevitability of his fate."

"Christiana," Marge's jaw dropped, "you cannot try to remove this book! You'll get caught. We'll both get caught." Panic seemed to have overtaken her as she tried to reach out for it.

"I don't think they'll catch me. I have a plan. If it works, I'd like you to come to Christmas dinner tomorrow at my grandparents' home. It's a family thing, but I'll be inviting a few other friends as well. If it doesn't work, I guess I'll be having my holiday dinner as a guest of the city."

"Christmas in the home of members of the Council of Elders? Christiana, do you think I could?"

I laughed a little, not at my friend but at the joy I saw flash across her face. "You have already been invited. Of course you can come."

"Wow, what a miracle. Now, we need another piece of gracious luck to get us through the hijacking of library property. How are we going to be able to get this book out of here?" Marge questioned. "You know they'll see us walk through with a book in our hands."

"I want you to walk ahead of me to Frank's station. You talk to him while I slip past. I'll put the book on the other side of the gate, then come back and walk through again." I had a plan I thought might work. "Frank always smiles more broadly when you come into the library, Marge. He watches you. With very few emotions in his quivery of arrows, Frank must save up all day for his brief encounters with you."

"Don't be silly," Marge blushed. "Besides, you'll beep when you sneak through."

"No, I'm sure I won't." I said as I gathered up the book. It wasn't large but it was thick. I was still able to carry it in my left hand, the side away from Frank. "I'll grab my hat but if you'll take my tunic and satchel, I think we can pull this off."

We walked into the hall and through the door that led to the outer library. No one was around. We kept walking, slowly, casually. When we emerged into the lobby, Frank saw us coming and smiled.

"Hi Frank." Marge positioned herself in such a way that caused Frank to turn his back on me to pay exclusive attention to her.

"Hi Marge," he grinned when we came up to his desk. "Are you going to stay here much longer?"

"Are you trying to close up early, Frank?" she smiled.

I took the few steps through the portal. It should have caused a beep from my chip. Nothing. *Good,* I thought.

They no longer tracked books with a bar code system, so the movement of the book alone would have not caused notice. Since people's bodies were now *bar coded* and their every move was tracked, it wasn't necessary to know what they carried in and out of buildings.

My heart was pounding when I found myself on the other side of the portal without being counted. Then, like a calming breeze, I remembered the words . . . *Silent night, holy night, all is calm, all is bright.* Those words blew away my fear and quieted my soul. I stepped back across the line, through the open gate, and slipped in beside Marge as she continued to talk to Frank.

"Thank you for carrying my stuff, Marge. I had almost forgotten. I can take my things now." I smiled and took my belongings from her, including the bag with my chip buried inside. "Walk with me over to the front door, okay?"

"Sure," then Marge turned to Frank, "if you have time to stop for coffee when you leave here later, let me know. I'll be going in about an hour."

Frank looked somewhat confused, so I walked back through the clearing station nonchalantly and beeped obediently. I moved over to the side table, picked up the book I had just placed there, and folded it into my wrap. When Marge caught up to me, we giggled a little.

"Marge, you made quite a sacrifice for the cause back there with Frank," I whispered through my laughter.

"That was no sacrifice, Christiana." She blushed and looked back at Frank who continued to follow us with his eyes. She patted the tunic-covered book. "Are you going home now?"

"I'm going to make a stop and invite another couple of friends for dinner tomorrow." I gave her a hug, and we parted. Out in the bright early winter day, I saw the transit approaching from the east. I hurried along, all the while remembering the calm melody of *Silent Night* that rang in my head at the library checking station. A new, hopeful spirit and calm peace rose and filled all the empty spaces, flooding my soul with joy. God had shown me a way to stop the madness. Then . . . I knew, and I knew that I knew why the angels sing.

CHAPTER TWENTY-EIGHT
Stoner Demands Answers

Over at the Headquarters of the Blue Guard, Inspector Ward Stoner was on another rampage. "Boone!" He barked as he charged past Chalky Boone's desk. "Come into my office."

"Right," she responded as she grabbed up her palm-held verbal steno recorder.

The inspector stood at the window seeing nothing. "I need as much information as you can get on Christiana Applewait."

"Lady Applewait?" she questioned.

"Yes, Christiana Applewait. Is she so far above us all that you can't get a dossier on her?" Stoner's body twitched as he hiked up his pants and smoothed his shirt trying to control his seething anger.

Chalky blinked in disbelief. "Yes . . . Ward . . . she is —"

Stoner certainly knew the law. He turned and glared at her. His valued assistant and First Lieutenant was perhaps the only person left in the city who actually knew him. "Chalky, I don't want to hear that answer."

"I know you don't, but it's the truth." Chalky stood her ground with feet firmly planted. She was the only person who could tell the Chief Inspector, "No."

"Boone, let's not talk about what's true. Let's grind out a little of what's necessary."

"Ward . . . she is a Legacy Citizen. You know the laws regarding the Council of Elders and those who will rise to that position. The Law of 2031 purged every file known to Society of even the name of a Legacy Citizen. None of our e-files have a word about the Wise Ones." Boone's tone was calming but firm. Educated as a lawyer, she knew the law.

"What about the little wise crackers, the second and third generations?" He hissed with sarcasm.

"Inspector —"

"Then how do we know she's Legacy? Tell me that." His face was red and the veins on his temples bulged with anger. "Can't anyone do their job around here but me?" he shouted.

"There is a paper file on each of the members of the Council, their ancestors, their descendants, and any pertinent information about them, including education, achievements, and their writings. But, there is nothing that we can access from our readers. It is not in the air, anywhere. It's on paper."

"Okay, okay, let's sit down and brainstorm." Stoner sat at his desk, leaned back and closed his eyes. "Applewait is her father's name. She is Legacy by linage from her maternal grandparents, Oliver and Constance Richly."

"Yes, that's true, Ward, but she is also Legacy through her paternal grandparents, Abraham and Claudia Applewait. They passed into the sleep several years ago following a house fire."

"Those wood frame houses in Oakwood should have been demolished a long time ago. They're nothing but tinder boxes waiting to ignite," Stoner said. "The fancy people think they are so great because they have so much space."

"Space and ambiance. I was in one once and it seemed so warm and friendly."

"Oh please," Stoner drew out his words with indignation. "Those buildings take a lot more maintenance than the newer, high-rise buildings."

"Yes Sir. There was a rumor that the senior Applewait's house was deliberately torched," Boone added.

"Why hadn't I heard about that?" Stoner snapped back. "Arson is a crime you know."

"That was about the time your wife went to sleep, Ward. You were off duty and probably weren't informed."

Stoner made no response. He had barely acknowledged the passing of his wife in his own frozen emotions. He was locked in a state of grief and anger and never spoke of her out loud.

"So, by linage, she is a Lady, Lady Applewait," Boone broke the silence.

"I'm not impressed," Stoner snapped back. "So, where are these paper files on the Legacy Citizens?"

"I . . . don't know how to access them," Boone said. "But, some place I ran across the addresses of a few Legacy Citizens. Those locations are stored here in my palm-reader." She spoke into her reader, "Legacy addresses." She selected a tab and the information was instantly available. "Christiana Applewait lives in the penthouse," she read, "in the Indian River Apartments."

A slight sneer crossed Stoner's lips. "Yes, I know."

Chalky looked up but said nothing about his comment. "Her parents live in the Lee Ridge High Rise and her grandparents, two of the twelve, live in Oakwood, at 721 Primrose Lane."

"That's all we have?" He growled. "That's it?"

"That's it."

"Who has access to the paper files if they're so secret?"

"The Council of Elders, Sir," she stated flatly as if she had just completed a circle. "And those files are stored in the vault at Fort Knox, Kentucky where the gold used to be stored."

"The gold is still there, Boone. It was never moved as they said it had been." Stoner's expression softened from the anger that was usually stored around his eyes. "I would be willing to bet that not even the current Council members remember what's in those files. We could say anything we wanted to about any of them."

"Yes, but if you spread lies about even one of them, are you willing to bet your career, maybe even your life, on getting away with it?" Chalky asked.

"Maybe not this time. For now, it may be enough to know where I can find them. As long as I know where these people are, they're as good as captured. They're not going anywhere. I'll keep an eye on Oakwood myself. It might be amusing to haunt the good little citizens who never have a worry, never have a care. Maybe I can shake them up a little bit."

"Ward, you just can't harass them." Chalky moved in a little closer and nearly whispered. "It's against the law."

"Boone, I am the law!" he shouted.

"Hold your voice down, Sir. You're sounding out of control."

"Don't you dare talk to me like that," he seethed.

"I'm the only one who can, Ward." She refused to retreat; she did not back down.

"You listen to me Boone, I don't plan to do anything now, just watch and wait. But, the time may come when the benefit of creating some chaos in Oakwood might far outweigh the cost. I don't know when. Maybe years from now. But, it would be fun if it happened in my lifetime." He spun his chair around and refocused his stare outside his office. "I have the time. Laws or no laws, power is everything. I can wait for the prize — when the golden nugget is ultimate control."

CHAPTER TWENTY-NINE
Gracie's Grief

9:30 a.m.

My conversation with Marge at the library had lifted my spirits. She had revealed her knowledge of the suppressed book and other forbidden documents hidden in the back rooms. I kept the book I had slipped out of the library wrapped in the folds of my cloak. As I rode across town to the medical center, I saw Sean, the man from the sing along—the one who delivered underground newspapers. He was sitting on the P-T side bench, and this time, I wasn't uncomfortable. He smiled but said nothing. I found that strange, since he had spoken out so freely last evening. Then, I saw that he was carrying a large bag of rolled up newspapers. I was amazed to see the papers out in the open! News sheets of any size had not been printed in years and the reality was, they had been forbidden. The Government Communications Agency, the GCA, hadn't initially banned them, but had corrupted the print outlets to the point they were no longer credible. Columnists and reporters were regulated on the most trifling detail, to the point they were eventually forbidden to report almost anything. Finally, newspapers were banned with the excuse they were no longer relevant.

Sean is delivering newspaper around town! He must have been delivering papers each time I had seen him on the bus. Since people hadn't seen newspapers in our lifetime, there was no danger. They didn't know what he was carrying.

I started to walk past him without acknowledging his presence but he stopped me. He spoke in a dull tone, like everyone else on the bus that day, but his eyes conveyed another meaning.

"I found that special high-mountain coffee we were talking about last evening. Do you know, it is grown at such high elevations, the snow caps look like grandpa's white hair," he laughed lightly. Others looked up.

His cryptic message was not well veiled but esoteric enough to slip past those around us. "Wonderful! Could we enjoy some at the Gift-giving celebration tomorrow?" I asked.

"That would be perfect. I could come by in the afternoon, after dinner." He smiled. We were just two causal friends talking about the little things of life.

"We will be at —" I couldn't mention my grandparents' home. "Well, here's my stop. Why don't you call me this evening and I'll give you the directions?"

Since grandparents no longer existed for most people in our age group, a mention of mine would have drawn curiosity. I saw my stop approaching, so I said no more.

I got off the bus near the huge medical center which housed several physicians' practices, various specialists' offices and labs. As I walked through the reception area toward the lift, I heard sobbing coming from the Women's Lounge. It was so strange to be drawn to the sound of sorrow. A few days before, I wouldn't have even heard it; or, if I had, I would have walked on past.

Cautiously, I pushed the lounge door open, not knowing what I might find. A young woman lay on the bathroom floor with her legs pulled up to her body. She was rocking back and forth, while moaning and sobbing like a wounded infant. She was gripping a partially opened pocket knife in her hand. I rushed in and knelt down.

"What happened to you? What is wrong?"

She whimpered and opened her eyes a little. "My Lady?"

"I'll get a doctor for you. Just lie still."

"No!"

"But, you need care."

"I just came from a doctor's office. They can't do anything." I saw her slide the knife under her body as she closed her eyes again.

I sensed her horrible plan and reached for the knife she had tried to hide under her clothing.

"No, I must have it," she gasped and grabbed at the knife as I pulled it from underneath her.

As she struggled to grab the knife from my hand, the blade popped open and slashed my arm a few inches above my wrist. I flung the knife out of her reach as she struggled to get up.

"Oh no, My Lady, no!" she pleaded when she saw my arm. She sank back to the floor.

I quickly wrapped a clean white cloth from my pocket around the slight wound and then turned back to her. "What has happened to you? Tell me, so I can get the help you need. Can you give me your name?"

"My husband and I love each other, My Lady." She started to sit up. She breathed more freely and the gasping stopped. "We have two beautiful children. Then, I got pregnant again so my doctor said we would have to abort the baby. Then the doctor was sick and my time went on." Her whispers bore testimony to the pain within her.

"So, your pregnancy continued?"

"Yes, there aren't enough other doctors in his practice to cover his patients when he's sick. I was seven and a half months along when they came for me. They terminated the pre-birth mass just this morning." She looked up at me with grief written on her face. "My Lady . . . I saw her. She was so tiny and pink and breathing. She wasn't a mass of anything. She was a baby—my baby." Her voice faded to a weak whisper. "It feels like my heart has slipped into a vast abyss. I am so lost and empty."

I felt so stunned that I couldn't find words to sooth her grief, so I sat on the bathroom floor with her and folded her in my arms. "Where is your baby now?"

"She . . ." the little mother sobbed in my arms, "she was

discarded. They said, since we already had our allotted two children, the third birth mass was unnecessary. They . . ." her words drifted off to a whisper, "just threw her away."

"What's the problem, Gracie?" A nurse startled us as she barged into the lounge unexpectedly.

"There's no problem," the new mother whispered with fear in her voice.

"You know what Doctor told you. If you can't pull yourself together, you will have to be hospitalized and that will put a point in your chart," the nurse said.

Gracie looked at me in terror and tried not to look at the pocket knife I had picked up and still held in my hand with the bandaged arm. She glanced quickly away. "No, I'll be fine. I was just a little weak and this lady spoke to me."

"We've called your husband. He's waiting for you in the hall. Are you coming?"

"Yes, yes of course. Stephen is here? Good," she smiled weakly and got up.

"Gracie, stop by the Main Library after the Holidays. We could have some coffee or something," I said as she started to walk away.

She turned and looked at me with amazement in her tired eyes. "You would have coffee with me?"

"I want to very much," I gave her a little side hug for reassurance. "My name is Christiana."

"I know who you are, My Lady." She smiled and then was gone.

When I got into the hallway, I saw Gracie disappear out the door with a young man. He had his arm around her as though he were both protecting her and guiding her unsteady feet. I stood there and watched them until they were out of sight. Grief was another emotion I was learning. And, sorrow often comes as its opposite, the joy of life. Little did I realize this was only the beginning of the horror stories I would encounter.

CHAPTER THIRTY

An Invitation and a Discovery

10:00 a.m.

I had come to the medical building to see Jason O'Reilly. I looked at my time piece. The encounter with Gracie, the tragic woman in the Women's Lounge, had happened so fast. I was still stunned when I walked into Jason's waiting room and looked around. It was empty and quiet. Even the receptionist was absent from her station.

"Christy!" Jason walked through the door from the inner hall and nearly bumped into me. "What are you doing here?"

His surprise would have put me off but when he gathered me in his arms, his reassurance made me feel wanted again. "Well now, that is better," I smiled.

"Oh yeah," Jason ran his fingers across my back. "I'll phrase it differently this time." He cleared his throat with dramatic flair. "I am so happy to see you Christiana. To what do I owe this visit?" He bowed slightly.

"I have come on the happy chance you have no plans for Gift-giving dinner, but I've just had a horrible experience."

"What on earth happened?" It was then that he saw the wound on my arm and the knife I still clutched in my hand.

"My arm will be fine. It's stopped bleeding. I cleaned it in the bathroom. But Jason, there was a woman." The whole incident raced through my mind. "She was so sad. I think she would have taken her own life with this blade if I hadn't heard her crying and found her on the bathroom floor."

He looked at the cut on my arm. "The bathroom? Here in this building? Where is she?"

"She had a pregnancy termination but, Jason it wasn't a cell mass at all. It was her baby they threw away."

"That's why I don't have maternity patients, Christy. It's the law. Thinning out the population has been legal, and even required, for a long time. I can't do it."

I looked around the room to make sure we were still alone and cleared my head of the image of Gracie and her only encounter with her beautiful baby daughter. "We've had the Length of Days policy for a long time, Jason. I'm hoping we can overturn it, including the section on *two for two,* two children for each couple. Maybe it will start a fresh reverence for life for all people. Let's talk about something else. I can't bear the pictures that are stuck in my mind. I have to think about something happy, something full of life."

"I know Christy." He hugged me again. "What would you like for a Gifting present?"

"To have a simple life again, like it was a few days ago. I haven't told you before about this strange little man who lives in my building. He turned up again, rumpled and unkempt."

"You have a lot going on in that building," Jason laughed.

"So it's turning out to be." All of the faces of laughing, singing people flooded my mind. My thoughts were overrun, like an unexpected infestation of vermin, by the foulness that Silas Drummond had described. "Jason, the man told me what really happens to those entering the long-sleep. It was too horrible to imagine."

"What did he say?"

"Their bodies are burned and their ground bones and ashes are used in things like building construction and fertilizer. Jason, today I saw that man being forced into a strata-car. He said that we were all in danger."

"Did you believe him, Christy?"

"I don't know. It all seems so ghastly, so preposterous. I don't even want to think about any of that. I want to think about Gifting Dinner."

"Tomorrow? Christmas dinner?"

"I'd like you to come for holiday dinner," I smiled. "It will be our family Christmas feast. Are you busy? Can you come?"

"Actually, I have no plans at all. Usually, I make rounds in the hospital so those who are stuck there on the holiday have someone to talk to. Right now, I have no patients in the hospital. What did you have in mind?"

"We will all be at Grand-mère and Grand-père's house. I would like for you to come to our family dinner with me."

"I get it, you want a ride in my car," he laughed mischievously.

"I do not need a ride, Sir. The transit will be running tomorrow." I gave his arm a little smack and then buried my head in his chest. "Don't make this so hard, Jason."

He tossed his head back in fresh enjoyment. "I would love to come to Christmas dinner with you. When can I pick you up?"

"Grand-mère serves holiday dinner promptly at twelve noon."

"Oh . . . I missed that. Dinner will be at your grandparents' home, two of the Wise Ones. I'll have to confess, I could feel a little intimidated around them." He teased again.

"Don't be. Grand-mère already knew who you were when I mentioned your name, Dr. O'Reilly."

"She knew me or had heard of me?" Jason's chest puffed out a little.

"She knew you. She called you by your first name."

"Perhaps she knew my parents or grandparents," he wondered out loud. "In that case, I would be honored to join all of you for Christmas dinner." He kissed my forehead and lingered there, close.

"Now, here's another thing," I approached the new idea more carefully. "I had thought I would invite Dahlia too. She could talk to my grandparents about the spiritual awakening she is experiencing. They could give her more answers than I could. I know Society doesn't approve of socialization between bosses and employees. Would you be uncomfortable if I invited her?"

"Christy, she would be your guest, not mine. Besides, joining someone for dinner at another person's house is hardly fraternization."

"Why do you think they initiated the non-mingling law in the first place?" So many laws were beginning to sound strange now that I was being detoxed and thinking with my heart as well as my head. "What could be the harm in enjoying someone's company?"

"Maybe enjoyment of anything was considered taboo. My parents had told me that marital relationships and loyalty to one's spouse had totally broken down in the past, threatening the emotional safety of nearly all of the country's children. Keeping people apart was a way of making sure that new alliances were not begun with people outside the family unit."

The image of Gracie and her supportive husband flashed before my eyes with the agonizing pain and desperate emptiness over the loss of her baby. I shuddered and wanted to crawl closer into Jason's arms.

He gave me a reassuring hug that let me know he was there. "Are you sure you're okay?"

"Yes, of course. I just want to have a beautiful Christmas. I need only lovely thoughts right now."

"Okay, a wonderful Christmas has been ordered for you and if you want to invite Dahlia, that would be fine with me too."

"Do you think she would come?"

"She came in for a few minutes today. Let's go ask her."

I looked around the room again and added, "Wait Jason, I want to show you something first." I pulled the book from under my cloak. I was trembling with excitement and fear. "It's all right here."

Jason pushed the book away, pulled my cloak over it and said nothing. He checked the door to the inner hallway and led me quickly through the complex and back to his private office. Then he turned around and closed the door carefully so as not to make a sound. "We have to be careful with any book in our possession, Christy." He threw his arms around me and drew me close. "Okay, what did you find?"

I placed the book on his desk and it fell open to the page I had marked. I turned the book around for him to read. "Jason, the law regarding our Length of Days can be changed." My voice shook and cracked as I forced out the words in an excited whisper. "A referendum can be scheduled."

"But Christy, how long would that take?" Jason sighed.

I felt my hope plummet again. "I cannot think about that now. The referendum will be in time. It has to be."

Jason looked toward the door. There was no sound, no movement. Then he began to quietly read. "A referendum in our government is usually in the form of a direct vote which is initiated by the legislature, the government itself. There is a second type of referendum, initiated by the citizens. The second type is an *initiative, ballot measure,* or *proposition.* This last form of vote is originated by the citizens as a petition. A *binding* referendum requires only a simple majority of the voters for it to carry. With enough signatures, the measure is brought to a vote by a citizens' referendum. If passed, it is binding."

"Don't you see, Jason?" I begged. "If we can get a majority of the citizens, right here in Capitol City, to sign the petition, perhaps the government will see the need to change the policy for the entire land." I held my breath as I waited for him to answer. He had to agree with me.

"Christy, I think you may have found the solution," he whispered. Then he paused. "There is a small hitch. There is a cover letter that must accompany the petition. If that official document is not with the petition, it won't be valid."

"An official cover letter? Where would we get that?"

"It says that one can be secured from the Office of Government Regulation."

"They won't be open until next Monday, due to the holidays." Again, my emotions plummeted. "There is so little time."

"Maybe we can intrude on a Constitutional Court judge this evening or even tomorrow. You're a Legacy Citizen. They will have to take your call."

I smiled. "I find it interesting how you can distance yourself from your own legacy, Jason. You are one of us."

"I know, I know," He admitted. "We can ask the judge together. Now . . . the next step is the petition. We have to find out how we can get a petition signed by a majority of the voting citizens without raising suspicion from the Blue Guard. I know they would stop us," Jason said.

"There will be a way. I know there will." It was done. "Now, Jason, may I see Dahlia?"

Jason took my hand and led me down the hall to a supply room and small pharmacy. Dahlia, a dark beauty, had her back to us when we entered.

"Dahlia?" Jason's voice was full of disappointment and surprise. "What are you doing?"

Dahlia was stuffing paper packets of the tiny white pills into her pockets. She turned, startled, when she heard her name.

"Dr. O'Reilly!" Dahlia jumped and staggered. Jason eased her onto a chair in the corner.

"Dahlia," I whispered and knelt down in front of her, "you are the one who has been giving the detox pills to the people in town, aren't you?"

"But, you reported the missing pills to me in the first place," Jason seemed confused and hurt.

"Since we finally had a patient who needed them, I thought it would soon be obvious that some were missing. I was afraid you would call for an audit of the pharmacy." Dahlia didn't say more. She merely nodded in admission. She swallowed hard then spoke with fear in her voice. "Yes, Christiana, I have started to pass them out too. I couldn't keep feelings of love and other emotions from my friends. Even if I would get caught, the gift of life was too precious to withhold."

"Dahlia, I understand." Not completely out of Jason's hearing, I whispered in Dahlia's ear, "The music stops when you don't have the pills, doesn't it?"

"Christiana, you know? You have heard the music already?" She wiped her eyes on the corner of her cotton office jacket.

"Yes, Dahlia, I've heard it. I wouldn't give it up for anything either." I gave her a hug. "Now, for the reason I came to talk to you. I've just invited Dr. O'Reilly to share Christmas dinner with me and my family. I want you to come too."

"Oh, My Lady . . . I am not worthy," she whispered.

"None of us are, Dahlia. I have contributed nothing to earn my place in society. I was born into it. I did not earn it. Please say you'll come."

"Yes," her voice was faint, and I could sense apprehension beneath the surface of her words. She looked at Jason.

Then I realized that Jason held the key to Dahlia's future at that point. I wondered what her fate would be in his hands. I was learning that he was a fair man, a man of integrity, but he also expected the same in return.

He took the pills from her pockets and placed them back in the cabinet. "We'll find another way to detox the people, Dahlia. It will be necessary to do it a little at a time in order to make sure they have no adverse effects." He helped her to her feet. "The chemical additives in our water supply have made illegal drug use a thing of the past. Drawing the police or Blue Guard into this would only raise alarm. No one else needs to know about this. We have to keep our circle small, but I will have to take the key to the pharmacy from you."

Dahlia handed it over with relief.

"For now, why don't you go on home and enjoy the rest of the day. Tomorrow, I'm going to pick up Christiana about fifteen 'til twelve. If you can be ready then, we'll all go together."

"Dr. O'Reilly," she sobbed, "how can I thank you?"

"By being the loving, caring person that you are," Jason said, "and the best healthcare professional I know. No one has been hurt. The pills weren't narcotics. They were neutralizing agents. The patients who became suicidal had abused the tablets you passed on to them. They detoxed too fast. Taken properly, they would have been fine." He took a tissue from the box on the table and smiled. He dabbed at her eyes and added, "You will have to blow your own nose."

CHAPTER THIRTY-ONE
Stoner Waited

Outside the Health Center, Ward Stoner waited in his car for his target to emerge. Her ID tag had told him she was there. He crouched in his vehicle like a thief, waiting to catch his next victim in a weakened state. He had always been able to dominate a situation, to use his mind and the weight of his office, to force his will on others. He could have had any of his Blue Guardsmen follow a young woman around town. But, he knew in his gut that this case was different.

A transit car streamed by overhead and he thought again about the ghost who had brought him into the hazy vapor of mystery in which he found himself. It was either one of the biggest cases of his career or someone was making a colossal fool out of him. *It had better not be the latter.* He tried to look at both sides of the paradox he called his life.

He inspected the old-fashioned timepiece he wore on his wrist. It had been his great-grandfather's, and for some reason he enjoyed wearing it. It had a tiny knob on the side of the case that he faithfully wound each night when he took it off. There was no one who would have dared to call him sentimental, any more than they would have called him Inspector Tombstone to his face. Besides, sentimentalism had lost all of it meaning.

Sentiment required emotions and most people had none. But, the watch brought a strange sense of continuity, a feeling of family. The hands on the face marched slowly on into the day. He looked again at the doors leading into the medical office building.

He wanted to leave but the whole thing mesmerized him. As he pressed on, in an effort to find answers to the puzzle he had started calling the Princess Case, he felt a strong force pushing back the more he pursued. He had to admit that the challenge made him angry. But, in the greater game he found himself in, he had finally met his match, an equal force to push against. Or was it equal? Still, the watcher watched.

CHAPTER THIRTY-TWO
Many Had No Joy

10:45 a.m.

As I gathered up my things to leave Jason's office, he wrapped me in his arms. "I'll meet you at the *Demitasse* in an hour? We could have some lunch." He gently touched my back, a gallant gesture of ushering someone along.

"Lunch would be fine," I agreed.

I soon walked back out into the wintery day and across the street to the shops I enjoyed so much. The library book was tucked neatly in the fold of my cloak.

The little shopping village was like something out of a Dickens novel, even if most people didn't know who Dickens was. I loved the little cluster of fancy shops and felt at home there.

Since I had an hour before I would meet Jason, I decided to spend my time shopping, something I rarely did. I passed the coffee shop and drifted into the boutique a few doors down. I hadn't bought new clothes in a long time. Clothes never seemed important before. I wandered over to the sale rack and shuffled through the hangers. Legacy Citizens have no need to shop from the reduced section since our personal fortunes and our annual stipend, allow us to live very comfortably, but I enjoyed saving money.

"Good morning My Lady," the sales clerk smiled lightly but her eyes were dull and unresponsive.

"Good morning," I replied then realized the woman was a classmate from secondary school. "Valley? Is that you? I haven't seen you in several years."

"Yes, Ma'am, it's been a long time. I didn't think you would remember me." Her eyes were looking away but there seemed to be a spark, a new measure of pleasure on her face.

"Of course I remember you. We managed to survive Mr. Funderman's advanced mathematics class together." I walked through life respected but alone when classmates no longer acknowledged my existence.

"Thank you for remembering," she added. "Is there anything I can help you with? We have a nice selection of holiday green caftogs over here. That color would look beautiful on you with your coloring."

Caftogs were long garments that took their design from a combination of the caftan and toga styles. They had a top with full caftan sleeves, under a wound skirt that then came around and draped up and over the shoulder. The display of fine silk garments, woven with threads that prevented the usual wrinkling, enticed me.

"Yes, Valley, they are beautiful." I ran my fingers over the delicate fabric and down the sleeve to the price tag. It was expensive but certainly not out of my budget. Ordinarily, I would not have considered such an extravagance. I was perfectly satisfied with more modestly priced garments but then I saw Valley's face and understood. She must have worked on commission and a sale of that magnitude, the day before Gift-giving Day, could have made her family's holiday more joyous.

"It is very lovely."

Valley didn't pressure me as it wasn't appropriate to push a sale on a Legacy Citizen.

"I'll take it," I smiled and took the garment without trying it on. "I'll wear it to my grandparents' Gifting Day party." It was bound to fit. The government established a uniform sizing system for all clothing many years ago. If you wore a size six, every six fit exactly the same way.

I casually slipped the library book into my clothing package and started to leave. To continue the comfortable contact I had with Valley, I asked, "Do you have plans for the holidays?" I waited for a response from my old friend.

"Plans?" she questioned with an emotionless expression except for an artificial, painted on pleasantness.

"You know . . . are you going to be with your parents for holiday dinner?"

"We always had gotten together but . . ." She paused as if she were searching her memory for a happy holiday with her family. "It's been so long since my grandmother was alive. She made the best date pudding."

"I always found the term, date pudding, a strange name for a cake." I hoped to get a real smile out of Valley, a brief reprieve from her dull life.

"What?" Valley blinked and stared. She was no longer with me but had drifted off to a gray existence among the colorless memories of her life.

I took my shopping bag with the book and package tucked inside and wished Valley a joyous Gift-giving Day. Outside, I saw the town clock and knew I was nearing my time with Jason and I smiled. A Blue Shirted Inspector looked at me sharply so I quickly wiped the smile from my face. He darted into the bank on the other side of the boutique and was quickly gone. I thought he looked familiar but dismissed him from my mind and smiled again. I had discovered that my face felt more relaxed when I smiled. And, the annoying pain between my eyes, I used to frequently experience, vanished when the corners of my mouth tuned up. Wow! Life was vibrant and new. But, when would the happiness stop? If I couldn't end the Length of Days terrible policy, my joy, like Valley's, might be gone forever.

CHAPTER THIRTY-THREE
Thackery and the Blue Guard

11:30 a.m.

Inside the *Demitasse*, I found a seat near the back where I could wait for Jason. Rather than facing the wall as I always did, I looked out over the people as they came and went and sipped their drinks. What looked to be a dad and his son were sitting at a table across from me. Even though their emotions were stilted, they were obviously enjoying each other's company. The boy, about ten years old, reached over and grabbed the last potato strip from his father's plate, then laughed. Dad rumpled the boy's hair and smiled. A couple in the corner were experiencing the beginning of an attraction neither seemed to understand nor felt comfortable with. He kept averting her eyes and stared into his cup with a hidden grin. I had to smile. Being part of the world was an amazing, new experience. Maybe I had been aloof in the past, just as Jason had teased.

Then, a man entered the café and looked directly at me without glancing away as most people did. He not only kept his eyes fixed on me, he continued to approach me from yards away. I squirmed a little in my seat as the bold, strange man continued toward me. In the present era, men simply do not openly watch a Legacy woman. When he got to my table, he leaned on it heavily with the knuckles of both his hands and whispered.

"Hi, Gorgeous, I haven't seen that beautiful, shiny hair around town before."

I was both irritated and afraid. Men not only didn't talk to Legacy women, they did not flirt—with anyone. The truth was, in our current age, men simply didn't have the emotional capacity or adequate hormonal level to flirt.

How was I going to respond to him? He frightened me in a way that made me want to run and hide. I thought of my grandmother and the kind words she had for everyone while maintaining a razor back dignity. Looking at the man with Grand-mère's royal authority, I spoke with all the confidence I could muster. "Young man, who are you and what do you want?"

He grinned arrogantly at my response. "Well done, My Lady." Then he leaned in even further. "I wonder if you have noticed how bright the lights are today. The reds and greens are great."

"Yes, but —"

"Thomas thinks the blues are casting dark shadows though."

"Who are you?" I demanded. A cold chill shot across my back and his mentioning Thomas's name offered no comfort. Maybe it was because my world had never been intruded on before and it was now being bombarded with stimuli from every angle. I sipped on the water the waitress had placed on the table, hoping to calm the sickening feeling that refused to be controlled.

"I'm Thackery, Ma'am. A friend of Sean's." Then he winked.

His brashness amazed me. "You also have a friend at the medical center don't you," I said. It was a statement, not a question.

He smiled mischievously. "You mean . . . well never mind. You may be talking about someone or something else."

"There are others?" I whispered.

"There are many of us, Christiana." Again he smiled and then suddenly became serious. "Are you with us or against us?"

"I'm just learning who *us* may be, Thackery." My discomfort had changed to interest but a measure of fear remained. I didn't know what to think about the man or of all the new people in my life. "I have one singular goal at this time. Nothing else can get in my way, Thackery. I can tell you that."

"I know My Lady," He whispered.

"What do you know?" I questioned indignantly. I didn't like his smugness. He seemed to know my mind before I knew it myself.

Thackery boldly slipped onto the chair next to me. "I know you have dear ones who will be celebrating their birthdays very soon."

"I don't think I like your knowing all about me and I know nothing about you." The feeling of being spied on crept in again.

"You and all the Elites, Christiana. We may not be able to print your pictures in magazines that were banned a long time ago, like the celebrities in ages past, but we still know. The underground newspaper announces your every move, each and every event in your life. You are our stars today, My Lady. It's just against the law for us to intrude on your privacy. You must not see us watching."

I suddenly had a need to rub the chill from my arms. "Being watched is just creepy," I said.

"Maybe. I wouldn't know. I'm not the focus of all that adoration."

"Adoration? Thackery, is it admiration? I thought it would be disdain, not respect." My thoughts wandered to the many times I knew I was being observed and my experience was not Thackery's experience.

"You don't have to be afraid of us, Christiana. But, have you noticed the increase in Blue Shirts on the streets? There had been fewer last evening, but now just before the holiday, there is definitely a stronger presence."

"Until the last few days, I don't think I noticed anything going on around me."

"I have. I don't know what it's all about, but you'd better be careful. No smiling in public, no laughter, no display of affection or emotion of any kind."

"That's hard to do." I thought of Jason.

"I know. When you have someone in your life like the Doc, it's hard not to smile all the time. Dahlia gives me the flutters."

"Dahlia?" I tried to show no surprise then stopped. What had he just said before referring to Dahlia? "Wait! Have you seen Jason and me together?"

"Many of us have, Ma'am." He lowered his voice to a whisper and looked around the room. "Do you still hear the music?"

My heart stopped its beating and my breath caught in my throat. "You know about the music?" I could not resist rambling on. "Isn't it the most miraculous sound you have ever heard?" Then I stopped.

"What is it?" Thackery asked without turning around. He slowly sat back in his chair, apparently not wanting to give away any urgency in our conversation.

"Some high ranking Blue Shirt has just come in," I whispered, then unobtrusively dropped a detox table into the water the waitress had previously placed in front of me. I held the glass to my lips, hoping I could block any expression of curiosity or fear. "I've seen him around town several times this morning, and I think last evening as well."

"A lot of people have." Thackery responded nonchalantly as if he were talking about the price of peaches in the winter season. He smoothed imaginary wrinkles from the table cloth. "Is he sitting down?"

"No, he's coming this way." I stopped and replaced my glass on the table.

The Blue Shirt touched his hat but didn't remove it. "Ma'am." He looked at me then at Thackery. "Is this man bothering you?"

I had to think fast. Was he asking me about my association with this man I had just met? I didn't know who Thackery's friends were. If I responded in the affirmative, I may have admitted to an association with those engaged in seditious actions or words. If I said I didn't know him, it might place Thackery in jeopardy.

"We have a mutual acquaintance," I said. "He was asking for a suggestion on a possible Gift Day present for her."

Stoner's facial expression never changed. With his steely eyes fixed on me, he demanded in a frighteningly friendly manner, "And who might it be, Miss Applewait, that you both know?"

"Dahlia Zoobamba lives in my building." I responded confidently, then added. "She is also my physician's nurse."

"Yes, I know. Dr. O'Reilly."

"You know when I've gone to the doctor?" I blurted out. I should have let the comment pass. I was close to revealing an emotion I dare not display. Novels described it as anger.

"No Ma'am. I happen to know that Dahlia Zoobamba is Dr. O'Reilly's nurse." He stared intently at me and then asked? "What have you suggested?"

"About what?" I stammered.

"She thought Dahlia might like a brightly colored silk scarf to wrap around her head in this cold weather." Thackery interjected.

"I wasn't asking you," Stoner glared. Then he turned to me again. "That sounds fine, Ma'am. Just where might one find such a scarf."

"I was just in the boutique down the street. They have a whole display of beautiful, brightly colored scarfs in floral and geometric patterns." Luckily I had just admired the scarfs as I was leaving the shop.

"Yes, Ma'am. I'll check on that." He looked at me again and stated flatly as if he were reading from a formal report. "You have had a busy schedule this morning, My Lady."

"Yes, thank you for keeping your eye out for me. I'm finishing my shopping for Gift-giving Day."

"Oh you are?" he stated doubtfully. "And what have you bought this morning?"

I felt uncomfortable. It was as though the hunted had turned and faced the hunter. A chill came over me that threatened to freeze out my fledgling confidence. Again, I could hear the faint sound of angel voices singing their calming songs. Peace warmed my spine and recharged the boldness battery I had inherited from Grand-mère. "I bought a lovely caftog just a little while ago at that same boutique. I'll enjoy wearing it at my family's dinner on Gift-giving Day." Then I added, because I rarely bought anything and had some sudden need to justify my purchase, "I haven't bought anything new in quite a while. Would you like to see it?" I reached for the shopping bag I had stashed under the table. I froze. The book, would the Inspector see it if I opened the package?

"That's not necessary, Ma'am," Stoner replied flatly. He turned and walked away.

I finally exhaled and sat back.

"That was interesting," Thackery whispered.

"What was interesting?" Jason came up to the table while I was still trying to shake the jitters I had just acquired from the inspector's prying comments.

"Jason," I gasped in relief.

"Calmly," Thackery warned.

"I can be calm," I assured him. "Did you see him, Jason? The Blue Guard officer that was at the apartment building last night. He was just in here. He was asking questions and trying to trip us up."

Jason stood for a second and then started to take a seat. "Are you all right?" Then he looked at Thackery. "Who is this man, Christy?"

Thackery jumped to his feet. "Here, Dr. O'Reilly, take my seat. I was just leaving and you two will probably want to be alone."

"How did you —?"

"Dahlia called me last night. I had hoped to get over to see her during the evening but I was helping Sean. I'll see Dahlia later." Then he bowed slightly. "I'm Thackery Swift."

Jason seemed to be shuffling through recent memories in his mind. "Oh," he restrained a smile, "Swifty. Dahlia has mentioned you, one or two or twenty times."

"Yes, Sir," he admitted.

Swifty's cheeks turned red and I remembered the warmth of my own cheeks the day before. *So that's what we look like when we blush.*

Thackery pulled the chair out for the doctor and leaned forward a little as he moved. "Dahlia will be at home on her piano bench again this evening if you want to join us."

"I would love to," I agreed with enthusiasm. "The music was so soul strengthening I long to hear and sing more."

"See you tonight," Thackery waved as he headed toward the door.

Jason frowned as I told him how the Blue Guardsman had almost threatened me. "I see him lurking around wherever I go, Jason."

"We must be careful not to give him anything to be suspicious about," Jason said. "But as Legacy Citizens, we should be free to move about the city, to take a walk, to have an uninterrupted cup of coffee. Are you ready to go?"

CHAPTER THIRTY-FOUR
Story Checking

Ward Stoner had accomplished little at the *Demitasse*. As he stepped out of the coffee shop, he looked out on the street and shook his head. No one had stood up to him in so many years he had forgotten how it felt. Chalky Boone always stood her own ground, but, she didn't count. That was her job. Besides, her keen investigative mind and her resistance to intimidation were two of the reasons he had kept her around. Now, there was a new person in his life who didn't flinch in his game of *political poker*.

Well now, we'll just see about you, Missy. He jerked open the door of the store his new opponent had mentioned. *There had better be scarfs near the entrance.*

"May I help you, Sir?" Valley asked as the inspector entered the store.

"I was told about these scarfs you have on display here," he began in his skilled way.

"Yes, Sir," she smiled and picked up one of the colorful pieces of silk.

"Perhaps you waited on her . . . Lady Applewait?"

"Yes, she was in here."

"Well, what did she buy?" Stoner had lost his patience years ago and raced through life on raw adrenaline charged by anger, excitement, danger, or any other experience in his day.

"Sir, I'm not supposed to gossip about our patrons and certainly not if they are Legacy Citizens." Valley smiled slightly and pursed her lips tightly.

"She just told me she had bought a caftog," he tried to mask his agitation and managed only a fair imitation of a real person. "That sounded like a good gift for my mother. She's young at heart and would enjoy wearing one just like Lady Applewait's."

"Yes, Sir," Valley perked up with the thought of another generous commission for the day. "They are right here. Lady Applewait chose this gorgeous green. I'm sure it will be lovely with her hair."

"Those things seem to be important to some people . . . not my mother." He ran his fingers over the fabric. It was exquisite, with hand embroidered details on the hem. "I'll take it. Wrap it up," he ordered.

"Yes, Sir!" she smiled. Valley didn't mask her surprise or joy. With that additional sale, she had earned more in one hour than she had all that day.

Stoner grabbed the package and started for the door where he passed the scarfs again. *You may have won the first hand, but I will win the game,* he snickered. *You don't even realize you're in a high stakes game with your own life in the pot.* The challenge of each hand he was dealt invigorated him. No one was clever enough to trump him. He would not lose for any reason. By the time he had reached that hand in the game, he would have marched into hell to win the match.

CHAPTER THIRTY-FIVE

A Dance in the Snow

12:30 p.m.

As we left the café, I shivered as I looked around to see if the Blue Guard might be waiting outside. I was still upset over the contact with the Guardsman.

"Are you cold?" Jason asked as he put his arm around my shoulder.

"No, it was something Thackery said."

"According to Dahlia, Swifty has quite an imagination."

Looking up ahead in the square, I saw a car pull to the side of the street. Two more men from the Blue Guard got out and stormed the area, running in cadence toward the hospital. I tried not to think about them or the cause of their increased activity. I wanted to enjoy my time with Jason.

Focusing on the season rather than the sinister, I turned back to what Thackery had said about Gift Day mentality. "They think the lights cause the little moths to cluster around so they can spend their hard earned money until they get burned on the bulbs." I snuggled closer to Jason as we walked along in the crisp air of the winter day.

"I guess they think if you have nothing in your life that brings you joy except spending money, you'll spend until you bury yourself in debt you can never repay, just to get a small reprieve from the numbness of your existence." Jason looked to the changing sky and the world around him. "Those who drink the water can't find happiness in even the smallest things around them."

"I understand now what you're saying," I agreed in amazement. "It's like I've never seen clouds before, and I want to take in every glorious image I possibly can, in case the beauty is taken back again. Do you have time for us to walk a while? I want to absorb all the color I see around me."

"I can't think of anything I'd rather do." He patted my hand as it rested on his arm. It fit there like we were made for walking together.

"How much time do you have?" I could have walked all day if I were walking with him.

He checked the clock on the courthouse tower. "About twenty minutes. I have to make two phone calls and do some paper work this afternoon and then I'm going to leave the office for the rest of the day."

"You'll come to the apartment so we can talk and then join the group for singing later this evening won't you?" I whispered.

"I wouldn't miss it for anything." He patted my hand again.

"If you come about three, I'll have a special concoction for you to try. Then, we could go down to the lobby —" I saw the inspector coming out of the boutique and didn't finish what I was saying. He eyed us suspiciously as we walked arm in arm, but I thought if I pulled away, it might raise more questions. I pretended not to see him. He walked on past us. *Is he checking up on me?* That thought made my skin prickle with fear.

Jason and I said no more for a few minutes until we got to the town square where the old octagonal, shake roofed structure stood in the center. Twinkling lights were artfully wound in and out of the white railing that surrounded it. The afternoon sky was overcast with fluffy gray snow clouds that dropped a linen-like film of shimmer over the day.

"I'm dreaming of a white Christmas, just like the ones I never knew," I improvised.

Jason took my hand and led me up the steps and onto the stage-like platform of the octagon. He pulled me near him and took me in his arms, like dancers I had read about in the books of old. He hummed the melody that streamed under the words, in my ear, "Where the tree tops glisten and children listen . . ."

"We'd better stop, Jason." I knew dancing would be just as forbidden as the music and the joy that the holidays had inspired.

"I don't know if I can stop anymore now, Christy. I know I'm moving fast, but I have waited so long for you to come along. Attraction is a powerful thing and without additives, it is like it was in the days of old. They called it *love at first sight.*"

"I've heard of such an emotion, and for the first time, I understand what that means." Being with Jason this short time had awakened me to the new emotions that had the power to make me understand risky behavior. "What will happen if someone sees us dancing, Jason?"

He stepped back and looked into my eyes. "Yes, I know it is best not to draw attention. It's best no one sees us. If our outward behavior gives away our inner emotions, people may notice. That could be dangerous."

CHAPTER THIRTY-SIX

Warmth from a Distance is No Warmth at All

It was too late. Someone had already seen the doctor and his Lady in an embrace. Inspector Stoner sat in his strata-car at a nearby curb. The frosty air was fogging up his windshield so he cleaned it with a small scrapper. It made him even angrier. Every small inconvenience was interpreted as a personal affront to his worthiness, his intelligence. The gods were against him. *Why does it always . . . ?* Then he would fill in any complaint to complete his protests against life.

Well, well, well, he mumbled to himself as he watched the happy couple dancing in the park. *I may have caught a really big fish. This little mermaid does anything she wants to do.* He sneered into the emptiness around him. *Why do they always think they can get by with breaking the law? And why are they so sickeningly happy?*

He had watched them with irritated interest from the time they left the café. He saw the couple laugh and twirl together in each other's arms. As he watched, he could feel his stomach tie up in its usual knot as he tried to process his loneliness without acknowledging his wife's death. Stoner had no one to smile with. No ear to whisper into. No love to hold next to his heart. His heart had ceased aching. He felt nothing anymore.

Stoner had seen enough. He pulled his car back into the street and headed in the direction of his headquarters. Still, he couldn't resist the need to watch the couple through the rear-view mirror until they disappeared when he turned the corner. He had to acknowledge the reality of his burnt out feelings but couldn't figure out why the romance between the Lady and the doctor fascinated him. Romance had died in the sleep chamber with Miriam. He preferred feeling nothing. It was easier. His heart beat only by habit. It had become like his name, a stone.

CHAPTER THIRTY-SEVEN
Eyes in the Apartment

1:30 p.m.

It was still early when Jason and I left the town square with the promise that he would come to my place later. In the evening, we would join the singing group again. The city had turned the holiday lights on earlier than other days. Now, it was the afternoon of Gift-giving Eve and the colorful lights seemed to encourage the shoppers to spend more money. Society liked to pretend that it was a time to honor one another with gifts and an opportunity to bring families closer together in celebration. But, there was little joy or meaning in any of it anymore, not like the old books had described. It was no secret that Gift-giving was a vital part of our economy and provided the financial support to keep stores and businesses open the entire year, based on the proceeds from gift purchases. So, the cities were brightly decorated to stimulate what fragile emotions remained, to prompt more and more purchases. At least that was my theory. I looked for the blue lights among the precious gold, and I shuddered a little.

2:00 p.m.

I had ridden the P-T back to my building. I hurried into my apartment and threw the curtains open to let in as much of the afternoon light as possible. It was nearly 2:00 p.m. so the long shadows of trees and buildings stretched out across the city. The holiday lights twinkled even brighter than I had previously noticed. I stood at the large wall of windows and looked out on the city I loved. With few private cars and the tremendous cost of air fare and high speed train tickets, very few people traveled beyond the boundaries of the city, since that was as far as the Public Transit system ran. And, it was forbidden to travel to the other zones. Mass communication offered a sterile education about other places but that was different from actually walking in their green woods.

I turned on the large wall mounted communications screen and curled up on the couch. Society reserved one channel that looped a video throughout the day. The scene was of softly pounding waves on a pristine beach.

2:30 p.m.

Suddenly, the doorbell rang. As I turned to respond, I noticed something strange near the bookcase. Was it something that was there that hadn't been there before? Or, something that wasn't there, that had been there before. But . . . what was it? What was missing? What had been moved? What had been added? No one could have been in my apartment. It was forbidden to enter the home of a Legacy Citizen unless treason, sedition, or other acts against society were suspected.

The doorbell rang again and interrupted my thoughts. I hurried to answer it, hoping it was he.

"Good afternoon Christy," Jason's speech was carefully measured there in the public hallway, but his eyes spoke bushels more.

I hung his coat in the closet with mine and then grabbed Jason's hand and almost dragged him into the room. He pretended to be surprised and stumbled in, then regained his balance once the door was closed. He whisked me nearly off my feet and hugged me long, with all the emotion his words could not express.

"It is so good to see you and I was just with you a few hours ago," I laughed softly. I found myself whispering in my own apartment. "Come out to the kitchen, I have made something special."

I led him into the food preparation area and ladled a full cup of cold creamy liquid into two cups. I handed it to him and waited for his reaction.

"Looks good. What is it?"

"Eggnog, Jason. I read about it in one of the books. It's made with eggs, cream, milk and nutmeg. It's a holiday drink they used to serve at Christmas parties. What do you think?" I was too excited to sip mine until I got Jason's reaction. When Jason smiled over the rim of his cup, as he savored the sweetness of the drink, I tasted a sip of my own.

"This is wonderful, Christy!" He closed his eyes. "I want to enjoy the entire flavor of the drink with no other distractions—just taste." He tipped up his cup and emptied the contents.

"Would you like more?"

"You know I would," he admitted as he placed his cup on the counter and dipped out another ladle full.

We took our drinks into the living room and sat them on the table in front of the windows. It was beautiful there. The late afternoon lights were even more magical than they had appeared earlier.

"This looks wonderful, Christy." Jason waited for me to be seated.

We talked and laughed and enjoyed each other, as red and green and gold lights danced across the scene beyond the building.

The events of the last day and a half raced through my mind like a collage of snippets and glimpses into a whole new world of emotions and color. Practicality was no longer the word that would define my life. But, I had few feeling-words in my verbal vocabulary to express my experience. I had read them but never expressed them. I was just a mass of sensitivity, and the raw nerves hurt at times.

I finished my eggnog as we sat in the quiet for a while. Later, I smiled at life, love and the cozy shadows that had settled into the apartment as I looked around the dimly lit room.

"Something wrong?" Jason asked as he followed my gaze into the corners of my space.

"I don't know." I looked at the bookcase again. "Just as you rang the doorbell, I noticed that something has been moved or added. I can't put my finger on what it would be."

We both looked around but couldn't see anything out of place. "I must have imagined it," I said. "Or, the kitten may have moved something."

"I am so sorry you've been frightened so many times lately. I wish I could take it all away." Then, Jason paused. "I know we forgot to finish something." He stood up and took my hand, guiding me from the table. "Our little dance was interrupted," he said as he gathered me in his arms in an old-fashioned waltz position. I remembered a well-written chapter in a book that described the dance and the music and the romance of it all.

We moved in a simple step in the silent room, but music soared within me. "The whole world is missing out on so much. I wonder why they banned the music."

"Emotions ride through the air and lodge in the heart on the strings of musical notes. If we weren't permitted to feel anything anymore, they had to ban that which stirs the emotions." Jason twirled me around. Then, like a grand ballroom move in an old book, he bent me back in a low dip.

"Jason!" I whispered a muffled gasp from my upside down position. It's funny how we see things differently when we view them from another angle.

"What?" he hurriedly pulled me up. "Are you all right?"

"Oh . . . yes, but I saw something." Again, I looked toward the book shelves.

Jason followed my gaze, looking for some clue, though neither of us knew what we were looking for.

I walked over to the books and searched up and down the shelves, pretending I was looking for a particular volume. The intruding object was there just as I suspected. I turned slowly and quietly, as if nothing were out of the ordinary. With my back to the bookcase, I winked solemnly at Jason.

"Well, now I'm ready for that ice cream you promised me this afternoon." I was glad I hadn't identified a time when we supposedly talked about ice cream. I had seen Jason during the early afternoon hours but I was so shaken, I didn't remember when. A misspoken time frame would have alerted whoever was watching us that a story was being fabricated. Would he take hold of the subtle thread I had tossed out? I could only hope that he had pulled together all the hints I had dropped.

He never missed a beat. "Ice cream it is," he agreed with a smile. I grabbed my hat and our coats from the closet and walked out the door. Jason looked at me seriously, quizzically.

"If we hurry, we can get to the ice cream shop while they're still open. I imagine they'll close early today, since it's Gift-giving Eve," I added to the impromptu conversation.

We hurried to the elevator, hopped in and said nothing. We rode to the first floor in nervous silence. My limbs were shaking from the anxiety I was feeling. We slipped through the front door and took long strides to Jason's automobile.

When we were safely inside, I began shaking totally out of control. I buried my face in my hands and screamed.

"Christy?" Jason's voice was full of bewilderment and concern as he rocked me in his arms. "What did you see on that book shelf? What was it?"

"Someone has been in my apartment, Jason." I searched my bag for something to blot my eyes. I couldn't believe I was crying again. Jason took a handkerchief from his pocket and tried to blot my covered eyes.

"What? Someone is watching you inside your apartment?" he gasped as he pulled me even closer.

"Drive, Jason, drive, move. I don't know who may be watching us." I was yelling through clinched teeth. I knew I dared not make any noise or draw attention to us but my restraint had dissolved with my tears.

He started the engine and pulled out into the street. "Christy . . . what . . . ?"

"Jason, there was a small camera of some sort stuck in among my books. I could feel that something was there. Someone must have been in my apartment, probably earlier this afternoon. When I saw the camera, I knew someone had been there. Now, someone may be outside too—watching our every move."

"You felt it? You didn't actually see it?" Jason eased slowly in and out of traffic like any other traveler on the road.

"Yes, I felt it at first, but then, when you bent me back, I saw it. So when I went over to the bookshelves to get a better look, I saw it clearly, Jason . . . like a camera thing I had seen in an old book. It takes motion activated pictures of anyone who happens to be in the room."

"How does something like that, an old camera maybe, continue to operate?"

"I don't know. I just glanced at it and kept pretending not to see it. But, some of the old cameras turned on and recorded when movement activated them. I read about them last week in an old spy novel." I sat back and tried to gather my thoughts. "Motion sensitive, I think they called them. The one in the book took one picture after another as long as there was movement within the range of the lens."

"I see another problem." Jason shook his head as he looked in the rear view mirror.

"What is it?" I turned around and tried to see what had caused alarm.

"No," Jason snapped and then added, "sorry. We'd better act like we don't notice it."

"What?" I asked but resisted my need to look.

"Maybe nothing but every time I turn, the car behind us turns too." Jason went around another corner to test his theory and looked in the mirror. "I was right. He turned again."

"With that camera in my apartment, if it had sound, they may have heard us. We'd better go to the ice cream shop like we said we were going to do, in case the camera had sound. Marion's Ice Cream Parlor is on North Main Street."

"Right," Jason agreed and turned the last corner to get us back on course.

"Who do you suppose would be following us and why?"

"I don't know but maybe they'll give up once we go into the ice cream shop." Jason said as he checked his mirror again.

Even when Jason stopped the car at the curb, I resisted the urge to look around. We had to pretend we were happily spending an afternoon out. By this time we both knew it was important to maintain that charade or we might be caught, accused, and tried for crimes against the state.

CHAPTER THIRTY-EIGHT

Ice Cream as an Alibi

4:00 p.m.

Luckily for Jason and me the little ice cream parlor was still open. I started to get out of the car but Jason touched my arm and stopped me.

"I'm not going to let whoever is back there, make me less than a gentleman." He smiled, walked around the car and opened the door for me. He offered his hand and I slid out. I resisted the temptation to look back to see if the other car had also stopped.

Once inside Marion's, we moved past the other patrons eating frozen treats. Their eyes told the Gifting Day Eve story. There usually was no life, no joy, no gift of Hope, but for the Gifting holidays, there was a faint glimmer of something beautiful. I wanted to find a shadow to hide in. My new happiness may have been dangerous to reveal and hard to hide among the walking dead.

We settled into a small booth in the back. I inhaled the sweet aroma of rich cream and chocolate. I used to think that some wise soul would finally make a perfume from those scents. "No, an aftershave."

"What? We came to the ice cream parlor, and you want to order aftershave?" He smiled but held in his laughter as a precaution.

"No silly. You must have read my thoughts. I was just thinking of a perfume fragrance, then realized the scent would be better put to use as an aftershave. What woman wouldn't be attracted to a man who smelled like chocolate?"

"Chocolate? You design the fancy bottle, and I'll invest in the company." He smiled.

"I would really be in trouble if you started using our new fragrance, *Chocolate Mystery*." I couldn't believe I had said it, but it was already out.

"Wow, that almost sounds like forbidden talk. Remember, women aren't attracted to men anymore. They have no libido."

"Well, most women don't," I teased.

We laughed softly and allowed ourselves to forget. Had we actually been followed? Was there someone—waiting and watching us?

CHAPTER THIRTY-NINE
The Shadow

From a parked car near a family ice cream parlor, Boone's voice came over Stoner's communication device. "Are you coming back to the office today, Sir?"

"No, probably not. I'm shadowing a suspect."

"A suspect in what?"

"The breach of security case, of course," he bristled.

"Sir, you're not following — ?"

"You know who I'm tailing, Boone. And, since you know, you're as much a part of this as I am. Are you going to report the situation?"

"Sir, you're on an unsecured frequency."

"Even the stalker has to take chances with the stalked."

"Your son will be expecting you to come home, Ward," Chalky coached.

"Are you manipulating me, Lieutenant?" he snapped.

"Is that possible?" She feigned an attitude of resignation.

"You're doing it again."

"Sorry . . . but I like my job so it's important to me that you . . . do well." She sounded cautious. Anyone tuned into the frequency would have been able to hear everything she said.

"A high tide floats all ships Boone and I'm riding high."

"Sir . . . you are very brave . . . but you have never been careless," Boone whispered, as if only the Inspector could hear the caution in her voice.

"Measuring caution with a larger beaker is sometimes necessary, Lieutenant."

"But a person can drown in a bigger pool, Sir," Boone returned without another word. Stoner had stopped listening. He was confronted with the greater challenge.

He sat back in his seat and scanned the road ahead of him but spent precious little time evaluating his options. The 281 Palm Device was on the seat beside him, waiting for his next bold move. He flipped it on. It glowed brightly; the hologram pulsed in front of him. "Call, Jonathon Fink . . . Fort Knox."

Suddenly, his old friend appeared in the middle of the glowing image. "Hi Ward. It's good to see you."

"You too, Johnny. Say . . . what kind of trouble would you and I get into if you were to look up some information for me on a Legacy Citizen?"

There was silence, but Jonathon's image revealed a restless man, uncomfortable with his friend's inquiry. "Ward . . . you know —"

"You know I know Johnny." Stoner watched the man intently as he shimmered in front of him. "Look Man, this is important."

"I know it is, or you wouldn't ask. What are you needing?"

"The fact is, I don't know. There is a young Legacy woman that is getting under my skin. She cannot possibly be as controlled as she pretends to be. She's brave and growing in self-assurance."

"Sounds like a great woman to me, Ward. How's that a problem?"

"There has been a breach of security here. I know she has something to do with it. If I can't stop what she's doing, maybe I can use some previous history to persuade her to cooperate."

"Persuade? You mean blackmail? Ward, I —"

"I don't see it as extortion, Johnny. I see it as evidence of a pattern of behavior, that's all. What do you say?"

"Okay Ward, I owe you. But, this whole thing had better not come back to me." Jonathon stated flatly.

"Thanks Man."

A little fish may drown in a big pool . . . but not a shark. Stoner's self-talk dripped with entitlement and confidence. *The great white always circles and waits before the attack.*

CHAPTER FORTY
The Evil at Howard Mountain

5:00 p.m.

Jason and I finished our frozen treats and were cautious in case anyone could see inside the ice cream parlor. I noticed the time. It was five p.m. Marion's was going to close at six. When we finally went outside, the early evening darkness had taken on an eerie glow. The holiday lights had grown halos from bouncing off a fog that had silently crept in, like a panther on the edge of a forest. I felt just as vulnerable as an innocent prey waiting for the pounce of a mighty cat. Eyes seemed to be watching from behind every dark window. It wasn't the same kind of curiosity I was used to. This was something else, something profoundly frightening to me.

Jason helped me into his car then paused at the passenger side door when his communications device vibrated.

"Dr. O'Reilly," he acknowledged. "Yes, well, it's late," he apologized. "Yes, I understand. I have someone with me and I'll have to bring her along. All right."

Jason hurried around and hopped in the car. He rubbed his hands as he tried to warm them from the cold.

"Sorry, Christy. I just had an emergency call from Howard Mountain. I'll have to go out there. I think I'd better take you along considering all that has happened this evening."

He looked around, but the parking spaces were empty except for a few nearby. "Must have lost interest in us," Jason said. "But, we'll still have to deal with that camera. If the building maintenance man is into spying on tenants, then he's in a lot of trouble."

"That's all right Jason. After a day like today, a ride in the country will be welcomed."

Jason's company blessed me more each time I was with him. Along the empty road to Howard Mountain, the rising moon was trying to burn a hole in the fog and cast an occasional moonbeam along our path. We arrived at the mountain at 5:30.

"Yes?" The speaker at the gate squawked when Jason buzzed for entrance.

"Dr. O'Reilly here. I've been asked to see a patient."

"Dr. O'Reilly, thank goodness you came." There was a rattle and then a screech. "The guard isn't on duty so I've released the lock. The gate will swing inward. Please come to the main entrance."

The gate swung open, and Jason pulled the car up to the front door of the huge stone facade at the entry to the chamber beneath the mountain. A gruff voice greeted us beyond the darkness of the vestibule. Jason assisted me from the car. Ice was rapidly forming on the front steps. He helped me safely over the threshold and inside the door.

"My Lady," the man whispered in surprise.

It was only then that I saw who he was and I shuddered. "Silas Drummond," I gasped. "I am relieved to see you are well. I saw —" I hesitated, not knowing what had happened or why Jason had been called to the mountain.

"Why have I been summoned, Mr. Drummond?" Jason was patient but sounded as confused as was I.

"Follow me." Silas led the way down a dark hall lined with unlit frosted glass display cases and into a brightly lit lounge area. He closed the door and leaned against it.

"We're supposed to be alone. Since it's Gift-giving Eve, I'm the only one here. But, I can't take any chances." He moved toward the light on the side table and displayed his hand which appeared to be seriously injured.

"That looks like a very bad burn, Silas," Jason observed.

"I'm sorry to interrupt, Silas, but I have to know what's going on," I said. "You tried to contact me several times in the recent days. You wrote an absolutely horrendous note to me and then I saw them take you away in a squad car."

"This is the man you have agonized about?" Jason's question was laced with anger. "Okay, Drummond, what is this all about?"

"The note was true, My Lady, every word of it. I tried to contact you because you were the only person I knew who might be able to get a word about this place to the right authorities." Silas waved his arms to indicate the entire surroundings.

"You mean . . . all the people who think they are entering the never-ending-sleep . . . are actually exterminated in a crematorium?" I shuddered with the thought of it and what that would mean to my grandparents.

Tears of anguish and exhaustion began to flow down Drummond's cheeks. "Multiple furnaces, Miss Applewait. More than I want to think about. It's my job to keep the flames lit and burning at a steady temperature. The other night, someone I knew was delivered, little Mari. You may remember her from the apartment building."

The image of a beautiful young woman, just a few years younger than me, came to mind. "She had an awful limp, didn't she Silas?"

"Yes Ma'am. Her medical advisor recommended a long rest but— there is no such thing, My Lady. It's all the same. Long sleep or extended nap, it's still death by fire." His voice trailed off to a whisper. "And most enter the chamber while they're still alive. I couldn't do it. I couldn't lie to her. I had to get her out of here, so I left before my shift was up. I needed to escape so desperately, I didn't even punch out and . . . I took Mari with me. I put a blanket around her, threw her over my shoulder, and carried her out with me. She was hidden near the edge of town at my sister's home. I got her out of the zone quickly. The next day, when I didn't show up for work, the Blue Guard found me in front of the library and delivered me back to this wretched mountain. They didn't even ask me about Mari. Since so few people know about our work here, and the agencies don't communicate with one another, no one was even aware that a soul had gone missing. They won't know someone has escaped until they count the pairs of shoes.

"When they brought me back, I was here alone so I had to hurry making my furnace inspection rounds. I burned my hand on one of the oven doors." He timidly turned the palm of his hand up and reluctantly showed the damage. "I was afraid my injury would be one insult too many to my safety here. I didn't know what they would do to me, so I called the only doctor I knew. Dahlia has talked about you frequently and has said you can be trusted. I didn't know you would be with Dr. O'Reilly, My Lady."

Jason hesitated for a moment, his jaw tense and a look of disbelief was on his face. "Silas, you mean—people are simply executed here at the mountain?" He clenched his hands as he leaned on the lamp table. "All of them?"

"Every last one of them." Drummond's voice cracked with emotion so heavy it seemed to weigh down his entire being.

"And, my own parents?"

"Your parents, Doctor? Who were they?"

"Charles and Stephanie O'Reilly." Jason's voice trembled to a whisper.

"Oh . . ." Silas hung his head and averted Jason's eyes. "I don't think I know about them."

"How long have you worked here?" Jason demanded.

"Almost twenty years, Sir."

"Then you would have been here when they were brought in after their accident," Jason pushed.

"I may have been on holiday, Sir." He hesitated in silence. "Can you do anything for my hand?"

Jason stared at the man for a moment. "Yes, I have some cream and a special glove to protect the hand while the burn heals."

"Will I be able to use my hand? If I can't, they may declare me unfit for work. That would be too much. They already gave me consideration for my years of service and the uniqueness of my job when they decided my fate after my absence." He closed his eyes and then added. "No one else would want this despicable position and . . . they've taken my car, so now I have no way to leave. I'm stuck here for at least a week, eating out of the food dispensers, during which time I'm supposed to be thankful that I have a valuable job that contributes to society."

"Who else knows about this place?" Jason prodded, as he tended the burned hand.

"Very few citizens, except for me and a handful of other workers, know about the wickedness here in the bowels of the earth. Those who had known about the mountain are gone by now. They left no notes, no files, no trace of anything." Drummond shook his head. He appeared to be in utter resignation to the part he had played in the atrocities under there. "All knowledge of the crematorium's activity has faded into the dust of time, but the Length of Days policy continues to function like a perpetual motion machine, going on and on with no slowing in momentum."

"You mean there is no one overseeing the work down here?" Jason asked.

"Once this horrendous mess was set into motion, it has just kept rolling on?" I couldn't believe it. "How is that possible?"

"That's what I've been trying to tell you, Miss Applewait. The only person who has ever come down here from above is Alister Bedlam."

"What on earth does Alister Bedlam have to do with all of this?" Jason's voice was curt and tense.

"He is the only one that I'm aware of, who has ever been down here or has ever contacted us from the surface."

"Silas, why does he come here? What has he said when he's called?" Bedlam is the richest man in the world, or at least the world with which we have communication.

"He calls to tell us when he has a display for the gallery. And, then he comes to see it once it has been delivered. Sometimes, he just comes to view the collection."

"Collection of what, Silas? No one has ever heard of a museum out here."

"Oh, I don't know. It's Bedlam's private collection."

"Why does he keep it way out here?"

"He wanted to keep it private and since no one knows anything about the process here, I guess he thought it would be safe under the mountain." Silas was growing more uneasy as he shifted from one foot to the other and avoided our eyes. "I'm not allowed to talk about Bedlam's museum. We are supposed to pretend we know nothing about it. Please don't ask me anymore."

"Keep the glove on until the burn is totally healed. Now, let's get out of here, Christiana. The stench of the place is penetrating my skin. But, you can be sure, Silas, we will do everything we can to put a halt to these evil practices as soon as possible." Jason took my arm and turned to leave.

"I will do what I can to close this place, Silas. You can count on me," I said. We started to open the door to the lounge, and I blinked in the blackness of the hall. I was a step ahead of Jason.

"Here, Christiana, you need a light." Jason reached for the bank of light switches on the wall beside the lounge door.

"NO!" Silas screamed as the lights blazed in the hallway.

We stepped into the bright hall and found that the cases we had passed were part of a long Galleria where glassed-in exhibits lined the area from the lounge all the way to the vestibule. Lights came on behind the frosted glass display cases as well. The objects of Alister Bedlam's art were grotesque beyond my ability to imagine. They weren't paintings or statues of fine marble. They were human beings, processed expertly for Bedlam's sole possession and entertainment. The maimed, the elderly people, the middle aged, the young, and even children were in the collection: their bodies forever preserved by a taxidermist and encased behind thick glass.

"Christy," Jason whispered in horror, "I know this man." He pointed to a figure in a pinstriped suit with a gray fedora hat perched on the side of his head. "He and his wife used to come over to visit with my parents and play games."

"I know him too, Jason. He was my Uncle Steven. He was one of the Wise Ones before he fell down his stairs and ceased to live." I recoiled in horror at the monstrous display of disrespect for the deceased. "Why would Alister Bedlam do this?"

"Power, Christy. What, or who, he didn't have power over in life, Bedlam gained in their death." Then I heard Jason let out an agonizing groan as he moved up the hallway. He reached out to the case on the right and collapsed against the glass as he sobbed great tears of deep sorrow. "This . . . is . . . was . . . my mother, Christy." Again he stepped back and took in the fully processed model of Stephanie O'Reilly. He looked with searching eyes for another exhibit and found it slightly behind his mother's glass coffin. "And, this is my father." He gasped as he shot a dangerously wild glance back at Silas Drummond.

"It's not my fault, Doctor. I had nothing to do with any of it. This is Alister Bedlam's total possession. We aren't to touch them or even look at them." Silas looked pleadingly at me with fear in his eyes. "Please Ma'am; get me out of this evil abomination. I had nothing to do with this exhibit. I had to follow orders and—I simply can't do it anymore." Silas dropped to the floor and reached out his hand to us, pleading. "You are the only people on earth who can help stop this evil," he cried.

"Don't look back, Christy" Jason gasped. "Let's get out of here before the vileness of this place corrupts our souls. I don't know if God even knows this place exists. If he does, he must flood these caverns with his own tears." Jason hurried me out of that place of horror and back into the air of the clear night.

As we stepped out into the air, we heard Silas calling. "Please," he begged, "don't forget me." He staggered to the doorway, "Please."

"I won't forget, Silas," I called out over my shoulder as Jason hustled me into the car. "We'll do something. Trust me, Silas!"

Once in the safety of Jason's car, both of us broke down in violent sobs. We grabbed each other and held on while the grief flowed from our spirits like a cleansing rain. Finally, we were able to talk about it. We knew that now, time had reached a vortex, whirling and churning and sucking all the forces of the world into a point of clarity where action would finally be required. Silas's warning had nearly cost him his life. Now that knowledge rested on our shoulders. It was ours to pick up and carry, or to cast aside.

If we were to keep our promises to Silas Drummond and to my grandparents, we would have to run fast enough to stay ahead of those who followed. Jason and I knew the evil in our society had the power to destroy us.

CHAPTER FORTY-ONE
Stopped

6:15 p.m.

The encounter with Silas Drummond and learning the awful secrets beneath Howard Mountain had shaken us with so much grief, horror and anger, that we sat in Jason's car, just holding each other for a while. Finally, Jason collected himself. "We'd better go back to your place Christy and think this out. Silas won't be left alone for long."

"You're right. No telling what Alister Bedlam might do," I said. "Jason, we will bring Bedlam to justice somehow."

Jason raced back to the city on a clear and empty road. Just as we crossed the line marking the city limits, the shrill sound of a siren pierced the night and was muffled strangely against the heavy air. The squeal of tires followed as three Blue Guard cars screamed to a halt in front of us. From inside the first car, I heard a loud shout. "We have them!" Then, Jason's car doors were jerked open.

I saw a tall man in a blue uniform, lumbering toward us and I froze. I could see as he stood beneath a streetlight, his jacket was emblazoned with the crest of the Blue Guard.

"Dr. O'Reilly," he touched his hat brim, "Ma'am."

"Good evening Officer," Jason responded.

I was exhausted with fear and too shaken to answer. The reality that I was being watched, even at my apartment and then the awful revelation of the ghastly murders at Howard Mountain left my emotions spent and numb. Now officials of the government—a government we were in profound opposition to—had stopped us. Had these men been monitoring us? Did they know we had been to the mountain? How was it possible that all of this was happening to us on our very first Christmas Eve?

"Get out of the car and come with me," the man ordered. The Blue Guard turned to leave and seemed to expect us to follow him without question.

"Why?" Jason stayed sitting with his arm holding me tight against him.

"Just come with me, Sir." The officer didn't turn around but kept walking to his car.

"I will know why and where we are going before I expose Lady Applewait to any more unknown situations tonight." Again, Jason did not move.

The man turned back toward us, obviously aware that his orders were not being obeyed. "Dr. O'Reilly, there is an emergency. You will have to bring Lady Applewait with you. There is no time to take her home."

"Where? What emergency?" Jason demanded. "Will I have the things I'll need to administer proper care?"

"Sir . . ." The Blue Guard's face grew tight and hard. "I will pull my weapon if I have to. Both of you are coming with me. Now, get out and get into my car."

"What is this emergency?" Jason began, again attempting to regain control of the situation.

"Sir, I am ordering you both to get into my car." The Guard placed his hand on his weapon holder and unsnapped the safety grip.

Jason helped me out of his car and into the back of the officer's vehicle without saying another word. I was wondering when we should take a stand. But, there are times when, for safety sake, talk must be abandoned. When we settled ourselves in the back of the officer's car, I saw no handles on the inside of the doors, and I panicked. I grabbed Jason's hand without saying a word, but my mind was flooded with fear. What was happening now? Where were they taking us? Were they taking us back to the mountain? Do they know we have been exposed to its secrets?

My mind reverberated from the screams I held inside and back to the words of my grandmother. "It won't be in time, Christy. We'll be seventy-five in two weeks."

As I clung to Jason, I kept thinking. How could we reverse the terrible Length of Days policy when no one remembered why it was initiated, or what the terrible processes involved? At the end of the month, my grandparents would reach the end of their Length of Days. They would then endure the vile death process that would only add more agony to their fate. Now, Jason and I knew that Alister Bedlam played a large part in the unspeakable acts and cruel disrespect for life at Howard Mountain. My mind couldn't hold any more. And, still the clock kept ticking.

As the Blue Guard's strata-car sped to our unknown destination, deep down, where fear takes root in all we are, I knew we could be racing to our own deaths. If we were to tell our abductors that we would do nothing to find a solution to the Length of Days policy, would they let us go? What did they know about Howard Mountain? How could we find the solution to unseal the fate of Grand-mère and Grand-père if we were held captive or exterminated like all the rest? I felt helpless and hopeless. I had never experienced those emotions before but recognized them.

I looked at Jason. His set jaw and determined look gave me courage. Together, we would find the solutions. Suddenly, above all the confusion and fear, I imagined that music filling the car with the power to calm my spirit, and I was able to think more clearly.

I had never thought of myself as a brave person, but for the first time in my life, I wanted to stand up for something, to have a cause worth living for. Overturning the laws regarding the Length of Days horror, I vowed would be the single focus of my life. But, while I knew I was willing to live for the principle, and to die for it if necessary, I didn't know if I could sacrifice Jason's life with mine for the cause ahead of us.

CHAPTER FORTY-TWO

Surveillance

Now what is this all about? Inspector Ward Stoner grumbled. *Why didn't I receive the APB first?* He saw the Blue Guard vehicle stop and force two people into their strata-car. He followed behind the racing convoy of heavily marked cars as they sped through the dark night. Stoner gripped the steering wheel roughly and his shoulders grew tight with tension. *Nothing came over the radio.* He couldn't believe the audacity, the arrogant disregard for protocol. *How is it that the Chief Inspector of the Blue Guard could be outside the chain of command, again? People will answer for this breach of policy.*

No one in the department had his finger on the pulse of every artery like Ward Stoner. He was usually the first to know everything, mainly because he was in charge of the unit but also because he never gave up or gave in. If he didn't have the answers, he held on until every nuance of the situation was revealed. He didn't care how long it took. He sped through the streets, mumbling curses at the colorful lights that twinkled brightly, while he felt dark inside his soul.

Without Miriam to go home to, there was little reason to end a work day. He still had Christopher, but the child only reminded him of Miriam and that made him miss her more. Her golden hair and bright blue eyes shone from the child they had shared. Recently, Stoner had been trying harder to be there for the boy. But, the more he attended to the child, the more inadequate he felt. Then like an exhausting, circular treadmill he could not free himself from, he pushed the boy away again to hide himself from the guilt.

Occasionally, circumstances outside his control forced him to face the reality of his relationship with his son. Now, it was nearly Gift-giving Day, and he wanted to make it special for the boy. Christopher had hinted about a new virtual game he wanted. In the game, the small child could place himself within several environments, like visiting a zoo where he could walk among the roaring tigers and brush so close he could count their stripes. In another scene, he could walk through a museum where dinosaurs loomed above and around. Within the holographic image, he could find a moment of joy and perhaps a brief experience of laughter. Stoner wanted that for Christopher.

The Inspector worked most of the time and the boy had only his grandmother to read the few approved children's books to him and interact with throughout the day. She was wonderful with Christopher, and Ward appreciated all she did. But, Chris was his son, and he knew that he should be more involved in his life.

Now, on Gift-giving Eve, Stoner was chasing around the city following his own men. He had also lost track of Lady Applewait some hours ago, like her chip had simply vanished from the tracking system. *How can that be? She started out toward the country then vanished from the grid,* he argued with himself. *My time is precious tonight, and I don't even know why I'm in pursuit of these cars and not following the little lady who has seemed to evaporate.* He growled on and on into the night.

The Blue Guard's cars flew through the streets at speeds that would have stopped other drivers. However, there was not a single officer of the law with the authority to stop a member of the Blue Guard, much less a posse of them. They sped through stop streets and traffic lights and whipped around corners at break neck speeds. They finally crossed the invisible line into Oakwood.

Well now, what do we have here? Stoner's sneer distorted his face and gnawed at his stomach. *Even the special, fancy people have problems do they? They're not above needing us, needing me.* His anger rose to the surface again and burst out every pore. *I will find out what is going on. The day after First-day, heads will roll!*

He slowed to the curb a half block down the quiet street from where the other cars had abruptly stopped and turned off his lights. The Blue Shirts got out of the front seat and jerked the curbside back door open. A man and a woman were pulled from the car and nudged toward a large old-style house. Once the authorities and their reluctant captives went into the house, the area was silent again. Stoner could hear the sound of his own breathing. His breath was visible on the chilled air, but he was far from cold. His anger shot hot blood through his veins. In the still of the night, he sat in silence and stared at the old house in the next block. He ground his teeth and clenched the steering wheel with fists of steel.

CHAPTER FORTY-THREE
Rebecca's Husband Michael

7:15 p.m.

Jason had kept his arm around me as the Blue Guard cars sped down the city streets. I knew where we were, and it brought me no comfort. We had crossed into Oakwood, the older section of town. My heart stopped with fear of what that could have meant. *Is this line of boot thumping Blue Guards racing to Grand-mère and Grand-père's house because of something I said or did? Are the dear ones' precious few remaining days at risk because of me? Will they end up on display at Howard Mountain?*

The cars had stopped, however, in front of a stately old red brick house two blocks from my grandparents' home. I felt both relief and dread. I was thankful they were not seeking out my grandparents. But, I wondered who lived at that house and what fate awaited them?

The driver stomped out of the car and jerked the door open. "Out quickly."

This time Jason said nothing. It was a command, not a request. We knew we had to play their game to the best of our ability, even though we didn't know any of the rules. A misspoken word or a misperceived movement could be taken as noncooperation, resistance, or even threatening aggression.

I was not sure that my legs would support me as I stepped from the car and staggered slightly. Jason grabbed me around my waist and held me firmly as I regained my footing on the ice. I kept my eyes fixed on the ground and didn't look toward my grandparents' home. The officers seemed to have more interest in Jason than in me. I didn't want to draw any attention to myself or to my family.

"This way," the Blue Guard leader commanded. "Follow me."

We walked quickly to the front door. The Blue Guard burst into the house without a word of warning. Were we forced into being part of this invasion into someone's personal space, perhaps a government official or a member of the Council of Elders?

"Back here," a man in casual slacks, open neck white shirt, bare feet and a grim look on his face, motioned for us to follow him. Only professional men continued to dress in the traditional garb of authority but it was easy to see that something had interrupted his attempt at relaxation. I didn't recognize the man. And, I felt a measure of relief not knowing him.

We followed him silently down a bright hall behind a grand staircase and pushed through a set of tall wooden double doors.

"Quickly," the man pleaded as he took Jason by the arm and led him into the adjoining bathroom. I saw a fleeting glimpse of a woman in white trousers spattered in blood, holding a fallen young man's head in her arms. She cradled him close to her body like a mother rocks her sick child, while streams of tears flowed down her cheeks. Her face was contorted in desperate fear. For the first time in my life, I could feel her pain, and it was nearly more than I could bear. *Empathy could prove to be a curse, not a blessing*, I thought. *Now, with all I know, my tender new soul will surly wither in the fire of evil.*

The guard held up a halting hand and motioned for me to stay in the bedroom while Jason went inside the bathroom. The sobs and groans of anguish were frightening to hear.

I couldn't focus on the pain. It was too much. I looked around the room and began to separate myself from the agony.

The room I was in was masculine in design, with muted tones of beige and brown. The bed was nothing like a normal bed, even an expensive one from a high-end store. The frame was metal, rather than wood, with shiny bars that came up one side and across and above the mattress. A festive red poinsettia plant sat on the corner of a large bedside table. A lamp, small bottles with lids, a pitcher and glass of water were also placed there. *Is someone ill?* A light blue bathrobe was draped across the end of the bed but I saw no slippers.

"Lay him flat." I heard Jason call out orders from the bathroom but the rest of the conversation was muffled. I could hear frantic movement but nothing more was said.

Someone was obviously struggling for his life in a society that no longer valued life. The thought came to me that, if the young man had been taken to the hospital, in his condition, he would have been permitted to slip into the permanent sleep. Yet, Jason had been captured in the hope of saving his life. Perhaps we were in a home that shared a reverence for life with my family.

The Blue Guard didn't stop me as I walked around the bedroom. A cluster of five pictures hung on the side wall, positioned so the one in bed could easily see them. In the first one, three young men, their arms linked in friendship, appeared to be celebrating their victory in reaching a blue sky mountain summit. The curly haired blond Nordic type appeared again in the next photo dressed in a fine suit. He held a beautiful young woman in a flowing blue gown in his arms. She looked familiar to me, but I didn't want to stare. Their happiness was written on their faces like a bold and beautiful advertisement of their love. The broad smile appeared again in the next picture, in a playful headlock with an older man. The mature one looked like the gentleman who had led us in through the house. I surmised it might be his father. The young man and the father appeared in the next shot with an attractive older woman, probably the one I saw bending over the man in the other room. The fifth picture was of a cozy log cabin in a deep woods with cloud-covered mountains stretching up toward Heaven. The same blond young man sat on the porch steps and smiled at the one who held the camera.

"Oh thank God, thank God," I heard the woman shout from the bathroom.

Then I heard what sounded like struggling, grunting and huffing. Then Jason's voice, "Your Honor let me help you."

Jason stepped out of the bathroom followed by the man I thought must be the father of the injured man. He carried the broken body of his son back into the bedroom. As the man strained under the weight, I could see that he too was covered in blood. The woman I felt sure was the mother, followed close behind, her hand gripped her chest and her face was etched with fear.

I quickly stepped aside in the shadows of the room and waited. I wanted to be somewhere, anywhere but there. I was unprepared for the powerful emotions that continued to pour over me.

Once the younger man was placed on the bed, I saw the apparatus that spanned above it. Even though he was obviously still weak, he grabbed the bar over his body and helped position himself in the center of the bed. As I watched, I could finally see his face. He was my friend Rebecca Brunner's husband, Michael, and Judge Brunner's son. I remembered that Rebecca lost her life in a mountain climbing accident less than a year ago. Maybe the fall claimed Michael's legs as well. It could have happened near the cabin in the picture. Rebecca was most likely the photographer he gazed at with loving eyes. I stared at the picture again and wondered why he would have placed such a memory in front of his eyes where he would have to look at it every moment of every day.

"How are you feeling now?" Jason asked Michael. "You'll have quite a headache for several days, and yes, that will include Gift-giving Day morning. But, if you're lucky, your stomach will settle by tomorrow afternoon in time for the Christmas feast." He chuckled and patted Michael's leg.

Jason had spoken the word out loud, *Christmas*, and in front of Judge Brunner and the Blue Guard. How did he dare to break the law in such a bold way?

"Vonny will be here at ten a.m. I'll be better by then, or I'll fake it." Michael whispered and tried to adjust his position again. "I wouldn't spoil Christmas for her for anything." Then he looked in my direction. "Christiana, is that you?" He strained as he looked back at Jason. He must have read our feelings. "Wow, Doc, I didn't know." He grinned as his light-hearted spirit seemed to fight through the fog of his pain.

I didn't know Michael well. Rebecca had introduced him to me.

She talked about him all the time. Rebecca had said that Michael had a sense of humor, which was a rare gift in those days. One had to feel in order to laugh.

"I didn't know either, Michael, until yesterday. Christy and I just met recently." Jason picked up Michael's wrist, looked at the clock on the side table, and took his pulse.

"I hope you feel better soon, Michael," I offered. "How old is Vonny now?" I approached the bed slowly and stopped a respectful distance away, not wanting to intrude on the family's joy of having their son back from the brink of death.

"She's three years old and looks just like her mother," he whispered.

I could see that Rebecca's death had left Michael's emotions raw and then I stopped and studied his face. Michael was experiencing feelings too, like some of the others around town. How many feelers were there? I wondered what else I had missed while I dozed behind the mask of additives. I had been walking around with my head wrapped in cotton all my life. I wondered if Rebecca too had been able to fully love before she died. I glanced back at her picture in the party dress and suspected that she had been a feeler long before her death.

"Vonny has been staying with Rebecca's parents for a few days since it's the holiday time. They love her so much. It's like having their daughter back again." Michael closed his eyes. It was easy to see his energy was spent.

"Is he going to be okay, Doctor?" Mrs. Brunner rubbed her son's foot, like she was afraid to let go.

"He should be fine," Jason answered.

A disaster had been averted, but I still didn't know what had happened to Michael.

CHAPTER FORTY-FOUR

A Little Understanding

I felt relief seeing Jason smile. It had been a medical emergency after all, not a threat connected to Howard Mountain. Jason and I still had to deal with that.

"Michael's fall has done no permanent damage. He will need a lot of rest if he's going to enjoy his Christmas dessert," Jason smiled at Mrs. Brunner. "Let's pull the shades to block the light for a while. Michael, you'll feel better if you take this medication for the pain and close your eyes. You should be better in a few hours."

"Thank God," Mrs. Brunner sighed like she hadn't exhaled for a very long time. "Let's go into the living room, and I'll bring in some coffee. I think a stimulant would be just what the doctor ordered right now." Mrs. Brunner smiled at Jason. "Am I right, Doctor?"

"That would be very nice." Jason sat down on the couch beside me and gave me a reassuring hug.

"May I ask what happened?" I felt like I was intruding into a very private part of a family's tragedy. But, I had been dragged into this situation, nearly at the point of a gun. I believed I deserved an answer.

Judge Carl Brunner sank down onto an overstuffed chair and buried his head in his hands. "Wow, that was close," he said when he finally looked up. "Yes, Christiana, you deserve an answer to all of this." He spread out his arms, gesturing toward Michael's room, to include an explanation for it all.

Mrs. Brunner returned with a tray of coffee cups and placed one in front of each of us. Then she turned and served the four guards I had nearly forgotten as they stood at near-attention against the wall. "You could use some hot coffee too, I'm sure." She came back and sat down in the chair beside the judge.

"Who are those men?" I asked. We were treated as if we were being kidnaped and brought here to find that Michael had nearly lost his life.

"They are a very special detail of Blue Guard that are independent of the entire division," Judge Brunner began. "After Rebecca died and Michael was hurt, he would have been immediately placed in the endless sleep. But his doctor, Roy Kundred believed that, given enough time, the nerves in Michael's damaged back could heal with proper stimulation and treatment with the newest procedures. Nerves heal, strengthen, and reattached with the aid of quantum radiation stimulation. But, there was absolutely no exception to the rule of termination. So Michael's Godfather, your grandfather, Christiana, assigned a loyal group of guardsmen to make sure no one got too near Michael or discovered his condition."

"My grandfather?"

"Yes, dear, and Connie, your grandmother, helped us as well. She would stay at home near the communication center to respond to any callers looking for Oliver while he came over here and prayed with all of us. Michael's wonderful guards, who are now his friends, were included." She stirred her coffee and sipped a little. "I would see Oliver walking past the house sometimes. He would pause like he was tying his shoe, and while he was down there, he would pray for Michael."

"He would . . . pray with all of you? My grandfather?" Tears came to my eyes as I thought of all I had not known, all of the love I had missed, all of the joy that had flown by while I was asleep in the shelter of my life.

"When you were younger, Christiana, it was dangerous for you to know of our beliefs, dangerous for you and for us. You had to be mature enough to know that you could not talk to anyone about it." Judge Brunner's reassuring words comforted me a little. I still felt I had been left out of the greatest secret ever held.

"Sir Richly handpicked each one of us, Ma'am," said the guard who had driven us to the Brunner's home. "I had felt very privileged at the time. Now, I know I was blessed with a great opportunity, to get to know and serve Michael and to learn about the Master."

"The master of what?" I asked.

"Not the master of just anything, My Lady, but the Master of my soul." As the guard spoke, his face seemed to glow with a mysterious radiance.

While I noticed, I didn't make a comment about the strange light that radiated from him. "And tonight?" I went on. "What happened to Michael that caused the crisis today?"

"Have his treatments not worked?" Jason questioned. He knew Dr. Kundred, but he had known nothing of Michael Brunner and the injuries that left him unable to walk.

"To the contrary, they are working very well," Silvia smiled. "This evening, Michael had swung himself into his wheelchair as he always did. Your dear grandmother had taken his chair from her own attic, Christiana. No one has had a wheelchair for a long time, except in the hospital for very temporary use. Since the severely injured or permanently disabled are not permitted treatment, there is no need for them. It would have brought attention to Michael if we had asked to use a hospital wheelchair. Connie's grandfather had used the chair and when he was done with it, it was stored in the attic and forgotten. When we needed it, Connie and Oliver put it in their own car, drove over here with it, and pulled right into our garage. We closed the door before the chair was removed. No one knows it ever existed. No one knows it's here." She smiled again as the color began to return to her face.

"But, what happened to Michael today?" I questioned.

"Today, Michael went through his bathroom door in the chair and tried something he shouldn't have." Silvia Brunner shook her head and closed her eyes. "His treatments have increased the sensations in his legs. They really have, and that's a good thing. This evening, he could feel his legs a little and decided to use his arms to lift himself out of the chair. He thought he could lean against the sink while he washed up for bed. He is improving, but he wasn't ready for that kind of move. His feet went out from under him and he struck his head on the basin on the way down. I heard the crash and found him unconscious on the floor. Blood was everywhere." She finally looked down at her slacks. "Oh my dear, I am so sorry. I look awful."

"You look like a mother who has gone through a trauma with her son," I reassured her. "I will have to be honest. . . ." I didn't know if I should share my thoughts with her or not, but, she knew my grandparents and she felt like family. "I wondered if he had attempted suicide."

Silvia's expression didn't change. The sweetness remained but pain came and mingled with it. "Michael has been through that dark period since the accident." She looked intently at me, and I could feel what she felt. My books called it empathy, but I named it heartache.

"Christiana, several times within the first month following Rebecca's death, Michael attempted to end his life. As soon as he was able to move around the house in the wheelchair, he tried to manoeuver himself out onto the porch. He hoped someone would see him and report the presence of a disabled person in the neighborhood." Silvia Brunner had dissolved into a whisper as fear overtook her again. "Our Blue Guardsmen were able to protect him from himself and brought him back in the house before he was seen. Then, a few days later, Carl found Michael on the floor of his bathroom, covered in his own blood. He had taken a sharp shaving blade to his wrist and, well, that was not the situation today. When Vonny saw her daddy's bandaged wrist and asked him what had happened, he was filled with shame. He vowed then and there that he would never try to take his own life again. Today was an accident, just an accident." Her eyes were pleading with me. "But, Christiana, now that he wants to live, he could have died tonight."

"It was a very close call, Mrs. Brunner." Jason agreed. "If you hadn't been there quickly, to apply a firm compress, he would have bled out before I could have gotten here."

"And thank you so much for coming, Dr. O'Reilly. Dr. Kundred is on a holiday with his family," she whispered, with a voice full of gratitude.

"I'm afraid their coming was our doing, Ma'am. They didn't actually have a choice," the Blue Shirt offered apologetically.

"Oh my," she gasped and looked back at Jason and me. "I am so sorry. I hope you weren't frightened."

"Well, maybe a little," I admitted a partial truth. "But, I understand now. The guards couldn't tell us anything in public."

"That's right," Judge Brunner agreed. "I'm afraid their insistence was my fault. I told them to find a doctor and bring him or her here, whatever it took. They weren't to tell anyone the reason. And, they weren't to take 'No' for an answer."

"Carl, you didn't?" Silvia scolded.

"That's okay, Mrs. Brunner. I do understand," I said. "Our family is facing a similar situation. I've been worrying over my grandparents' birthdays coming up in a few days. They will both be seventy-five years old. Their birthdays are only days apart. You know what that means."

"Oh Christiana, not Oliver and Constance," the judge gasped. "I had been so caught up with Michael's needs, I hadn't even been aware that they were coming near the end of their Length of Days. I'm sorry I've been preoccupied. They helped us so much and still support us with their prayers."

I thought of the risks we were all taking that night. I thought about the glass cases of loved ones, Jason's family, someone's family. The images brought a nausea that rose and swelled within me and spoke out more boldly. My insides rattled with fear, excitement, and overspent energy.

"This evil act, the Length of Days policy, must be dissolved. Tonight, Jason and I have learned more about the despicable practice than anyone knew. It's deceivingly called the never-ending-sleep, but it isn't sleep at all. And, I may have found a solution for overturning the policy regarding terminations based on the Length of Days."

"Christiana, praise the Lord! What have you found?" Silvia threw both hands in the air. "It's all so dangerous. Bless you for doing this."

"Grand-mère and Grand-père mean everything to me." As I spoke their names, I felt a renewed strength and reason for the fight. "I used to sit on Grand-mère's lap as a small child while she read books to me. It was magical. She would play out each part, changing her voice to match the characters. Someday, I'd like a child of my own to sit on that same sweet lap while Grand-mère reads to them."

"Ah, my dear, the French word for grandma, Grand-mère. That is lovely."

"And . . . Mrs. Brunner," I continued, "I am waking up to a new spiritual awareness and a reverence for life. No one cares about life anymore. It's being disposed of like yesterday's trash. And for the rest, life is more to be endured than to be lived. Life is . . . God given and its worth is God validated." I could feel hot tears gathering in the corners of my eyes and stream down my cheeks. "I will fight for the overturn of that Godless law before it's too late, too late for my grandparents and the unnumbered others who await that fate. Jason and I have just learned some horrible information about the process of termination."

"We'll share more about the process another time," Jason added. "Tonight is Christmas Eve, a time for beauty and rejoicing."

"That's right, Jason. Thanks for reminding me," I said. "But, we will try to stop the policy and put an end to it all."

"You don't have much time, Christiana," Judge Brunner warned. "What on earth can you do with only a few days remaining before their birthdays?"

"Judge, I may need your help."

"Anything," he pledged sincerely. "I owe your grandparents so much. And now, today, I have added another debt, to you and Dr. O'Reilly. Besides, a change in the law could help more people than just your grandparents and my son. How do we do it?"

"Sir, a law can be overturned by a citizens' referendum. I have done the research. With a petition signed by a majority of the population, a law *can* be changed." I didn't know if I dare say any more. But, I didn't have time to play it cautiously. I leaned in toward the Brunners and whispered. "I have heard a rumor about a petition that is already circulating, but I don't know yet if it pertains to Length of Days legislation or . . . detoxification, or both."

"All of us here have been detoxed for several years now, Christiana." Judge Brunner spoke with the seriousness worthy of our cause. "I said I will do anything, and I will. If you can get enough signatures on a petition before your time runs out, I will institute a stay order, suspending all terminations until signatures from all across the country can be secured. This affects Michael too, you know. And Christiana, God bless you and Dr. O'Reilly for your bravery and dedication."

"Thank you, Sir."

"Judge Brunner, we need something else," Jason joined in.

I was baffled. I felt like our cause had been assured if the petition signatures were there.

"The cover letter, Christy," Jason reminded me.

"Oh, Jason." I felt my hopes slip into doubt again, but I shook off the easy way out, of giving up. Maybe Judge Brunner had a solution to the cover letter as well.

"What cover letter?" the judge asked.

"A formality put in place many years ago. A citizens' referendum must be accompanied by a cover letter. It is an official form that must be filled out exactly according to the directions given."

"And where do you get that?" The judge asked.

"The forms are buried among some old papers in the records office in the Capitol building," I sighed as I thought of yet another hurdle to leap. "The offices are closed until the Monday after the holidays. We'll have to turn it in that day." I got up, feeling I wanted to flee. I was tired of hearing the problem. I wanted to talk about the solution.

Judge Brunner jumped to his feet and reached into this pocket.

"The records and forms office is on the second floor of the Capitol. The lift won't be working until after the holidays, but you can go up the steps." He fished out two keys. One looked new and the other was dull and old. It had a scrolled and fancy head and a thick, warn shaft.

"This newer one goes to the door in the back of the building where the judges can enter out of the watchful eye of the public." He then handed me the antique key. "You can get in the records' office with the newer key. It's like a master to all the other locks. But this old one goes to the back file room where old records and forms are stored. Your cover letter and instructions must be in there. Try looking under *Old Order* or simply *Old Forms*. You should be able to find what you need. That's the only place I think, that type of material may have been filed."

"Oh, Judge Brunner, thank you." I flung my arms around him without hesitation or thought.

He patted my back the way my father used to soothe me when I fell. "Your courage tonight will benefit us all, Christiana. God's speed and safety to you both." Then he turned to Jason. "You are going with her, aren't you Doc?"

"Absolutely," Jason assured him and put his arm around my waist.

Then the judge reached out his hand in friendship to Jason. "Bless you, Jason O'Reilly. You saved Michael's life tonight. Tomorrow, when I have pulled my wits together, I will thank you properly."

"I'm glad your Guard contingent could find me, Sir," Jason smiled broadly, "even if your Blue Shirts did kidnap us in the process of getting us here."

We turned to leave then Jason stopped. "I think we will need a ride back to my car."

"One of the guards will take you anywhere you want to go—the moon and back if that's your desire." He waved in wide sweeping motions.

I started toward the door, but I could not let my question go unasked. "Ma'am, I hope this doesn't seem too nosy but—if

Rebecca's accident happened near the cabin in the picture, why does Michael have the photo hanging where he has to look at it all the time? I would think he wouldn't want to be reminded of his loss every day."

Silvia Brunner put her hand to her mouth and smiled softly. Gathering her composure, she said, "Let me see if I can explain this to you, my dear. He said, others may forget her, but he will make sure he never does. Michael doesn't have to see the picture every day, Christiana. He wants to see it every day. He told me that it is a privilege. He said it's because . . . his heart is buried there."

At that moment, I knew why angels sing. When love overflows the heart, it spills out in song.

CHAPTER FORTY-FIVE
Michael Was Saved

8:55 p.m.

While Jason and I were being driven back to his car by one of the Blue Guards, Jason asked me how I knew Rebecca Brunner, and I told him.

> Rebecca Brunner was my friend. She was older, but we had a similar interest, painting. Rather than talking about my love of words and how authors can paint alphabet pictures that can place the reader in another time, another place, we talked about the breathtaking vistas around us.
>
> Rebecca and I would take our artist palettes, canvases, and brushes out to the foothills of the mighty peaks and paint for hours. I enjoyed painting, but Rebecca was the real artist.
>
> "Christiana, that is a beautiful color," she would encourage my efforts. "How did you see that particular yellow tone in that green? It makes it sparkle like a jewel. You have a talent buried inside you. I see the fluidity, the sweep of movement. You have an inspired gift that you are holding back for some reason."
>
> I only smiled. Now, I wish I could have simply said, "Thank you."
>
> One late-day afternoon, she was talking about Vonny. "She is beautiful. She must get her good looks from her daddy."

"She looks like you, Rebecca," I said.

Rebecca had thrown her head back and laughed.

"Where do you two get all that elation? It must be in the water," I had laughed

"You know, there may be something to that. Michael puts little pills in his water so we keep a pitcher of it in the kitchen. Vonny and I drink it too. It doesn't taste any different, but we seem to have more energy after we drink a glass."

At the time, I didn't know what Rebecca was talking about. Now, Rebecca and Vonny's unheard of happiness made sense. Michael's detox pills, that they all took, were the key that unlocked the flatness of life for them and opened them to a full palate of emotions.

That evening, Mrs. Brunner told us, Michael and Rebecca had built a cabin near where we had gone to paint. The young Brunners would hike and wander through the forested area near the base of the mountain. Occasionally, they would mountain climb with ropes and harnesses and all the equipment. That was how it had happened.

Michael had led the way up the last face of the mountain and helped Rebecca to the summit where her hands grew cold and stiff. She lost her grip and fell. Michael reached for her, lost his own footing, and plummeted from the top. After several days of unresponsiveness, Rebecca's life was terminated.

"That would be awful, to see your loved one slip through your fingers," Jason whispered.

"Oh Jason, maybe being in love isn't so wonderful after all. Maybe, not feeling is better than broken feelings."

"Christiana, you wouldn't want that. Not now," Jason said.

"No, not now. Not now that I have experienced feelings and now that I have met you." Somehow I knew that Jason was smiling.

"It took a doctor dedicated to life to give Michael the opportunity to live. I'm surprised the hospital went along with it,"

Jason added.

"The hospital wasn't consulted," the Blue Guard driver said. "I'm sorry, I shouldn't have interrupted," he apologized.

"No, please, tell us," I answered.

"I know the judge wouldn't mind if I tell you. He tells it proudly to those he trusts." He paused. "In the morning of the second day of Michael's stay in the hospital, his physician, Dr. Kundred, came into his room. Michael's eyes were closed; the doctor just patted his leg.

"Good morning, Mountain Climber," the doctor said, then he laughed as if Michael had just responded to him. "Well, that's great," he said to Michael, still comatose in his bed. "Your dad will be here to take you home in a few minutes, so you just rest for now."

"What if they got caught?" I wondered out loud.

"They almost were. A nurse who started to enter his room questioned, 'Home, Doctor? He was unresponsive the last time I checked on him.'

"A few minutes later, Doctor Kundred and Judge Brunner whisked Michael out of the hospital. He began to recuperate in his room on the first floor of the Brunner residence. When he regained some strength and heard that Rebecca was gone, life no longer had any meaning. Later, he knew he had to live for Vonny."

"Thank you, officer," I said. Finally, I understood these new feelings. With the sunshine comes the shadow. If I wanted to experience love and joy, I would have to accept sorrow and grief that accompany them.

CHAPTER FORTY-SIX

The Capitol at Night

9:14 p.m.

It was nearly 9:15 when the Blue Guard pulled up to where Jason's car was still parked. The Guardsman opened the doors for us, and I jumped out quickly and into Jason's car. I knew full well that time was precious. My heart pounded in my chest so loudly I wondered if Jason could hear it above the sound of the motor once it was started. Would we be able to follow Judge Brunner's instructions with the keys to doors and files in the Capitol? Would we be in time?

As we raced toward the Capitol through the darkened night on our Godly mission, I noticed that Jason kept checking in the rear view mirror.

"Is someone following us again? Will this ever stop?" I was exhausted from running, from feeling, from being exposed to evil. "Will we be hunted for the rest of our lives for what we are doing tonight?"

My thoughts rushed back to words I had read. The framers of the Constitution risked everything, and many lost it all. I would have to be willing to stand up and be counted among them, regardless of the cost.

"Let's see if this guy stays with us even if we . . ." Jason jerked the steering wheel and snapped around the corner just seven blocks from the Capitol. On a side street, we buzzed through a grocery dispensing window where runners picked up food to distribute. Then we dashed down an old alley behind the shops that serviced the inner city and darted into an open, single car garage behind an apartment building. Jason turned off the lights and engine. Everything about the night was still. The traumatic energy in the car felt explosive. We sat there in the darkness so as not to draw attention to ourselves. We nearly held our breath as silence overtook the night. Hyper-vigilant, we scanned the empty alley. We waited in fear, yet prayed in hope.

The black strata-car I had seen around town all day sped through the narrow, one way, one lane passage behind us without slowing. It appeared he was still on the chase, not the careful search.

The night suddenly seemed too quiet and still, as we sat there in the dark. Jason took my hand but said nothing. I was afraid the people who owned the parking space would come home, find us there, and report us as intruders. We already knew the fate of those judged to be unnecessary or dangerous to Society. My eyes darted from the door that led to the entrance of the residence, to the alley behind us. Nothing stirred except my stomach as it churned with anxiety. Strange. I suddenly felt hungry and the humor of that clanged with the reality of the danger we were in.

"Here we go," Jason whispered as he backed out of the parking space and into the back alley. He allowed the downward slope of the driveway to carry us silently out of the garage. Rather than turning left and onto the thoroughfare again, he rolled across the street and continued into the alley. He crept along and allowed the momentum of the descent to carry us forward without gunning the engine. He slowed as gravity no longer propelled us forward.

"This won't work from this spot on," Jason spoke with measured caution.

At that point in the city, all of the roads and alleys took an upward grade. Generations ago, the city planners had placed the Capitol on a mound in the center of the city to insure the safety of records and other materials in the event of flood. As the need for space increased, existing, adjacent structures were torn down as the Capitol's wings spread out across the city like tentacles that reached out and touched all the areas of the citizens' lives.

A transit bus went silently above the street that ran parallel to the back lane but few other vehicles were on the road. I wondered what had happened to that black car that had been following us. But, thinking about it only made fear rise within me, and that fear could corrode my resolve. I had to calm down or our cause could be lost. Our own, personal fate would also be sealed if we were anything less than totally successful.

"Let me see . . ." Jason mumbled, as much to himself as to me.

I saw the back entrance to the Capitol waiting ahead like a refuge from a rolling storm. We eased through the narrow, lower level entry into the huge complex via a valet-hosted entrance to the parking garage. We were inside the basement but not yet all the way in the structure. The entry-bar was down and blocked the way since there was no attendant on duty to raise it. I gripped the keys Judge Brunner had given us tightly in my fist. The mechanism that raised the bar hummed slightly as if it had been activated. I panicked again as a new wave of fear gripped me.

"Is someone nearby, taunting us with the parking bar?" I whispered as I gripped the key ring more tightly. Again the mechanism hummed. Then, I realized I had been slightly depressing a button on a tab attached to the set of keys. I held my breath and pressed the button firmly again. The bar jerked and then rose.

"It's a remotely activated, electronic tone to open the garage gate when an attendant isn't on duty," Jason said as he shot through, under the raised bar, and drove around the ramp. I pushed the tab button on the key chain again and the gate lowered. He parked the car in a space out of sight from anyone who might pass in the alley.

It felt a little safer, parked there in the vast cement cavern of the empty garage. Without saying a word, we carefully opened our doors and slipped out. We checked in all directions for the exit. I grabbed Jason's hand as we hurried across the wide expanse of driving area. The sound of our footsteps echoed as we walked. I tried to elevate onto my toes but that only slowed me down. When we got to the door, Jason peered through the glass cautiously and then used the master key to open it. We slipped silently inside.

We were on the lowest level of the parking garage, so we began walking up the two flights of stairs that took us to the main floor. Again, Jason checked for any movement before opening the door into the large rotunda. It looked different at night. No light streamed through from the stained glass dome above the great hall. But, the wall of windows to the front of the building, which looked out onto the holiday lights of the city, allowed festive beams to shine in.

"Up the grand staircase," I whispered anxiously. We crept up the steps against the inside wall. It reminded me of mice as they scurry through a maze while hugging the walls of the partitions. *I'm endowed by my Creator with a right to life, liberty and the pursuit of happiness,* I rehearsed in my head. *I am not a mere mouse. I have a righteous obligation and duty to complete the task at hand, not only for Grand-mère and Grand-père, but for Michael Brunner and who knows how many others who may be hiding in back bedrooms of silent homes.* I knew they were worthy of living their lives to the fullest, by virtue of God's precious gift of life.

The second floor, our destination, was a few steps away. I started to move ahead of Jason, when I noticed in the dim light, a bracket attached to the wall near the ceiling. "One of those cameras," I whispered. It was facing the doors on the opposite wall, including the door I needed to enter, and it wasn't stationary. The camera slowly panned the area, back and forth. If we moved, we could be seen. My eyes also caught the now familiar people-detecting device that was embedded nearly unseen near the base of the door, another monitoring portal. Then, I had an idea. I reached in my pocket and removed the chip that was still wrapped in the tissue.

"I can't be detected," I whispered and returned the chip to the pocket of my cloak. I took it off and handed it to Jason. "You wait here with my cloak, and I'll take the keys and go inside."

"Christy, no." Jason protested. "It may not be safe."

"Then it won't make it safer if we are both in there and set off buzzers. Besides, we may have already sounded an alarm for all we know," I insisted. I thrust my cloak into Jason's hands and waited until the camera had panned to the left. Then, I darted across the hall, undetected by the people-buzzer and out of view of the camera. I put the newer master key into the lock and felt it turn the tumblers with quiet ease. Once inside the room, I waited until my eyes adjusted to the semidarkness. The room was windowless except for one small window, which, along with the open door, let in enough light for me to move around. I felt more secure in the smaller space. Scanning the far wall beyond the desks and files, I saw another door, an older one. It looked heavy, with raised panels and fancy millwork.

The old key with the ornate head fit easily into the lock, but when I tried to turn it, it didn't budge. I was afraid the shaft would snap off if I forced it. I panicked again. My heart began to pound so loudly, I could feel the beat of it behind my eyes. My hands began to tremble, and I nearly dropped the keys on the concrete floor.

I must use this fear as an ally if I'm going to succeed, I demanded of myself. My panic had to be translated in my mind to a motivating force for good.

Go ahead and panic, I thought. *The more the panic, the more worthy and justified my cause.* I felt calmness overpower my fear. Now, I had to think of a solution for the key.

I remembered something from an old book. A woman was using fancy scissors called pinking shears to cut some cloth. The sheers were dull and would not cut, so she folded a sheet of material called waxed paper and cut it with the shears. The wax made it possible to cut the fabric. But where would I find wax? I looked around the room and saw a desk with a lamp. I turned the light on and opened the lap drawer and several side drawers until I found what I hoped would be there, a small cube of wax. I had seen file clerks use wax to lightly tip their fingers, making it easier to leaf through a stack of paper.

It flashed through my mind that electronic devices were supposed to have eliminated the need for paper and filing, but when the chaos of the past century hit the country in a vast array of safety breaches, including the crash of all computer servers and systems, it became necessary to file important papers in cabinets again. There had to be a paper trail of the events and contracts we needed to find.

I touched my finger tip to the wax and gently applied it to the shaft of the old key. When I placed it back in the lock . . . it turned. *Praise the Lord,* my heart sang, and I smiled as I thought of Silvia Brunner.

Once inside the old records room, the file cases were much different from the ones in the outer office. Rather than numbers on the end of each drawer, there was a brief account of its contents. I looked for the words, *Old Orders*. There was nothing. Then, *Old Forms* appeared like a miracle.

I riffled through the files frantically, aware of the time. There it was: "Referendum Cover Sheet." I snatched it out and held it to my chest. It had to be in time. It just had to be.

CHAPTER FORTY-SEVEN
Chasing Phantoms

Out in the night, Ward Stoner pulled to a stop outside the Capitol and parked in the security parking space. He stared at the glass fronted building, the interior of which was illuminated by the Gifting lights. He shook his head. *They have to be in there somewhere*, he whispered into the frozen air. *Their chips say so.* Suddenly, he thought he saw a movement inside the building near the staircase. It was fleeting, as a shadow of someone or something ran down the steps. He waited. No one emerged.

At first, the ever present anger that constantly gnawed at his insides, flared like a fanned flame. He fought with the negative thoughts that bombarded his professional self-concept. *No one will believe this. They'll say, "Old Inspector Tombstone is exaggerating again, casting aspersions on someone as fine as Christiana Applewait." They won't listen to me. Why do I even talk sometimes?*

He shook his head as he tried to clear his thinking. *Stop it Stoner,* he demanded of the demons that haunted him. *They'll have to listen to this tale. This is real and it's happening right here in front of me. They will learn who has the power, and they'd better not cross me.*

As he watched the door to the Capitol, Stoner rolled the old argument over and over in his mind. He had believed that everyone thought he was wrong since he was a young boy and had cowered at the fierce criticism of his stepfather. When he was in his late teens, he had taken an internal stand. *I am not wrong, you worm. You are!*

From that day until the night he found himself chasing phantoms through the city streets, he had done battle with the specter of his stepfather whom he saw in anyone who challenged him. He still fought for power constantly, while he held one of the most powerful positions in society. Only with Miriam was power not part of the relationship.

Stoner continued his vigil, but still, no one emerged from the Capitol. Time seemed suspended. He thought he could hear the tick of a distant clock. He translated the long wait and the loss of the one he had chased, as a personal affront to himself.

So, it's a game of hide-and-seek is it? He jeered. He pulled his car back into the street and drove slowly around the building. Nothing. He shined a flood light into the private parking area, but no one was there. The bar was down, intact and obviously undisturbed.

"Where did you go, Little Ghost?" he mumbled into the darkness.

Stoner pulled the strata-car around to the side entrance and parked. A set of concrete steps with a pipe-style hand rail ran up to a platform that provided an entry apron for the non-public entrance. With a hand-held tone controlled master opener, he sent a signal into the lock and opened the door. The inspector emerged into the rotunda. He found it still, silent and empty. He could see well enough with the glow of the festive lights outside coming through the windows and illuminating the great hall.

From what he had seen from the car window, he believed someone had been on the stairs, so he mounted the steps, and inspected each, one at a time. He searched the marble treads for even a bit of disturbed dust. *The cleaning crew is too good for an investigation like this.* There was no sign of a living soul having passed that way.

Ghosts, he mocked in the dimly lit space. *I guess I'm becoming a ghost hunter rather than a Blue Guard Detective.*

At the foot of the stairs, he pulled back a mirror-like panel that hid a person-sensor. He taped the portal monitor that counted and announced anyone who might step onto the upper floor. Two beeps counted two intruders. Midway up, he tapped another monitor. One beep. At the head of the stairs, there was nothing. He stopped and smiled. *Well, well, little spook. I have found you.*

He opened the door to a supply closet around the corner on the second floor and took out a step ladder. Placing it beneath the camera he had mounted earlier that afternoon, one of several he had placed around the city, he climbed up for a better look. *Well now, we will just see what we have here.*

In the back of the camera was a modest sized viewer. Stoner pressed the rewind button and zipped it back far enough to reveal the activity in the previous half hour. The hall was dimly lit but the screen was bright.

Okay Pluto, let's see who is not here. He watched the screen that showed no activity at first. *If Clyde Tombaugh could find a planet in 1930 by studying the images he took of the night sky, and discovered Pluto by noticing what was not there . . . so can I. There is the hall.* The next few seconds of the image revealed the door to the records' room across the hall from the steps as it closed the final few inches. A few minutes later, the lower leg and heel of a woman's shoe were seen as she crossed the hall back to the staircase. He tapped the top portal, no beep. Again, mid-stairs, two beeps. *Well, well, well, she was not there at the portal . . . and suddenly . . . voila, there . . . there she is. So Miss Daring Spook, I don't know how you did it, but you are my holiday ghost.*

CHAPTER FORTY-EIGHT
A New Emotion - Rage

We had left the Capitol at 10:27 p.m. I had grabbed the paper and hurried to the door of the records room. Jason had given the signal that the camera had panned out, so I could slip past safely. When it was clear, I had darted out. We had carefully and quickly made our way down the staircase, around through the grand hall and out the back door to the private parking garage where we had come in. We hadn't known if anyone was out front when we pressed the button on the key ring and drove back out into the back streets of the city. We had gotten away and had not seen anyone. No one was in the building. No one had followed us.

• • • • •

"A blessing for your thoughts," Jason whispered once we were back in his car.

We rode toward my apartment in near silence. I was thinking about how much had happened. So many memories stirred. So much pain and horrible evil had been exposed.

"I've been thinking about Grand-mère and Grand-père." I looked out on the ice that sparkled on the trees and bushes. Everything was so beautiful, and I felt so ugly and dirty from the filth I had been exposed to. "This is no longer about me and the loss of my grandparents, is it Jason?" I looked at the enormity of the world around me. I had never really noticed it before. If I wasn't checking the weather to determine how it would affect me and my own needs, I

239

didn't even see the blue sky or feel the soft rain. "I don't know if I'm big enough for a task of this magnitude. I don't know if I'm brave enough. I guess I think in micro-bites. I have no big picture panorama inside me."

"You may have seen the smaller picture in the past, Christy. But, you have been called to a larger cause, bigger than your grandparents, bigger than any one of us." Jason squeezed my hand to reassure me.

"How is that even possible, Jason? Nothing ever happens to challenge anyone anymore. We live on railroad tracks, never steering right or left, never going backward, never hitting a bump, always rolling toward . . . nothingness."

"Christy, there is a strength you can call on. I know how new you are to the Kingdom, but trust me we are not marching toward nothingness. For those who believe, we are always moving toward home. The porch light has been lit, and they're waiting for us."

"Who, Jason?"

"All those who have gone before . . . and Jesus."

"I've started reading about him. It's like I'm learning about someone I always knew." Suddenly my eyes flashed on a movement up ahead. A woman and a small boy ran out of a building and across the lawn in the direction of the road. They had no coats and the boy had no shoes. "Jason, what —"

"Hold on," he commanded as he slammed on the brakes just as the two ran to the edge of the road.

I grabbed the safety strap above the door and held on. The road was icy and the surface shone like a giant diamond, beautiful but dangerous. With the help of the DSR 210, Distance Safety Restraint that detected the presence of others in the periphery, Jason was able to control the vehicle and swerve past them to the curb.

"Please," the woman begged as she clawed at my car window. "He's coming."

I left the window safely closed but spoke into the side communicator opening. "What's wrong?"

"He's coming, please let us in," she implored as she checked over her shoulder for what was chasing her. The small boy clutched her leg.

Who was this woman? Was she an operative of the government? Had they found out that we had discovered their evil? Had they come for us, in order to keep their secrets?

At that moment, a large man, sweating, shirtless and wielding a wooden bat above his head, charged out of the apartment building like a raging bull stampeding out of the pen. I eased the door open to let the woman and child climb in, but the burly man pushed them aside and grabbed at my wrist. He jerked me from the car in one motion, so fierce I was almost lifted out of my shoes. I struggled to stay on my feet as the man tightened his viselike grip on my arm.

"Christiana!" Jason yelled as he jumped from the car and flew over the hood and landed on the man, jumbling all three of us to the ground in a scrambled heap.

"Charles, no!" The woman screamed and clutched her son close to her body.

The man looked at her without releasing his hold on me. "Ruth?" He looked wild, bewildered.

Then, I saw Jason, unconscious and flat on the ground. Fear seized me when I heard him moan and saw him try to move from under the huge man's foot. He had pinned me down also, and I felt helpless. In that instant, I knew the man's mind would not be reached with more struggling.

The man got to his feet and dragged me with him. "Charles," I smiled as casually as I could muster, "something is bothering you. Can I help?" Suddenly, I felt at peace and words came forth I had never known before.

"What?" he stammered, still grasping my arm.

"You were chasing this woman and boy, Charles," I said. "What's the problem my friend?" I patted the man's hand where he held me tight. I hoped he would release his grip.

"No . . . that's Ruth, my wife," he stared at me with wide, blank eyes.

"Christy? Are you okay?" Jason gasped as he regained consciousness and tried to get up, but the man had planted his foot on Jason's chest.

"I'm fine, Jason. It's Charles here who needs our sympathy. I want to help him." I swallowed my panic and spoke softly, hoping to calm him down. "I think Charles is just having a really bad day."

"Bad day?" He waved the ball bat he was still holding over his head; his eyes flashed and he raised his voice wildly again. "No. I was showing my son how to play baseball, with a bat like this one."

"Have you been taking little pills lately, Charles?" I asked. "They're great, aren't they? Did you get them from a friend?" I knew this had to be the answer.

"Yeah, from a friend of a friend." He lowered the bat and blinked like he was trying to see everything more clearly.

"Hey, should I call the authorities?" A man yelled from the doorway of the apartment building across the street.

I looked at Charles and his little family as we stood in the snow on Christmas Eve. We were all held by a man who didn't even know he was out of line. "What do you think, Charles? Are you going to be able to calm yourself down on your own? Or, should we have this man call the Blue Guard and have you put in jail on Gift Day Eve?"

"No, no," he protested and stood back a little. He took his foot from Jason's chest. By this time Jason was aware of the situation and slowly got to his feet.

"Should we ask your wife if she wants you to go back in your home with her and your son, Charles?" I asked.

He looked over at his wife. I could see fear on her face. He looked at her in shock and grief. "Ruthie, you're afraid of me? Of me?"

Charles took one step in her direction. She jumped back and dragged the frightened child with her.

The man's face froze with sorrow and shame. "Ruthie . . ." he reached out to her again. She recoiled and tightened her embrace around her son. Charles stopped and looked at the bat in his hand.

"What . . . ?" he looked at his family again and then at Jason and me, the two strangers he had threatened.

"That's right, Charles. You're not well this evening. What should we tell your neighbor?" Jason said. "Are you going to be able to get yourself under control on your own? We believe in you. I think you can."

I felt Charles' hand release my arm, but I did not pull away. The touch seemed to quiet him. The medication he had taken may have worn off.

"I'm fine. I'm okay." He turned to his wife with pain in his eyes. "Ruthie . . . I am so sorry."

"Charles, I'm a doctor, and I think you will be fine if you get some sleep. We can help you," Jason said.

"I think we'll be all right," I called to the neighbor who had offered help. I hoped we had made the right choice.

"I'll stay at my brother's home tonight, Ruthie. Or, I'll sleep in the jail if you would feel safer." His voice was softer, calmer.

"That might not be necessary," Jason offered. "How many of the white tablets did you take today?"

"Ten," Charles admitted, looking down as if he knew he had overdosed.

"I have some medication in my bag that will counter the effects of those pills, Charles," Jason said. "Take them right away with plenty of water. The white tablets you had taken will dilute quickly and drain from your body immediately." Jason went to get the medical bag from the trunk of his car.

"We'll come in while you calm down," I suggested. "If that's all right with you," I asked Charles' wife. She looked at Jason as he came back with his bag. Then she looked cautiously at both of us as she motioned for us to follow her into the apartment.

Charles responded to the medication Jason administered just as he had predicted. We sat for a while and talked with the family about the holiday. Charles admitted he had been overdosing for days. He had started taking the medication on the promise that he would get back some energy he had been lacking. After Ruth put their son to bed and knew what had happened to her husband, she assured him she was no longer afraid and they would be fine. Soon, he was ready to settle down for the night.

"Thank you both so much," Ruth said as she escorted us to the door. "I don't know what would have happened if you hadn't been here."

"I've taken the rest of Charles' supply of white pills with me. Have him make an appointment right after the holidays. Do not let him go out on his own. He will be feeling tired and may go in search of more pills. He cannot do that."

"Yes, Doctor," she assured Jason. "And, thank you My Lady. You were like an angel. Bless you Miss."

"An angel, Ruth?" I was surprised to hear of heavenly beings again.

We wished each other the happiest of Gifting Days and made our way back out into the snowy night. We were soon back in Jason's car, heading home one more time.

"You are most definitely brave enough, Christy." Jason assured me as we drove through the night. His words filled me with added warmth.

"I was brave?"

"You don't know?" Jason's voice sounded like he was surprised.

"No, Jason. I was afraid, not brave."

"Bravery doesn't mean you're not afraid, Christy. It means you do what needs to be done in spite of the fear or anger you may be feeling. You weren't thinking of yourself this time. You were more focused on that couple and their little boy and making Christmas Day happy for them, than you were concerned about yourself."

I thought about all that Jason had said and held the words close to my heart. Everywhere around me, my life was changing, coming alive. I was now seeing the world with different eyes, and I didn't even know when it happened, when it changed. Regardless of what Jason said, I had not felt brave or up to the task when I was talking to

Charles, but I had felt the presence of something powerful in my life that seemed to counter balance the self-doubt. Yet, the thought kept coming back. *Would we win the battle against the evil that had gripped our country for so long? Would we be able to save my grandparents? Or, would the glory of the victory be meaningless without my grandparents to share it?*

CHAPTER FORTY-NINE
Stoner Panics

"I'm done for now," Inspector Stoner stated with finality as he made his way out of the Capitol back to his car. He put the camera on the front seat and slid in out of the snow. The follow-up could wait until morning. Confronting Lady Christiana Applewait and starting an internal probe of the activities of a clandestine unit of the Blue Guard would both come in due time. In the morning, Gift-giving Day would have to share the clock with his never-ending responsibilities. It would be more than just a morning of gift exchanges with his son and family and a breakfast of hot chocolate and homemade pecan rolls. He would have to go over to Oakwood and intrude on Oliver Richly and his family. Never mind that it was a holiday. Stoner shuddered at the thought of the extreme breach of protocol, wound up and bound in the career-ending step of invading the home of one of the Council of Elders. That was not something he looked forward to. He wasn't afraid of Sir Richly. He admired him and, in his mind, there were very few people who deserved his admiration.

He drove along the streets of the city, his streets, and for the first time he wondered how long it had been snowing. He hadn't noticed. Stoner didn't mind spending time in his car. He felt he was surveying all that he owned.

Because of Ward Stoner's job, he was privileged to own a single family dwelling. As head of the Blue Guard, it was necessary. He could be called at any time to inspect a situation. He couldn't disturb other people as he would if he lived in an apartment building. An efficient workforce required eight hours of uninterrupted sleep. Stoner owning his own home was for the greater good of the collective.

As Stoner pulled onto his own street, he saw that the lights were still on at his house, and he felt good for the first time that day. He had to have nerves of steel and the bearing of a tyrant all day long. His job demanded it. But, if he couldn't lay down the facade of the archfiend of Capitol City at the end of each day, he believed he would turn to dust and blow off into the barren dessert of his own soul. Miriam had helped him shed the mantle of aggression in the past, but she was gone now.

Twinkle lights beckoned him to the front room window, and he smiled. His mother may have let Christopher stay up until Daddy got home. Gift Day Eve had always been a special time of family games and laughter. Even though Miriam had been placed in the sleep chamber, his son deserved a Merry Gift-giving Day. Somehow, he had to pull together the remaining acting talent in his playbill of fictitious characters to create a happy day for his son, and it was late.

He drove the car farther into the driveway. Suddenly, it felt like he had hit a bump. *Christopher, what did you leave in the driveway this time?* He chuckled to himself as he thought about all the toys and tools he had mangled under the wheels of the car in the past. A fairly new wagon, a red tricycle, and a black tool box were recent sacrifices to Christopher's play.

He opened the car door and came around to the walk that led to the house where he saw Christopher laying on the ground near the edge of the driveway. Stoner's heart fell from his chest and landed on the small broken body of his son who sprawled between the lawn and drive.

"Oh, my god!" Ward screamed in agony.

The front door burst open and Stoner's mother ran out into the night. Fear gripped her voice as she tried to scream but no sound came from her throat. She rushed to Christopher's side, fell down on her knees on the snow covered ground, and gathered him in her arms, rocking him the way she had rocked his father when he was a child.

Christopher must have snuck out to surprise his daddy, thinking he was standing on the edge of the sidewalk. He often got a little too close to the drive and Stoner had warned him about staying back. But, it was dark and foggy that night. Perhaps Christopher had not been able to judge his position on the grass.

Stoner's blood froze within him. Damaged children were discarded. He knew that all too well. Christopher's condition was not important to the authorities; an injured child could always be replaced. Stoner had to hide the child immediately.

"Hurry, Mother, hurry! Let me carry him inside. He can't be seen out here like this. The authorities—" Ward Stoner reached for his son.

Sarah Stoner hung onto her grandson's bleeding body and brought his sweet cheek next to her own. "You," she screamed, "you are the authority that you now fear!"

Stoner was stunned by her words—shocked to face the sudden truth of his life. He was the one who hunted people down who were just trying to live their lives as fate had endowed them. He was the intruder. He was the ghost of this life, hiding in the shadows, waiting to snatch away the breath and shorten the lives of others. Now, the broken body was Christopher's. Now it was his family's tragedy. Now, he held the entire span of his son's Length of Days in his own blood stained hands.

Sarah Stoner would not relinquish her grandson, not even to the child's own father. She struggled to her feet, carrying the child's limp form as she moved. Ward ran ahead of her and held the door while she took Christopher inside and placed him on the couch. Stoner fell to his knees beside his son and listened to his chest. "He's breathing," he whispered.

Sarah soothed the child's cheeks until he opened his eyes. "Hello Sweetheart." Then she turned to Ward. "We have to take him to the hospital to be checked out."

"Come on Big Guy," Ward said as he scooped up his son and carried him into his own room. He placed him comfortably on his bed then turned. "I'll be right back, Christopher."

"The hospital? No!" Ward hissed through gritted teeth as he returned to his mother in the living room. His face was strained with worry and twisted in fear at the thought of anyone knowing that his son had been hurt.

Sarah's face was ashen and the grip of fear was already etched there. Suddenly, she raised her arms with hammer-like fists and slammed them down on Stoner's back and head. Blow after blow landed on his shoulders.

She lashed out with her inner rage at all that was evil in the land, embodied in her own son.

Ward did not fight back. He seemed to welcome the attack. Perhaps the mortification of the flesh imposed on him by the little woman who beat him, like a necessary whipping from a devoted mother in the ancient past, might cleanse his soul.

Finally, Sarah let out the raging screams that had been mute when she held her small grandson. Then, completely spent, she ceased the thrashing.

"Mother, Mother, shh." Tears Stoner could not shed when Miriam died welled up within him and broke forth in great sobs and pains of anguish. He cried uncontrollably, his body heaved with emotional pain. Ward's body went limp and weak and the agony drained all life and meaning from him.

When Sarah saw her son, broken and weeping, she called out to him. "Oh Ward, I am so sorry," Sarah sobbed. "I have hated your job from the very beginning . . . but I never hated you."

"Daddy? Grandma?" the soft little voice of Christopher called out from the bedroom through his injuries.

"Christopher?" Sarah gasped and hurried to his side. "Oh thank God."

Stoner wiped his eyes and rushed to his son's room. He put the back of his hand on Christopher's forehead. He wasn't hot. "Where do you hurt, Son?"

"I don't know."

Ward went numb. Was his son paralyzed? Could he not feel his body? "What do you mean?" Stoner ran his hands down the child's arms. "Can you feel this?"

"Yes," Christopher laughed as he started to get up. "Why can't I feel my legs? They feel like they're asleep."

"Christopher, you can't feel your legs?" Sarah's tone was calm but her timbre was weak and shaken.

"Tell me about those legs, Son," Ward coaxed, longing to hear some words of hope.

"I can feel them, sort of, like they're prickly but they're not awake either." Christopher didn't seem to be in pain, just curious. "Why, Daddy?" He placed his small hands on his father's face and patted his cheeks.

Stoner's facade crumbled into rubble at the touch of his son's gentle, innocent hands. With fear and dread he asked softly, "Well . . . did Daddy's car run over your foot or anything like that?" Stoner dreaded to hear the answer. How could he live with himself if he had actually struck his own child?

"No, the car bumped me over and I hit my head and bottom on my new wagon," he admitted sheepishly. "You told me to put it away this morning. I'm sorry Daddy."

"You know you aren't supposed to be that close to the car and driveway don't you?" Sarah smiled. "It's okay this time. Just be more careful the next time, Honey." Sarah looked away, perhaps so Christopher wouldn't be able to see the fear on her face.

"Maybe it's just a pinched nerve," Ward suggested.

"What if it's permanent?" Sarah breathed low. "I know what you said, but maybe we should take him to the hospital, now, tonight."

Stoner turned his back and tried to mouth and whisper the words that had to be said. "We could, but let's think this through. Even if he heals, and he's just fine in the morning, this is serious. He would have one strike against him. With very many strikes, he would be declared defective."

"But, if we wait," Sarah tried to keep her voice low and muffled with her hand across her mouth, "what may not be a permanent injury now, may become one without proper treatment."

"I know someone who may be able to find a doctor for us. I'll call him." Stoner reached for his personal communication instrument and touched in the number. It rang several times.

"Hello?" the familiar voice answered. Stoner explained his need for a doctor with integrity, one he knew would have compassion for an innocent child. The person gave him a blind phone number, a contact without a name, and Stoner placed the call. It was a frightening moment. He wondered how much he should tell the doctor. Yet, how could he withhold information the doctor may think could be pertinent to the case? Either way could be disastrous for Christopher. Up or down could be the wrong move. He didn't know which way to bounce.

Stoner knew that physicians had one main object in mind, to protect his own family and career. He didn't know if the person he was calling would be the genuine healer he hoped for, or someone who would place his Christopher's health and needs far down on his own priority list. But, for Stoner, the hunter needed his son to survive before he became the hunted. Stoner's truths, so ridged in the past, could turn into lies in a matter of seconds if necessary.

Stoner placed the call which connected within seconds. "This is Chief Inspector Stoner, here. Someone gave me your number."

There was no sound at the other end of the connection.

"Doctor?" Stoner questioned.

"Yes? What can I do for you Inspector?" a deep voice answered.

"It's my son. He . . . fell a little while ago. At first he was unconscious. When he awakened, he said he had fallen on his head and bottom. Now he says he can't feel his legs like he should. He said they tingle."

"Perhaps you had better take him to the hospital. I could meet you there."

Now it was Stoner who was silent with apprehension and fear. "Do you think that's wise?" He hoped his veiled words would be understood.

Again there was silence. "Are you afraid of . . . never mind. If you decide to keep him home tonight, you'll have to try to keep him awake in case he has a concussion. Does he complain of a headache?"

"Does your head hurt Christopher?" Stoner asked his son.

"No, I don't think so," the child patted at the side of his head and paused like he was listening for a slow leak in an inflated ball.

"He said 'No'." Stoner leaned low and covered the mouth piece with his hand. "I would like to avoid the record of an injury if at all possible."

"I understand," the doctor concurred. "If I don't see the boy to treat him, I don't have to make a report. Well, I'm here at the end of this communication line. If you are refusing treatment tonight, there's little I can do. Watch him for twenty-four hours."

"I would have done more in similar circumstances and have already done as much in the past," Stoner admitted like an accused man admitting he had committed a crime. "I would have had the authorities take over the care of an injured child if the parents refused treatment."

"Yes, Sir . . . I imagine you would have. But, I am not you," the doctor on the end of the line responded crisply.

"No, Sir, you are not. I want to thank you for that distinction. My wife is gone, but my mother and I will stay up with Christopher tonight. We will call right away if he takes a turn for the worse."

"How old is the boy?" the doctor asked.

Stoner's eyes filled with tears as he thought of the possibility of his son being labeled defective. If he were anyone else's child, Stoner would not have valued the boy's life at all. Suddenly, he felt that blood seemed to drip from his own hands, and he wrung them in an attempt to wipe away the guilt that justifiable clung there. Ward Stoner cleared his throat and tried to speak. Finally he whispered, "Doctor, my son is only five years old." Stoner's heart crumbled into gravel at his feet.

CHAPTER FIFTY

The Eyes on Christy Are Closed

11:45 p.m.

Jason parked the car a short walk from my apartment building. "Hopefully, whoever was following us has gone home for the night," he whispered into the frosty air.

My body felt heavy as Jason escorted me to the door. I wanted to get in out of the darkness and evil that seemed to wait at every turn.

"I know it's late Jason, but can you come in for a while? I'd feel safer," I said.

"Of course, Christy."

We walked quickly toward the door. I felt exposed, like many eyes followed our every step.

Inside the building, firelight danced on the faces of our new friends who were gathered again in the large room, like families I had read about in my books. "Look at this, Jason. I hardly recognize it as my apartment building."

"Many of those people are the carolers from the last sing-along," Jason smiled. "Dahlia is still at the piano. I guess I really never knew her at all."

"Do you think it's safe to join them?" I motioned to the group and patted my satchel which still contained the precious lifesaving papers. "What if we're still being followed? I wouldn't want to put these people in harm's way."

"I haven't seen anyone behind us since we came out of the Capitol. Not even when Ruth and her son stopped us in the road near her home, there didn't seem to be anyone around except for one neighbor." Exhausted and filled with fear, Jason and I wondered if eyes would still be watching our every move. He took my hand and led me over to the group who was still celebrating. It was nearly midnight.

I took off my cloak, draped it carefully over my arm, and watched that the paper was secure. Removing my hat, I placed it on the piano.

"Come sit beside me," Dahlia patted the piano bench and kept up the melody with her right hand.

It looked like fun and I needed a peaceful moment before trying to sleep. I knew I would toss all night with all I had seen. I had to bring my soul back from the brink, the edge of utter hopelessness.

Oh Holy night, my heart soared in ways no spoken words could. *Fall on your knees, Oh hear the angel's voices,* the golden melodies threaded the words that linked Heaven with my wounded heart.

After a few songs, Jason and I went over to the coffee pot on a long side table. With cups in hand, we found a place to sit and talk while we enjoyed the group.

"Jason, these lyrics are not threats to the people's health as Society had said they were," I said. "Look at their faces. Peace and joy shine in their eyes. Their emotional health is not being damaged by the musical threads of these songs."

"I don't see any primal instincts being stirred," Jason smiled. "I do see raw emotions rising. Love is in the room."

Finally, sleep began to overtake me. "I think I need to go to bed," I yawned.

We walked over to say goodnight to Dahlia. Jason stood behind me at the piano. I could feel his warmth on my shoulder. "I'll walk you up, Christy."

"Wait," Dahlia got up from the piano and put her hand on my

arm. "I have wanted to talk to you, Christiana," she whispered.

"I know you have Dahlia, but I don't see how I can be of help. I'm newer to these feelings and experiences than you are."

"I realize that, but there is something different about you. You are growing in understanding and love so fast, Christiana. It's like you knew before, somewhere in time. I need to know how you took fire so fast."

"I don't even use feeling words yet," I protested. "I have no idea why feelings are accumulating all around me."

Dahlia smiled. "I remember how that felt. None of us had experienced emotions before, so there didn't need to be descriptive language to talk about it."

"But, I'm a person of words, Dahlia, many words, beautiful words. I have to know my feelings' names."

Jason patted my shoulders in comfort and support. "I think what Dahlia is asking, Christy, if you can think of a pivotal point when suddenly you knew what you didn't know before, on a level where language isn't needed."

Suddenly, I knew. I knew a few of the words that matched my feelings. "I heard the flutter of angels' wings and the breath of their song." I smiled as words poured forth from my heart where knowledge is stored before there is meaning. "A strange warmth filled me, like Jason's warm hand on my shoulder, and a flame was lit deep inside, Dahlia. That is all I know."

"That's all you know?" Dahlia smiled with awe. "I want as much as I can get. Is there anything else you know?"

"I know that, in the very beginning, Dahlia, there was God and that is all I need to know." I wondered if I should cite the source of my certainty. Would I dare? "Dahlia, can I trust you?"

Her expression was pained, but her words were sure and true. "Christiana, you can trust me."

"I have an old book . . . a very old book. When it's safe, I'll let you read it."

"When will it be safe enough for me to read a book that's not already on the approved reading list?" She shook her head at the futility of the existence in which we all lived.

"When the time is right . . . I will tell you." Then I stood. I was afraid to say more. "I'll see you tomorrow?" I gathered up my hat and cloak. I patted my satchel and compulsively wanted to open it to see if the paper was still there. I had to leave it alone, or risk revealing it to someone who might report that we have it.

"Yes, indeed, I will see you tomorrow." Dahlia's smile was sweet and genuine.

Jason walked me to the elevator and we rode up in silence. It was a comfortable silence in a language that spoke louder than words. There were so many things on my mind, all mixed with a new joy I had never known and a fear I had never experienced.

"The camera, Christy," Jason whispered at my door. "We have to take care of that. I can step inside where I can't be seen by whoever is watching, while you investigate. But, I'm not going to leave you alone while that thing is still in there."

I stepped into my apartment. Everything was quiet and still, but I was uncomfortable. My library stepladder still stood against the book case. I knew I would have to do something about the camera that lurked above my head. It seemed to hover above me like a vulture ready to attack the weakest one on the ground. But, I was not weak anymore.

I walked past the bookcase, first going to the windows as a diversion to my true destination. Perhaps whoever would view the film later might think my plan was an accident. I stood looking out onto the city and stretched my arms above my head as casually as I could. Then, I walked to the small table beside the couch and picked up a book I had laid there earlier. Pretending to leaf through the small volume, I scanned several of the pages then laid it down as if it didn't hold my interest. I looked up and down my bookcase wall, then climbed the ladder near the camera but avoided looking at it.

"There it is," I whispered as if talking to myself and pulled a book from the shelf with a jerk. Swinging my body wide, as one might if they were steadying themselves against a fall, I flung my arm out and knocked the camera to the floor with my elbow.

"What on earth?" I spoke to myself again and hurried down the ladder. Pretending to trip near the bottom rung, I stomped the heel of my shoe down with a thud on the small camera as I landed squarely on the floor.

"Oh my goodness," I added in case the camera was still functioning. The object was even smaller than it had appeared while on the shelf. I carefully scooped it onto a piece of paper that was lying on the table and tossed the entire thing into the trash.

"That will be the end of it for tonight. I'll worry about the *who* and *why* another time," I said as I dusted off my hands.

"Good job, Christy," Jason said. "The trash is a good place for it," he laughed.

"Well it certainly is trash," I agreed.

"Are you okay?" Jason asked. "I could stay—on your couch—tonight if you would feel safer."

"Thank you Jason. I appreciate that but . . . it wouldn't be proper. And—I think that I'll be all right. Whoever placed the camera did so when I was out. I don't think he'll come back while I'm home."

"He seems to sneak around rather than confront," Jason reassured me. "You've been through a lot this evening. We both have. I can be here in minutes if you become frightened."

"I know you can, Jason." We walked slowly to the door. "You would think I would be eager to sleep and free my mind of all that has happened. But—I do hate to see you go."

"Christy, I—"

"I know," I finished his thought with thoughts of my own. "Good night," I whispered as he kissed me. I leaned against the door after he left and smiled.

Alone on the couch, I sat looking out at the city, brightly lit with holiday lights. It was late. The day had been traumatic. Evil was discovered beneath Howard Mountain. A foul, wickedness dwelled there. Tomorrow, Christmas Day, would be as different as joy is from sorrow. Celebrating awaited and the huge task of starting the petition loomed before us. I had to remain positive, or fear and disgust would drain all of my energy. I now knew what vileness lay at the bottom of the souls of some. We would not be safe, and we were only weeks away from my grandparents' final days.

I panicked when I thought of the number of signatures we would need for our petition to stop the Length of Days laws. "Will we have the signatures in time?"

CHAPTER FIFTY-ONE
Christy's First Christmas

8:00 a.m.

In spite of the fact that my energy had been depleted from all the joys and horror of the previous day, I awakened on my first Christmas morning, feeling like a child, anxious to open the biggest present under the Gifting Tree. I finished dressing myself in my beautiful new, green silk caftog and looked in the mirror. I smiled and dabbed a little color on my cheeks.

Jason came early. He was going to take Dahlia and me to my grandparents' home for my first Christmas gathering! When I opened the door, he immediately swept me off my feet and into his arms.

"Merry Christmas, Christy." He held me close and added, "You look beautiful!"

"Thank you, kind sir. Jason, this is my very first Merry Christmas," I squealed. "I can't get enough of hearing those words. And, I wish for you a very Merry Christmas as well, Jason O'Reilly."

"We took care of our little spy last night," I said triumphantly as I pointed to the trash receptacle in the kitchen.

"You know that won't be the end of that little chapter in your life, don't you?' Jason put his arm around my waist and kissed my forehead.

"I know, Jason. But, the thought of someone being able to watch my every move on Christmas Eve was more than I wanted to think about."

"Whoever put it there will be back as soon as the holidays are over, looking for their equipment," he whispered and sighed in my ear.

"I know. I realize I've only postponed the inevitable. I also know that they might have placed it here on a previous night when I was asleep. But, I will not think about that, not today. I'll think about it tomorrow."

"Now you sound like Scarlett O'Hara," Jason said.

"Scarlett who?"

"You haven't found Margaret Mitchell's book yet? *Gone With the Wind* is required reading in my mind. At the end, a whole race of people was freed."

"Now, a whole nation must be set free." I thought of the enormity and the danger of it all. "Oh Jason, I hadn't even thought about how I've pulled you into all this intrigue. I've only been thinking about myself and my grandparents. I have not meant to be so selfishly unaware of other people's safety and reputation that I would risk a physician's professional standing to help me with my family's problem?"

"This isn't a family problem anymore, Christy. It's a national disaster," Jason insisted. "And, those were my parents in those cases beneath the mountain. They were on display like dinosaurs at the museum. Christy, you have abandoned all concern for yourself. You are selflessly focusing on the needs of your grandparents, and everyone else too, because we are all affected by the Length of Days policy."

I saw the sadness in Jason eyes and felt we needed to focus on the holiday.

"Well, I am certain of one thing. I am not going to think about it today. I am too tired and burned too deeply from the atrocities at the mountain to think about anything." I gathered up my cloak, my hat and bag and squared my shoulders. "I will not think of it today. I am ready, Sir."

"Good," Jason smiled and checked his watch. "It's earlier than we had originally planned, but I got your message about the schedule change."

"Good, I hope Dahlia did too."

"I got the holo-memo but didn't get your reason for the change."

I put on my holiday red hat and Jason helped me with my green cloak. "Wait until you hear about the developments, Jason."

"It's only nine-thirty, Christy. Will your grandparents be expecting us at this hour? Will they be up this early on Christmas Day?"

"Yes, I called Grand-mère and told her that I was expecting someone to stop by their house this morning. She said Grand-père has been up for hours." I laughed to myself as I thought about my grandfather. "He's like a child on Gift-giving Day. He's too excited to sleep. I've seen him sneak into the gathering room and dig around under the tree, looking for packages with his name on them. He shakes them gently and makes sure he doesn't break anything. Then, he'll write down on a small piece of paper, his guess about what's in the gift. Later, after the presents are opened, he'll produce the paper to prove he had guessed correctly. He likes to be right." I smiled. Remembering the dear ones was always a joy.

"It will be sad when they die, even from old age. But, Jason, to purposefully cut their lives short while they're still healthy should be criminal, an act of homicide."

I reached in my cloak pocket for the key to lock my door and found the other two keys from the Capitol I had put there the day before as well. "You mean," I gasped as I stared at the keys to the Capitol, "that was just yesterday?" I whispered.

"Just a few hours ago," Jason smiled and shook his head. "It's hard to believe isn't it?"

"Oh, wait," I remembered. "I want to take the book from the library and the paper from the Capitol." I started to dart back inside.

"I have them, Honey. I knew you wanted to take them."

"Honey?"

He threw his head back and laughed softly. "If that's okay with you?"

I smiled and took his arm. "I like it. It is very okay, in fact, it's charming." I nearly skipped along beside him. Then I remembered . . . caution . . . slowly. "We'll get off on the fifth floor and pick up Dahlia."

The ride down on the elevator was relaxing. Jason stood with his back to the door and we talked. A few minutes later, with Dahlia in our company, the three of us burst onto the morning streets where snow had dusted a powdery white on everything. The day looked clean and pure. Since it was winter and the car windows were up and tight, no one would hear us, so we sang Christmas Carols as we rode through the empty streets.

Everywhere I looked, lights were glowing from holiday homes. Festive, Gifting lights brought more color into most people's lives than there had been all year long. Gift-giving Day had always been a happy day for basically unhappy people. But now, Christmas Day brought a new, holy meaning to my heart and made it a sacred celebration. It all seemed beyond my wildest imagination, outside the limits of all possibilities that a small child could bring such peace and hope to a gray and lifeless people, even though I had read about Christmas in the books I loved. While I had enjoyed the holiday in seasons past, I had never been blessed before by the song of the angels who heralded the Christ child's birth.

CHAPTER FIFTY-TWO

A Referendum, Some Petitions and Christmas Joy

10:00 a.m.

"Wow," Dahlia expressed with awe when we crossed over into Oakwood and drove up to my grandparents' house. "I never dreamed that I would be invited to a home like this. The white clap board is beautiful. Your grandparents' home is a real Victorian." Dahlia sat forward in the backseat of the car and took it all in. "Just look at that wide veranda across the front. It wraps all the way around the side of the house. I didn't know anyone lived in houses like this anymore."

We all got out of Jason's car and started to walk up the sidewalk. Dahlia held back a little as Jason and I moved toward the house. "They are both on the Council of Elders, aren't they?" Dahlia asked in a whisper.

"That's one of the hats they wear, Dahlia. But the chapeaus I like the most, are the ones that go with their grandparent costumes," I laughed.

We walked up onto the wooden porch floor and the boards had a happy, hollow sound under our feet. In my usual fashion, I put my hand to the door latch and pushed it open with my hip.

"Grand-mère," I called toward the great room as we let ourselves in. "I would like you to meet my friends."

I led Jason and Dahlia through the wide entry hall and into the large sitting room that was furnished with overstuffed chairs and decorated with wonderful paintings and pottery of bygone days.

"Grand-mère, I'd like you to meet Dahlia Zoobamba and Doctor Jason O'Reilly," I sang out an introduction.

Constance Richly rose with the bearing of a Grande Dame in a royal court. She reached out both of her hands and embraced my friend Dahlia. "Then, this gentleman must belong to you," she laughed. "Mr. Swifty has already arrived."

"Swift, Grand-mère, Thackery Swift," I corrected her.

"Yes, my dear, I know. But Swifty and I have already had an understanding, haven't we young man?" She wrapped her arm in Thackery's and patted his hand.

"What kind of understanding do you have with my grandmother?" I teased Swifty.

"She will feed me part of that goose I helped put in the oven, and I will tell her about my Grandma Rose. It seems your grandmother and mine were school friends." Swifty smiled proudly. Perhaps because his grandparents were now asleep, he seemed to like being close to mine, borrowing some of their warmth.

Then Grand-mère turned to Jason. "And, I am thrilled to see you again, Jason O'Reilly," she smiled. "Your parents were long and dear friends of Christy's parents, Elizabeth and Robert Applewait."

"Yes, Ma'am. They talked of them often," Jason took my grandmother's hand, then bowed and kissed it gently.

"Happy Gift-giving Day," Mother called out as she and my father came through the door.

"We're nearly all here," I said. "When Marge arrives, we will gather in a cluster in the great room." I expected Sean, the newspaper deliverer from the tram, to arrive in a few minutes.

Just then, my father answered the doorbell and Marge came in. "I've asked all of you to come early because Jason and I have some news."

"Jason?" Mother questioned.

"Oh, Mother, Daddy, I would like you to meet Dr. Jason

O'Reilly, Marge Cummings, Dahlia Zoobamba, and Thackery Swift, A.K.A. Swifty." Everyone laughed.

"Jason O'Reilly? I knew your parents, didn't I?" Mother asked.

"Yes, dear," Grand-mère smiled warmly at her. "Jason's parents were Stephanie and Charles."

"Stephie? Oh Jason, I miss her so much." Mother put her arms around Jason and gave him a hug as one comforts the bereaved.

"Yes, Ma'am, so do I." Jason responded.

The vision of Charles and Stephanie O'Reilly, encased in glass in Bedlam's gruesome museum, flashed through my mind. I shook my head to free my mind from the dark memories of the previous night.

As we gathered in what Grand-mère called the parlor and after everyone was seated, all their faces turned in expectation to me. I had called each one to come early, before the meal. Now, the floor was mine.

"You all know by now that Grand-père will turn seventy-five at the end of the month and Grand-mère will follow him a few days later."

Each face in the room grew solemn. No one seemed to know what to say and the silence grew heavy.

"We believe we have found a solution." Jason handed the book and paper to me.

"Any law can be overturned by a citizens' referendum," I began.

"A referendum?" Grand-père snapped to attention and leaned forward to the edge of his seat as he waited for more details.

"Yes. A citizens' referendum requires a petition bearing the signatures of a majority of the population. The petition would call for the eradication of the law concerning the Length of Days policy for termination of life," I explained. "We will also include a reversal of the laws concerning chemical additives in the water supply."

Grand-père stood up quickly and paced back and forth, crisscrossing the room. Then, he sat down on the arm of the chair beside Grand-mère. "Connie, is it possible?"

The doorbell rang and everyone jumped. We were excited and edgy. The government could claim we were practicing sedition right there in my grandparents' home on Christmas morning if the wrong person found us there with incriminating documents.

Thankfully and surprisingly, the new visitor was Judge Brunner. Jason invited him in. Judge Brunner came into the parlor and greeted Grand-père with a hearty handshake and kissed Grand-mère on the cheek. He turned to Jason and then to me. "Were you able to get it?" he asked.

"Yes," my voice cracked with the excitement of our accomplishment. I handed the paper to Judge Brunner and added, "The cover form for the petition."

"Where did you find that document?" Grand-père asked. "I am amazed. I haven't even heard of a special form or a citizens' referendum."

"You don't want to know where it came from, Oliver," Judge Brunner warned. "Just let it be."

"A petition will not be received without an official cover letter or form." I said. "It is a necessity."

"But . . . Christy," Mother whispered, "half of the signatures in the whole country . . . by the end of the month? How?"

"Well . . ." But before I could answer, I heard the door again. I was expecting Sean at any minute.

Jason jumped up and let him in.

"I hope I'm not late," Sean apologized as Jason led him into the room where all eyes had turned to him.

"You're just in time." I rushed to greet him. "And, Sean, I would like you to meet my grandparents and my parents."

"I am honored," he smiled broadly and offered his hand in friendship to all.

Sean carried a black leather valise in his left hand. My love of books drew my attention to the bag and I wondered if the dramatic case testified to the importance of the contents. A character in one of my old suspense novels would have carried such a serious looking grip.

"Sean, I'll have to ask you to respond to my mother's question, because, I don't know the answer. She wondered how we would be able to get the signatures of half the population before the end of the month."

Sean opened the valise and pulled out a tall stack of papers. "The heading on each page identifies it as a petition, or citizens' referendum as Christiana calls it, to overturn the New Bill of Rights, in particular, the policies regarding the Length of Days law and the additives in the water supply." Sean took a deep breath and continued. "We have been secretly gathering signatures for months. We're going after the termination of the entire New Bill. Citizens signed the petition below the heading and included their address and contact information as required. This is a representative sample. We have boxes and boxes of signed petitions, all carefully preserved and filed."

"Weren't people afraid to sign their name, knowing it would be presented to authorities who might misunderstand the petition's meaning?" Grand-mère's words mingled concern for their safety with deep appreciation. "These heroic neighbors who put their name to such a document could be accused of treason." There had been no protests against the government in many years, since words spoken against the current policies or laws were forbidden.

"No, Ma'am, there was no fear at all," Sean said. "They felt privileged to be counted, excited about being able to actually participate in something as large and noble as this." Sean spread the pages on the table. "The petitions we have, account for seventy-five percent of the adult population of Capitol City."

"Oh Sean," I gasped as tears filled my eyes and tightened my throat. "We have the required number of signatures already?"

"But, that's not the whole country." Mother shook her head and her eyes glistened with tears, but they were not tears of joy.

"My wife, Silvia, and I knew that we probably wouldn't have a full sample of the population," Judge Brunner spoke up. "We believed if enough names could be produced to represent a trend, even if it isn't a completed work, we hoped it would be recognized as the will of the people. With the proper signatures, and the required cover paperwork . . . we think we can still make this happen. I have no doubt there will be enough signatures when this effort is completed." Judge Brunner cleared his throat and added, "As a Zone Judge, I can issue a stay order on all those who are to be put to sleep due to the Length of Days policy, until the entire country can be canvassed." Carl's eyes fell to the ground and he spoke another truth. "You have to know that I have a conflict of interest in this. My son, my only son, Michael . . . is slowly improving from paralysis. But, he would have been terminated if we hadn't hidden him. He hasn't been out of our home for nearly a year. Not even the neighbors know that he's there."

"Carl," Grand-mère offered in her own soft sweet way, "Michael is a wonderful young man. He deserves to live . . . just as all people everywhere have a right to fight for their own lives, no matter how difficult the strife or how long the battle. It is their own personal battle to fight . . . or surrender to . . . but it is their decision alone."

Daddy had been silent up until then. He was a man who used words sparingly but when he spoke, his message was profound. "We will stand behind you, all of you, at every turn this cause may take. Together, we will regain liberty for the weak, as well as for the strong, for the sick and broken, as well as for the robust and hearty. This cause must succeed."

Before my father could finish expressing his thoughts, we heard a loud crash coming from the front door. Who would dare barge into a private home of Legacy Citizens—unless? Had he found us?

CHAPTER FIFTY-THREE
Unlawful Entry

10:45 a.m.

I gasped as the front door of my grandparent's warm home burst open and the coldness of the Christmas morning swept across the floor like a flood of ice water. Sean shoved the petitions back into the valise in a subtle, protective action. Then he caught my eye, silently stepped toward the door, and slipped out unnoticed, into the winter morning.

I quickly placed the cover letter back in my bag. I had seen what people were capable of. I knew the danger we were in. My blood froze with the blast of arctic air.

Inspector Ward Stoner stormed into the room, his eyes fixed forward. He didn't even glance at Sean as he quietly slipped out. Stoner shattered the sanctity of my grandparents' home, with one apparent aim—he was looking for someone. "Christiana Applewait, Jason O'Reilly, you will have to come with me, both of you."

"Why?" Jason jumped to his feet and stepped between me and the inspector.

"You were seen in the Capitol after hours." The Inspector's voice was hard, brittle.

"Seen?" I questioned. I knew there had been no one around.

"The heel of your right foot was evident on a surveillance camera, Missy," he hissed, evidently quite proud of his detecting work. "I'm sure a careful comparison of the image we have, with your foot, will reveal a match. You were there, Miss Applewait. Any unauthorized presence after hours in a government building is against the law."

"Unauthorized?" Judge Brunner rose to his full six foot-four inches. "Inspector, these two dedicated people were there under my authority. I am Judge Brunner. I gave them my keys."

I pulled his keys from my pocket and handed them back to the judge. "I'm returning them to you now, Sir," I announced.

Stoner glared at me. Evidently, he was not used to being trumped in the little spy game he played with a tremendous amount of gusto.

"There is also another situation," Stoner proceeded in his game, as if the previous hand had not been lost. "There appears to be a secret group within the Blue Guard of which I have not been kept informed. Somehow, and I don't know how yet, but I will, you two have some knowledge of these men."

"I have the information you seek, Inspector," Judge Brunner interrupted again as he squared his shoulders and straightened his back to rebuff the Inspector one more time. "I ordered a small, select contingent of Blue Guard to protect my home."

"It was at my suggestion and authority," my grandfather affirmed.

"Why?" Stoner snapped.

"I beg your pardon," the Judge replied with authoritative indignation. "I owe you no explanation, Inspector. It is well within my authority to do so."

"Perhaps you had the authority, but politically it was not very wise . . . Sir," he spit out the words like they had left a nasty taste in his mouth.

"I am not political," Judge Brunner edged toward the inspector. "I am a judge by birth and Legacy by the grace of God," he shouted.

"God?" Stoner yelled back, but there was a change to his expression. "If you are going to hold up a deity as your authority, Sir, can you prove to me that there are gods?" His voice was shrill, not commanding, not controlled. He had lost the moral authority of his position.

Something was stirring within the Inspector. I could see it trying to free itself from his soul. However, the tortured look on his face seemed to be evidence of an evil to come, that blocked the path to freedom.

"I am not defending the gods, Sir," the judge declared with power and strength. "I am bearing witness to the one true God."

"Then call him to your witness stand Judge. Let him defend himself." Stoner was icy in his gaze, but his shoulders lost their square, as one who has already lost confidence in his own argument.

"God does not defend himself, Officer," the Judge replied more softly than before. "We, all of us, bear witness to his existence in our lives and the work he performs in our own hearts. He heals and pardons each one of us. That is our testimony."

Ward Stoner's expression grew weak, and his face was suddenly ashen.

Grand-mère approached the head of the Blue Guard, reached out her steady hand and touched his shoulder. "Inspector Stoner, what is wrong? Has something happened? You were all worked up before, and now you look broken, my son."

Stoner stepped back, out of her reach, as though Grand-mère's touch condemned him, rather than soothed his spirit. "Broken? No never," he insisted with uncertain command. "I am the sole authority in the Blue Guard." His face was twisted and drawn with emotion that seemed to come from deep within his gut, raw and razor-edge sharp.

Grand-mère's love reached out again and would not let him go. She put her hand on his shoulder and drew herself even closer. "But your control stops with your office, doesn't it? Tell me what's cutting your heart so deeply."

"My only son Christopher, Ma'am," he whispered. The Inspector's eyes darted back and forth wildly as if he were looking for a place to hide from the reality of his pain. "My little boy, I . . . didn't know he was there in the dark last night. The car bumped him, and he fell." Ward Stoner couldn't hold back the secret any longer, not in the cradle of love Constance Richly was offering him. Then his voice melted and could barely be heard. "He couldn't feel his legs, except for some tingling. My mother and I were up all night with him."

"You should have taken him to the hospital or doctor's office," Jason said. The healer's heart within Jason dismissed the inspector's accusations when he first roared into the house and responded only to the need of the man's son.

Stoner's eyes were pleading. He looked at Jason with agony on his face. "I couldn't. He might have been labeled *defective*." Ward's shoulders were racked with pain as they heaved under his stifled sobs. "The . . . never-ending-sleep."

I knew he was begging for mercy and understanding. "How is he this morning?" I asked.

Stoner rubbed his eyes. His display of grief appeared to embarrass him. "He's a little better, thank you. He's stiff but feeling is beginning to return."

"But, he could have gotten a strike placed in his life file if you had taken him to a health professional," Jason said.

"I called a physician. A friend gave me his number—but not his name. He said he wouldn't have to report a telephone call." Stoner looked around the room at all of us, studying each face. "Why do you care?"

"I am that physician, Officer," Jason admitted. "The one you called."

Ward Stoner's face was gray and drawn as if he had been dragged heart first into Hell. He had nearly arrested the man who had shown his son compassion and had helped him during the second horrible crisis of his life.

"Someday soon, Mr. Stoner, I will tell you about the Special unit of the Blue Guard that is attached to me and my family," the Judge offered. "As far as the doctor and Lady Applewait are concerned, they have done nothing wrong. They have simply retrieved a paper that I needed."

"Don't you worry now, Inspector," Grand-mère soothed as she

directed him to the door. "You go home and take care of your son and enjoy your Gift-giving Day. We will all be around tomorrow."

"Thank you Ma'am," Stoner murmured low.

As she guided the inspector toward the door, Grand-mère said to him, "Maybe someday there will be a rescinding of the law about termination through the never-ending-sleep. Perhaps someday, life will be valued again and joy will return to our people." My grandmother boldly stated what was becoming true, even if the inspector wasn't aware of it.

Ward Stoner stopped and took both of Constance Richly's hands in his. "Ma'am, do you think so? Do you know something? Are you all . . . ?"

"We are enjoying Gift-giving Day, Mr. Stoner. Please pass on our well wishes to your son. Perhaps God will bless him with complete healing if you ask him," my grandmother said.

Then Stoner turned, as a small labored smile crossed his lips. "Something strange has been happening to me lately, and I—." He stopped and shook his head. "I just don't understand any of it. I cannot change. I cannot be soft. I cannot bend."

"You can't, or you won't Officer?" Constance Richly asked with a piercing tone of voice.

"I would . . . dissolve. I would cease to be," Stoner stammered.

"The you who is not *you*, would cease to be, so the *you* who God intended you to be, could be born again within you." Grand-mère smiled lovingly. "Don't be afraid, my son. God wants only all of you and no more."

Ward Stoner studied the little grandmother as his personal communication device signaled an incoming message. Quickly, he straightened his back with a snap. "What?" he demanded.

His face contorted as he tried to find the side of life he belonged on, the world of power or the world of love. He turned his back to the happy holiday group and hissed into the communicator. "Bedlam is missing? Did someone call in a report or what? How do you know?"

He paused to listen, his jaws flexed with anger. "What do you mean, 'People are looking for him?' Who? What people?" His voice was harsh and full of rage. "I am *the people* who would have been called and this is the first I have heard of it. First it was that Drummond fellow, then Mari, the end-traveler went missing, now Bedlam himself."

Again he paused. His fisted flexed and clinched as he listened. "He has left the zone?" His voice grew hard and shrill.

"Inspector, please . . ." Grand-père cautioned.

Stoner's entire body seemed to be fighting between the spirit that pulled at his heart and the power that dominated his mind. Then, a flash within his eyes changed his surrender to power-hungry anger again. He stepped toward me with a cold, steely gaze once more. "Don't forget to read the handwriting on the wall, Missy." Then he smiled a sinister grin. "Have a very Merry Christmas and may God's richest blessings or his most impoverished curses, be on all of you."

We all stood there in silence. The display of good and evil from the soul of that one man stunned us. I wondered how safe we all were now. Evil stalked the streets and buried life beneath a mountain of blood. There was Silas Drummond's warning and our witness to the evil at Howard Mountain. The monster had escaped to a different zone, so evil was loose in the whole world. Yet, amid all that darkness, the Christ child beckoned us once more to the manger of life, where love was born again in the hearts of those who would believe.

CHAPTER FIFTY-FOUR
The March to Freedom

4:00 p.m.

The Christmas goose had been picked to the bone and the leftovers put away. Some played something that afternoon called *Monopoly*, an odd game of buying personal property and ransoming others' ability to make passage around the game board. If a player landed on another's space, they were taxed with rent payments. The game's rules were old fashioned to all of us since taxes were no longer levied on the citizens. And, for the most part, people didn't own their own homes or property. They rented space in high rise apartment buildings like the one I lived in. Most individually owned homes were in and around the Oakwood area of town, a little oasis where an expression of individuality was enjoyed.

"Oh, no!" Mother shouted as she and my father tried to beat Grand-mère and Grand-père at the *Monopoly* game they loved. Since that type of game had been replaced with individual, solitary games in past years, we all felt lucky that my great-grandparents had saved many of the favorite old ones of their day and stored them in the attic.

"I want to buy this property," Marge sang out when she landed on a square she coveted.

Thackery and Dahlia were enjoying the lavish grounds that were still beautiful even though it was early winter. In December the icicle show on the bushes and trees sparkled like cut glass and filled their eyes with beauty.

Jason and I spent our time talking. We interspersed our conversation with comfortable periods of silence in front of the fireplace.

"It's cozy here," Jason whispered, as if we were in an old sanctuary with stained glass windows smiling down on us.

"I have always loved it here. But Jason, even as we relax, I can't help thinking . . . in a few days . . . well, my grandparents' birthdays." I shook my head. "Their termination just isn't going to happen like the Length of Days law says it must. I am determined that we can win this."

"You are an amazing woman, Christiana Applewait," Jason smiled. "Absolutely amazing."

I thought about my few days with Jason, and imagined spending many more with him, talking, walking and traveling. "Jason, have you read any of the books that have described travel around the country and even abroad? People used to get in their cars and just drive, for hours, for days."

"Yes, I've read many of them. People would fly in huge air liners across the oceans and take trains to distant towns," Jason answered.

"Wouldn't it be wonderful to travel out of the country and touch the lives of people in other places? I've read about the South Sea Islands, countries on the continent, France, Italy, and the British Isles. Most of us have traveled no more than a few miles from our homes. Jason, I found large picture books in the library with photographs that took my breath away."

"I've seen some too, Christy and . . . I've traveled a little." Jason sounded hesitant. "Wouldn't it be nice to go to New York, Boston or maybe Philadelphia? The books say that these are the places our country used to hold in reverence."

"Jason!" I squealed with muffled glee. "It would be marvelous!"

Mother looked over in our direction and smiled. She looked content, even beautiful that late afternoon. She seemed to be enjoying my growing relationship with the son of her old friend.

Jason and I shared descriptions and recreated the word pictures from the books we had read. The firelight sent golden shadows that danced across the room and animated the scenes in my head. The wintery darkness had come on early, gathering familiar forms into her snowy shadows and nestled them there.

"Oliver, dear, please turn on the lights. It's getting dark in here," Grand-mère called out.

"I can see fine Connie."

"Well, yes dear, but I can't seem to see a thing."

I laughed quietly. Those two dear old ones. They fit together like two pieces connected in Heaven, then separated at birth, only to find each other again. I wondered if Jason would be my soul companion, and it frightened me a little. All my life, I had only thought about myself.

"Yes, dear, do you have enough light now?" Jason teased.

I looked at the firelight reflected in his eyes. They were as warm as the flames, and I knew I was home. "Yes, I have enough of everything."

Suddenly, there was a pounding at the door and banging until Grand-père flung it open. "Sean?" He gasped as our new friend stood there in the dim, late day light. Sean wore no coat or hat and appeared to be short of breath. "What's wrong?" Grand-père asked.

Sean burst into the house. His eyes searched each face. "Christiana, there you are," he called out, his voice sharp with excitement.

"Sean? What is it?" Fear gripped me again as the memory of that morning's brush with the Blue Guard flashed through my mind.

"Christiana . . . Jason, it's wonderful! You won't believe it. They're marching, right now. They're moving out across this city and gathering more and more people as they go!" He dashed from one side of the room to the other.

"Who, Sean?" I couldn't grasp what he was talking about.

"Everyone, Christiana, everyone. They are marching to the Great

Leader's home, President Alexander, to deliver our petitions. They're doing it now, as we speak."

"No, not yet!" I cried.

Sean staggered back. His high mountain of joy seemed to crumble with confusion and surprise. "Why not? Christiana, what is wrong?"

"All petitions require a cover letter, or special form, to accompany them, Sean. You left this morning when the inspector came in. I was showing everyone that Jason and I had gotten the form. Here it is. We have it!" I jumped up with excitement and waved the precious page in front of him.

"Where did you —" Sean darted about the room and bounced off nearby furniture.

"Don't ask," I cautioned as I followed him. I tried to get into his line of view so he could focus on what we were telling him. "Before our Christmas dinner, I filled it out with everyone's help. We made sure there were no mistakes."

"We prayed earnestly for all the courage we could muster, and to know God's will as we put the words on the paper," Grand-père whispered.

Sean stopped pacing long enough to process what was said. "You have the form? You are very sure you have the right paper?"

"Don't panic, Sean," Dahlia cautioned. She and Swifty had come back into the house in time to hear the discussion and witness the wild emotions.

"Yes, we are positive," Jason assured him.

"Then get your coats and that paper, and follow me to President Alexander's house." Sean shouted over his shoulder as he started out the door. Then he turned. "Well, are you coming?"

Sean had run all the way from the transit stop. Time was vitally important. We had to get to Alexander's house before the crowd handed over the petitions. My parents and Marge rode with Grand-père and Grand-mère. Dahlia, Swifty and Sean were with us in Jason's car. Jason called Judge Brunner and his wife Sylvia on his communications device and let them know about the people's walk to President Alexander's home.

There were few other cars on the streets at that time of the evening on Gift-giving Day, so we covered the first several miles rapidly in spite of the gathering fog. As we came within the last mile along the corridor leading to President Alexander's home, people were everywhere, in the streets, on the lawns and sidewalks. There was no place, where the citizens of our community had not marched to take back their freedom. Even members of the Blue Guard had abandoned their cars and were walking with the people.

"We might have to go the rest of the way on foot," Jason said as he tried to look past everyone to see what waited down the street.

"We can't." Sean warned. "The people have the petitions. If it's like you said and they give the petitions to the Great Leader without the cover form, Alexander may dispose of them immediately, on the spot."

"We have to get through," I cried. The tension rose within me like a drowning wave. I was worried about my grandparents and the pressure they would be feeling. Finally, I did something I had never done before. I prayed to a God I had only recently heard of, to protect my dear ones, and to make a path through the people so that life could win over death.

"I know." Sean immediately snapped to attention, opened the car window, and pushed back the people who pressed against it. He swung his body, headfirst, out through the window and then used the opening as a stepping stone to lift himself up onto the car's roof where he sat down. "Clear the way," he shouted at the people ahead of us. "We have a piece of the solution. Move, move . . ." he called every few feet as both of our cars inched toward the home of Nathan Alexander, the President and Great Leader.

When we got to the president's home, Sean stood on top of the car and held up both of his hands. "Everyone, listen . . ."

The crowd stilled. A hush fell over the evening. Lights glistened off the snow and made the spot a hallowed ground where freedom had taken a stand once more.

"Nathan Alexander," Sean called to the house, "President Alexander, please come out."

"Let me go up and invite him out," I suggested but didn't wait for an answer. "I'll make sure he knows we mean him no personal harm." I tried to squeeze out through the car door, but people everywhere pressed against it. I opened and closed the door inch by inch until I could wedge myself through and started up the walk to the house.

"Christiana," Jason called after me. "I'll go with you."

As I neared the steps, Grand-père had worked his way out of his car. "Christiana, wait, I have an important message for you." He came near and whispered gently yet firmly in my ear with all the confidence I knew my grandfather had.

"Sweetheart, there are some verses from the Bible you must hear. From the book of Luke, chapter twenty-one, verses fifteen through nineteen:

> For I will give you words and wisdom that none of your adversaries will be able to resist or contradict. . . . By standing firm you will gain life."

I hugged the dear man I loved so much, then, I turned. Jason, Sean, and I stepped up onto President Alexander's porch.

CHAPTER FIFTY-FIVE
Accusations Turn to Revelations

6:30 p.m.

My parents and grandparents had maneuvered out of their car, stepped up on the porch, and stood to be counted on that historic night. Even Marge joined us, front and center, no longer afraid who might see her. To the contrary, she was eager to be seen, to be numbered with us as a freedom marcher.

"Are you sure you want to do this, Missy?" Chief Inspector Stoner had pushed his way forward and touched my arm as he whispered in my ear. But, his tone was not one of concern or comfort. It felt threatening. I recoiled at his touch.

The President's porch was wired from one side to the other so the president could broadcast from there, both over the communication waves and to throngs of people who might gather there for a special event. I was careful to guard my words that I did not want everyone to hear.

"Inspector, I'm not afraid of you." I looked at him with increasing confidence, my eyes fixed on his. My feet planted firmly on the solid surface of the presidential residence.

"What seems to be the problem?" Jason put his hand on my shoulder. I could feel his strength and knew I was not alone.

"You two have stirred up a hornet's nest of mistrust and rebellion. Look at all these people. We call it sedition," Stoner hissed.

"The people have a right to make their voices heard," Judge Brunner stated with the authority of his robes as he too stepped onto the porch. "These people are doing no harm. They aren't threatening anyone. They are here for one purpose, to deliver something to the President."

"And what might that be? Is it so important that it has to be done tonight?" Stoner asked.

I wanted to shout, "Yes, tonight!" But, I said nothing. I did not want to give away the cause of our sacred mission before it had been completed.

"There will be plenty of time to talk about their purpose for being here another time, Inspector. Lady Applewait and Dr. O'Reilly are here merely to present their material to the president," the judge said.

Stoner stared at the judge, determined to not back down. "I am talking to Miss Applewait, Sir. Not you."

"Lady Applewait will talk to you at the first of the week," Judge Brunner stated with firm resolve. "I'll accompany her to your office myself."

The judge's strength gave me courage, and I was determined to press forward. "Excuse me, Inspector." I tried to move beyond the man, but he continued to bar my way. "I have come to speak to the president tonight," I insisted, my eyes fixed on Stoner's.

"I told you to pay attention to the writing on the wall. It may be something you don't want these folks to know about."

Stoner spoke low, as if he were attempting to reveal a secret.

"I don't know what you're talking about, Inspector." I couldn't get past him and had no idea what he was saying.

"There is something in your past that your entire little Legacy club has been keeping from everyone and possibly even from you." Stoner seemed to be getting a great deal of satisfaction from dragging out his accusations against me, whatever they were.

"There is a record of you being involved in a work of sorcery," he sneered. "Do you want these people to hear about it? He studied my face and then added, "Or, nothing needs to be said, if you and your friends and family just go on home."

"Sorcery?" My father advanced and wedged himself between Stoner and me. There was a power in Daddy's stance I had rarely seen.

"Keep it up, Mr. Applewait. If all of you don't go home now, I will tell everyone about your little girl and the handwriting on the wall. Then you can watch how fast these fine people turn into a mob."

"The handwriting on the wall?" Mother moved onto the porch and into the inner circle. "I think I may know what he's talking about. Christiana, we never told you about it and this man should never have found out."

"Told me what?" I couldn't fathom what I could have done that the Inspector would be able to use against me.

Daddy stepped forward to talk to the huge group that had grown silent as they watched and strained to listen to the confrontation. "Ladies and gentlemen," he held up his hands to address the people, "my wife and I have something wonderful to share, not something to hide." A hush fell over the people as they stood in the silent night.

Mother wrapped her arms around me as I turned to face the people.

My father paused for a moment then spoke with power and confidence. "Our daughter, Christiana, is a marvelous young woman. She has been blessed with a holy presence since an early age. The inspector would like to call it sorcery, something out of black magic." My father looked at me with the love I had always received from him. "No, what Christiana has, is a blessing from God."

"What is he talking about Mother?" Then, I looked at Jason to see if he had been shaken by Daddy's words. Jason was smiling lovingly, knowingly.

"Let's just listen to him, Honey," Jason smiled and took my hand.

My father looked at Jason and me and patted my cheek. "When Christiana was seven years old, the Council of Elders was meeting in the Grand Hall to listen to requests from many people. The hall was full."

"You'd better think this through." Stoner growled angrily at me as he saw my parents take his ammunition against me and turn it back on him. He tried to move closer to me. "You don't even know what they're going to say. You could be a laughing stock or a freaky curiosity."

I just looked at Stoner for a minute then turned my eyes back to my father. I would not believe that my own father would do anything to harm me.

My father looked at me as he continued speaking to the people. "Your mother and I brought you into the Grand Hall so you could have your first taste of the Legacy you will inherit, Christiana. We sat in the back so we wouldn't disturb anyone. Your mother gave you some coloring sticks to keep you entertained."

Suddenly, I remembered the sticks. I hadn't seen them since I was young.

Mother wiped her eyes. "We thought we were watching you, Sweetheart, but we got caught up in the proceedings."

"I saw it first," Grand-père smiled at me as he stepped forward. "You were standing up on your chair so you could see the proceedings better."

The inspector turned to all the people gathered there and shouted. "It was sorcery I tell you. What are you—sheep? Do you follow wherever these people lead and believe everything they tell you?"

I heard murmuring as a restlessness spread throughout the people. Feelings of fear began to rise within me. Would the crowd turn on me and stop what we were trying to do?

Then Grand-père's voice rose above the throng, clear and strong. "People, Christiana is no sorceress. She is a messenger from God!" Grand-père raised his hands to the people as they gasped in amazement.

"God?" someone asked. Most just listened intently, their voices hushed.

I was stunned, stricken by fear and wonder. A messenger of God? How could that be? I had never heard of God as a child.

"God?" Stoner yelled. His eyes flashed with rage at the name of the Holy One. "There is no God!" He shouted into the darkened sky. "Only the blackness of the night." Then he whirled back to face Grand-père. "Sir Richly, you expect us to accept your statement that this woman is a messenger from God?" He turned to the people and strutted back and forth on the President's porch, as if on his own small stage. "I demand that you produce your god!"

Grand-mère smiled her knowing, sweet smile and opened the locket she wore around her neck so Grand-père could see the contents. She embraced him and waved a calming, royal hand to the people. Then, she kissed my cheek.

"If you will wait a moment, we will produce our God." Then she asked, "Does anyone have a 281 Palm Device with you?"

"I do, Connie," Jason spoke up. "It's in my car. I'll get it."

"Will you all please let Dr. O'Reilly through?" Daddy raised his arms to the people.

Jason squeezed his way through the people and returned with the Device. "Let me open it for you, Oliver," Jason said, as he handed the Palm Device to my grandfather.

Grand-père raised his hands to the people again and they grew silent. "Christiana was very small the day we took her to the grand reception room, so she had to get up on her chair and stretch as high as she could. She took her color sticks and began to draw on the back wall, that's why I saw it first. I was facing her masterpiece and it was magnificent! Little Christiana worked fast, like someone else controlled her creation. What burst forth from her hand was . . . the very face of God."

He turned to the inspector and added. "Just like the writing on the wall in the Biblical book of Daniel when a detached hand appeared and wrote on the plaster during a wild banquet. Daniel interpreted the words for the king. He told King Belshazzar that his reign was over. I believe Christiana's drawing and writing, tells us that God's reign is never over, regardless of what government may rule. But you, Inspector, have asked to see the face of God."

Grand-père turned and took Grand-mère's locket. "My wife, Lady Richly, has kept a miniature likeness of the wall art Christiana drew that day, here in her locked. I will project the image against the fog for all of you to see."

Jason helped Grand-père place Grand-mère's locket in relationship to the Palm Devise so it could register on the small device screen and project a hologram onto the wide expanse of Heaven above our heads.

I had seen Grand-mère's locket many times and had asked her what was inside. She always said, "Something holy, my dear. I'll show you one day."

There were gasps and murmurs of awe from the people as the hologram shimmered in the cold night air, then formed clearly against the fog. As it burst forth, the memory of that day took shape in my mind.

"There," Grand-père's voice rang out with might and power, "there is the picture of God you wanted to see, Inspector. Christiana drew it when she was only seven years old. She is seeing it tonight for the first time since the day she drew it, the same as all of you."

Tears flowed like healing waters as I was bathed again in the same spirit of holiness that had touched me so many years ago. Against the canvas of Heaven, like a mighty, holy colossus striding across the firmament, was a completely formed drawing of a being. With the breath of life flowing from his mouth and nostrils, the being looked as if his spoken word had just caused the whole world to leap into creation. His powerful muscles declared his strength and his eyes revealed his love. His hair blew across the night sky like a field of tall wheat in late July. There it mingled with the tails of winter clouds as they stretched across the canopy of our world. The light from his eyes was as glorious as the dawn of a new day. His gaze was as strong as the towering oaks and as sweet as a field of wild flowers after a spring rain. It looked like all of creation laughed and loved within his gaze. There was so much glory emanating from his countenance, it was nearly impossible to look upon him. Across the bottom, under the drawing, were the words and letters, "Ego sum Dominus sum ego"

"What does it say?" a voice called from the crowd.

Stoner kept his back to the sky and would not turn to the face of God illuminated there. "Can't you see what they are doing? It's a trick," he yelled. "There is nothing there you need to see," Inspector Stoner ordered.

"You asked to see our God," Jason reminded him. "Look into an innocent child's magnificent depiction of his face, Inspector Stoner. Go ahead . . . or don't you have the courage to look?"

Stoner turned slowly to face what he did not believe in, and yet, there he was. He glanced at the sky and his expression fell like shattered glass. "What does it say?" he whispered.

"The words, 'ego sum dominus sum ego' is Latin. It says, 'I am Lord am I.' And the hand of a seven-year-old child had drawn and written it, my granddaughter, Christiana Applewait. How she knew what God looked like or what words to write, we had no idea. I don't know the mind of God but—he obviously knew her—before she knew him."

I was astonished to hear Grand-père's explanation. I finally remembered the drawing and the words, even though no one had spoken of them since.

"Why didn't you tell me?" I asked.

"The inspired drawing was obviously a miracle, Christiana," Mother reassured me. "We believed the people might not understand your special gifts. We had to protect you from stares, even adoration."

"Christiana, you were a child prodigy." Jason was as awed as I was. His eyes stayed fixed on the portrait of God.

"Maybe that's what Rebecca meant when she said I had a talent that I was holding back." It made sense to me now.

"I am sorry," Daddy apologized. "We were all so amazed. We probably made a fuss over the art and you. Then, we became frightened that people would give you too much attention and adulation that would harm your growing spirit. Maybe you didn't understand our intentions and thought you had done something bad."

Daddy kissed my cheek. "We only wanted to protect you."

"I know, Daddy. I have always trusted you and Mother . . . and all of you," I added as I turned to my grandparents. "I have always felt safe and protected."

My struggles to paint what I saw and not what I felt came to my mind. I will admit I was aware that I was holding back on my paintings, afraid to express myself through it. I could see wonderful images that couldn't be expressed in words on the blank canvas, waiting for me to bring them forth. Society does not permit creativity. My visions were far beyond Society's approval. I smiled as I thought of some compositions I had wanted to paint but didn't have the nerve to do it.

Stoner turned his eyes from the masterpiece in the sky and stared at the dirt near his feet. He shook his head and added, "I will not believe such nonsense."

As the Inspector turned to leave, Grand-mère touched his arm and he jerked away as if he had been burned. She reached out again, "But, you want to believe, Inspector."

Stoner did not reply nor turn back to the light. Nor did he return the life and love that were being offered to him. With his shoulders slumped, he stomped away into the night.

CHAPTER FIFTY-SIX
A Holy Night

Grand-père closed the locket and the vision disappeared. "The people understand that you are not a sorceress as Inspector Stoner accused. As a child, Christiana, you had drawn an impression of a God no one knew anymore." Then Grand-père turned to the people and offered to hold future gatherings to explain and teach more from the scriptures.

Now, we had to confront President Alexander. After calling his name again, the massive front door of the Central Zone president's home opened.

President Nathan Alexander came out into the confines of the clear, attack-proof Ceremonial Reviewing Chamber, a security bubble to the left of the main entrance. Members of the Capitol Secret Guard surrounded him. Alexander stood with closed, folded arms, obviously in protest to what he heard we were doing.

"I was expecting you," he announced through a speaker. "I received a call," Alexander said.

"Sir," I began, "I am Lady Christiana Applewait."

"I know who you are." His voice was edgy as he looked beyond the porch at thousands of people who had straightened their backs and had come here to say by their presence, *No, not anymore.*

The moment was breathtaking as the citizens gathered in closer to be counted before the world. There were so many people with us that cold, yet holy night, the people in the back could not possibly have heard what was being said, but that didn't seem to matter. What was important was that they were there. Perhaps they believed, we will stand together or we will fall together, but no one had to stand alone that night, on that very first Christmas Day evening in one-hundred years.

"We have a petition," Sean began, "bearing the signatures of 75 percent of the citizens of this city."

"I don't have to accept them, young man. Things must be done in the proper way."

"We know that Sir," Sean agreed.

"No, I don't think you do. You can have signatures from every person in the entire country, including all quadrants, but if it isn't filed properly, I can throw them in the rubbish pile."

"But, we do have all we need," Sean explained. "You have these boxes of petitions."

"And we have the proper cover letter," I added as the glint in President Alexander's eyes faded with my statement. "This citizens' referendum is calling for an end to the policies regarding Length of Days terminations into the never-ending-sleep, the control of the population through chemical drugging, and the reversal of the New Bill of Rights."

"This will still be too late . . . Ma'am." Alexander shot a glance at my grandparents. "I understand, Your Excellency, that you and your wife will be seventy-five years old in a matter of days. A few days aren't enough. Your referendum must include signatures from a majority of citizens of the entire country, not just this city or even this zone."

"That's right," Judge Brunner announced with authority as he stepped forward. "I am Judge Carl Brunner and this display of citizen action has been heard. The referendum they have completed for our city will be expanded and put to a vote of the entire population at the next election. Between now and then, freedom loving people will ride out across this land and gather support from every village and hamlet, from every state and quadrant in the entire country. This citizens' referendum will pass. I guarantee you."

Alexander's eyes narrowed and his face grew red with stifled anger. "But it will still be too late," he spit out with a full measure of satisfaction. "The elections you are talking about will take place months after Oliver and Constance Richly are dead and buried. Your little scheme to oust me from office and overturn the entire government will be months past your deadline."

"No, Sir, it will not be too late," the judge rebutted. "We have accepted the inevitable, as if we had no other choice, for far too long. I am issuing a stay of execution, halting the judicial writ regarding Length of Days legislation. I'll file the papers on Monday, suspending the carrying out of all termination procedures and halting the use of chemicals in our drinking water, for the next two years. This will give Christiana and Jason, Sean and the rest of them, all the time they need to complete the task of gathering every signature necessary to make it law."

"It only took one brave man to step out of the silence and testify to the horrors of our society. I see him now." I spotted Silas Drummond as he made his way through the crowd.

Silas moved to the edge of the steps so as not to be seen by the entire group and whispered, "I got your message on my communication device, My Lady. They took my car, so I ran all the way to the transit line. Thank you. Thank all of you for what you are doing."

"You broke the silence, Silas. We all owe you the thanks," I said.

"You won't have to go back to the mountain, Silas," Judge Brunner assured him. "The stay will stop all work there for two years. Come and join us on the porch where your presence can also bear witness."

Silas placed his foot firmly on the first step as tears streamed down his face. Timid by nature and bold by necessity, Silas waved to the people with his bandaged hand, burned by the fire of the despicable furnaces.

Then the judge turned back to President Alexander. "It doesn't matter if you choose to be behind our cause or not. We no longer need you or your government." Judge Brunner took a step forward but still maintained a respectful distance. No one would be able to say that he had intimidated the president of the zone.

"Besides the referendum, at the next election, we will also be voting on a new president," Judge Brunner continued. "We will reconstruct the representative convention system and call for delegates. I plan to help these young people develop a political platform that will drastically change this country, not into something different, but back to the inspired and inspiring nation it was originally designed to be."

"Oh Judge Brunner that is fantastic," I shouted over the cheers of the crowd.

"Beginning tomorrow," Sean announced, "you will find a free news sheet on every transit car so that all may know of our plans." Then he pointed to the people clustered at the president's residence. "You, here in the front, spread the word to those in the back. They will be informed by the free newspapers available to all."

Those near the front of the group cheered, then turned and passed the word back through the crowd. Each group respectfully stood in silence so the word could go forth to the entire gathering of citizens.

Then, from somewhere among the people gathered on that wonderful night, someone called out, "Christiana Applewait for president! Christy . . . Christy . . . Christy . . ." they began to chant.

I was stunned! And flattered! And for a moment, the thought of power was overwhelming. "Thank you, thank you," I called to the people. "You have honored me beyond any aspiration I could have ever dreamed. But, I'm afraid I have read the founding fathers' papers and, my friends, I'm just not old enough."

The people laughed and called out words of teasing and support. "Lower the age!" some yelled. "Kids can make more sense than adults!" another laughed.

I felt loved and accepted. I raised my hands to silence the people and called out above the crowd. "I nominate Oliver Richly to run for office as our new president."

The throng erupted with an uproar of cheers and hugs and

laughter. Again, the repeated message of what had just been said spread like a child's party game, from one person and one group to another, beyond the sound of my voice. Suddenly, chants of, "Richly . . . Richly . . . Richly," rang out above the throng.

Grand-père stepped forward and raised his voice to the people assembled there. He was calm and full of strength. "We are at the dawn of a new day, when free men and women will rise up to say, 'I am loved. I am of value. I am blessed by the Lord our God with the right to life, liberty, and the pursuit of happiness.' Join us, one and all!"

Cheers resounded again with laughter and praise. Even the majority, who had never heard of detoxification, hugged each other and danced with joy for the first time in their lives. With their hands raised in praise, they frolicked like children who were not inhibited from expressing their joy. That night, the human spirit had risen above the evil efforts of others to hold it down.

Jason swept me up in front of everyone, swung me around in a continuation of our dance and kissed me with power and love. I could feel joy and the thrill of the night of new beginnings. The gift of a new life had been offered to everyone on that Christmas Day Eve.

When the people saw our display of tenderness in public, they cheered again and clapped wildly. Such simple pleasures had not been seen or felt in many years. Regardless of the laws that had robbed them of joy, there seemed to be a deeper knowing that touched their hearts. They were starved for love, and they didn't even know they were hungry.

A hush fell over the group as someone in the back of the crowd began the words I had just learned, but many of the people seemed to know already. "Silent night . . ." they began, "holy night . . ." and it was holy. Like the hum of an angel choir, even the trees swayed to the melody as we sang. It all seemed right and good.

It would be hard, but I knew, with Judge Brunner's stay, we had the time to get all the signatures necessary. As time went on and the people overcame their dependence on the drugs they hadn't even known they had been taking, there would be even more support for the cause.

I knew, once people began to feel, they would lay down their very lives to continue in the joy of living. We would all regain a reverence for life. A battle had been waged that day and victory had been declared. On that day, Life had won.

EPILOGUE

Ward Stoner stood in the darkness on the front edge of the crowd on that cold and sacred night, when the country was reborn—and said, "No more." He didn't cheer nor did he sing. A smile never crossed his lips. His job demanded the exercise of power and a total disrespect for life. Silas Drummond had defied the orders of his position, the end-traveler, Mari, was missing, the Legacy one had managed to get by him, and Alister Bedlam had left the zone, illegally, even for him.

Out of the Zone are you? And, you little petition peddlers are going to try to escape the zone as well? I will reactivate my National credentials and pull my Federal badge out of the drawer. None of you will escape from me.

But, Inspector Stoner was torn between the dictates of his job and the distant call of something else. He didn't know what had been pursuing him, what had been tugging at his heart.

That Christmas Day evening, those who passed by or stood near him paid no attention to the stoic figure who hugged the shadows. But, the dark figure was keenly observing all of them. At times he jotted down the names of those he recognized or overheard a name being spoken. Other times, the joy and display of love actually mesmerized him. But, in the end, even the love he saw for the first time on the streets of his town had no influence on the inspector. In fact, it had an opposite effect on him. The love of his life was gone. There was no more humming in the kitchen or flowers on the table.

The scent of her cologne had finally faded and no longer floated on the air of their home, even though Stoner had done all he knew how to do to keep it alive.

Christopher had been the happiest child Stoner had ever known before his mommy was put to sleep. But, after her death, most of the time, Christopher's lethargic gaze looked out on his play yard and saw no joy in any of it. The moments that managed to coax out a little happiness in his day, were the hours after his daddy got home.

Hoping it would help Christopher, Ward Stoner had prepared himself. He had taken a few minutes at the end of each day to reframe his experience. Before going inside his own home, he would sit in his car and try to reconstruct the dirty and evil thoughts of the work he had to do, into upbeat positives that would benefit his small son. He looked for a humorous moment to retell him. But, Stoner was getting more and more discouraged with his attempts to bring happiness into his home at the end of the day. Out on the streets, where others saw needy citizens and offered help, Stoner saw lazy slackers who offered nothing to society. When a small child fell from his bicycle the other day, a man stopped and helped him up. Where someone else may have seen a kind man, the inspector saw a child molester, trying to show enough compassion to lure a child from the protection of his home.

Stoner was a man with a bruised soul, who used to come home to a loving wife who had the power to reknit his wounded interior with a smile, the song she sang while cradling their son, and the soft words of endearment that were forever on her lips.

But, now the light in her eyes was gone and the hope in his heart had died with her. All he had left was his son Christopher. What would become of him? Was he now broken and damaged, a flawed child unit? Perhaps Christopher would leave him too. Then Stoner would be utterly alone in a world of anger, fear, and silence.

Blessed by the Lord God, Stoner sneered into the darkness. As with some men of old, he was a man whose own might was his only god. For that moment, he surrendered to the emptiness of his own heart. *Little Lady Applewait,* he hissed, *you will soon learn the true meaning of the word Tombstone. I will chase you to the ocean's tide if*

I must.

Stoner watched and listened. He heard the wonderful music, but there was also a whisper of something else. What he heard could make him kinder, or it could make him more dangerous, depending on which voice he listened to.

And, the people sang on.

BIBLICAL REFERENCES

THE HOLY BIBLE, NEW INTERNATIONAL VERSION®,
NIV® Copyright © 1973, 1978, 1984, 2011 by Biblica, Inc.™
Used by permission. All rights reserved worldwide.

Page 2 Proverbs 3: 1-2　　My son, do not forget my law, but let your heart keep my commands, for length of days and long life and peace they will add to you.

Page 127　Genesis 1: 1-3.　　In the beginning God created the heavens and the earth. Now the earth was formless and empty, darkness was over the surface of the deep. And the Spirit of God was hovering over the waters. And God said, "Let there be light, and there was light."

Page 128　John 1: 1-5.　　In the beginning was the Word, and the Word was with God, and the Word was God. He was with God in the beginning. Through him all things were made; without him nothing was made that has been made. In him was life, and that life was the light of men. The light shines in the darkness, but the darkness has not understood it.

Page 283　Luke 21: 15 & 19.　For I will give you words and wisdom that none of your adversaries will be able to resist or contradict. . . . By standing firm you will gain life."

Book ORDER Information

Length of Days - The Age of Silence

ORDER (paperback) **at any bookstore** or online at:

Most any on-line bookstore - also

http://www.directbuybooks.com

Download eBook at:

www.amazon.com

Other sites where eBooks are sold.

Also by Doris Gaines Rapp:

When available: Order at any bookstore:

Smoke from Distant Fires – available in the spring 2014
Hiawassee – Child of the Meadow: available in late summer 2014
Length of Days – Beyond the Valley (2 of 3): available in late 2014

Available now at any bookstore:
Escape from the Belfry - Order from any bookstore or Archway Publishing
from Simon and Schuster: www.archway.com and other online book stores.

Those below can be ordered at www.danielshousepublishing.com and
eBooks at www.amazon.com and www.b&n.com
Holding on to Sand – From the Interactive Journal of James Rapp
Prayer Therapy Primer

Weekly prayers at: www.prayertherapyrapp.blogspot.com

Doris Gaines Rapp is a novelist/author, Psychologist, Prayer Therapy Leader and Speaker.

Length of days - The Age of Silence is book one is a three book series. Book two, ***Length of Days - Beyond the Valley*** will also be released in late 2014. Go to www.dorisgainesrapp.com for information.

As a psychologist, Dr. Doris Rapp understands people and her characters. She has directed the Counseling Centers at Taylor University, Upland, Indiana, and Bethel College, Mishawaka, Indiana. She has worked as a Christian therapist at two comprehensive mental health centers.

Doris Gaines Rapp posts a devotional and prayer every Monday at www.prayertherapyrapp.blogspot.com

She has been the President of Northeast Indiana District United Methodist Woman and continues to be interested in the needs of families and children.